# Cemetery Stalkers

## Horror Collection

### Holly Copella

To Ruth Meredick

# CONTENTS

# ACKNOWLEDGMENTS

Copella Books: First Paperback Edition 2017
Cover Artist: Daniela Owergoor
Dani-owergoor.deviantart.com
Printed by CreateSpace, An Amazon.com Company

# PUBLISHER'S NOTE

# Night Creatures

# Chapter One

It was a cloudy, dreary day with more thunderstorms approaching in the distance. The airport runway and planes remained wet from a previous downpour. There was a small passenger building toward the back of the airport where those catching private planes could wait in limited comfort. The furniture was worn and the coffee station was in need of a good cleaning, but it served its purpose. The airport was mostly used by pilots who owned private planes and a small pilot training facility. Unlike most of their usual clientele, a well-dressed man in an expensive suit stood before the counter while arguing with a heavy-set man, who stood behind the desk eating a sandwich.

"I can appreciate your need to get to that boat, Mr. Stiller, but we don't fly our choppers in weather like this," Gus informed the well-dressed man. "Our insurance is high enough."

"I have to get out there. It's urgent," Rob Stiller informed him, now becoming frustrated.

"Someone needing an organ transplant urgent or business urgent?" Gus asked with a curious look as if suspecting the latter.

Rob frowned at the question since the answer was obvious even to the man behind the desk. Rob was a lean, wealthy looking man, who more than likely hadn't worked a manual labor job in his life.

His expensive haircut was no different from cheaper haircuts, but there was nothing low-maintenance about him. Even his fingernails were professionally manicured. It wasn't as if he was an unattractive man, but his expensive wardrobe gave the illusion of a more handsome man.

"I'm willing to pay whatever it takes," Rob informed the man behind the desk.

"I'm sure you would, but it's still against company policy," Gus informed him. "I can't help you."

"There must be someone--?"

Gus seemed to consider something that had previously come up in their conversation. "Wait," he announced with a curious look. "Which cruise ship was that?"

"*Queen Ariel.*"

"Well, this must be your lucky day," Gus suddenly chirped then pointed outside to a nearby hangar. "See that hangar over there? That crazy bastard is flying to that same ship. Must be picking up some rich guy." Gus gave Rob a knowing once over, almost mocking him. "For a price, he may let you ride along, but you'd better hurry."

Rob looked across the waiting area to an attractive, dark-haired woman in her mid-twenties dressed moderately fashionable in a basic black dress with a smart black jacket. Jasmine Manning paced the lobby while on her cell phone. She was almost as stressed as Rob was, indicated by the way she paced and constantly ran her fingers through her once neatly pinned-up hair, leaving it moderately messy. She disconnected the call then looked at Rob and frowned. There was about to be a backlash, and Jasmine knew she'd be on the receiving end. Rob urgently motioned for her to join him. She realized he must have found something, grabbed her bag, and hurried toward him.

The hangar contained a few small, private planes. Most were only two-passenger puddle jumpers. A tall, distinguished looking man in his mid-thirties stood alongside a man in a brown mechanic's uniform. The two men studied an oceanic map spread out on the wing of one of the smaller planes. Max was a ruggedly handsome man with dark nearly black hair worn business short. His blue eyes beyond dark lashes were almost hypnotizing. There was no denying he'd look just as good in a pair of jeans and a worn t-shirt as he did in his khakis and collared shirt beneath his black, leather jacket.

"Based on its coordinates and destination," the mechanic announced while studying the map, "your ship will be somewhere--" He pointed on the map with a grease stained index finger. "--around here."

Max circled the spot then looked at the mechanic and offered a grateful smile. "Thanks," he announced cheerfully. "You're a lifesaver."

"You got some sort of death wish, Max?" the mechanic asked while giving him a strange look.

"No, just need to rescue a friend," Max replied, although he did seem to find the question humorous.

As Max walked away, the mechanic smiled and shook his head, apparently coming to his own conclusion. Rob and Jasmine ran through the light rain and into the hangar. Both were moderately wet already. Rob hurried past Max without giving him a second glance and approached the mechanic. Jasmine waited by the open hangar doors and shivered from the dampness of her wet clothes against her skin. Max approached the bay doors near Jasmine and looked outside. A strange grin crossed his face as he cast a look at the shivering woman.

"Beautiful day, don't you think?" he teased.

Jasmine politely returned the smile. "All things being equal, I'd rather be at home in bed."

Max placed a baseball cap on his head and grinned while looking into her eyes. "I wouldn't mind that myself," he remarked while grinning his hidden meaning. "Good day."

Max ventured into the light rain and headed for a moderately expensive helicopter. Jasmine stared after Max a moment, saw where he was heading, and then looked back across the hangar to Rob. Her boss was attempting to talk to the busy mechanic, who didn't seem interested in conversing with him. Jasmine ran from the hangar as fast as her one-inch heels would carry her and hurried after Max as he prepped the helicopter. She reached him as he opened the pilot's door and climbed inside. When he saw her approaching, he stopped his pre-flight check and watched her.

"Must be that new cologne," he teased while grinning with boyish charm.

Jasmine was cold and wet, leaving little enthusiasm for small talk. "The man at the desk said you were flying out to the *Queen Ariel*."

Max finally took his eyes off the attractive woman and flipped several switches, prepping the helicopter for take-off. "So I am," he casually replied and barely glanced at her. "Why the interest?"

Jasmine pointed to the hangar with some embarrassment. "My boss and I need to get to the *Queen Ariel* right away," she announced. "It's extremely urgent. Could we fly with you? He'd pay you very well."

Max looked at the dark, stormy sky out the open door and made a face. "It's not a very good day to play taxi," he remarked then looked at her. "I shouldn't even be going myself. I couldn't risk anyone else."

"He's very determined," she countered then felt her entire body sag with defeat. "Please, at least make an offer."

"Dinner?" he replied without hesitation while grinning playfully.

She frowned. "To my boss--"

"I doubt he's my type."

"Please," she again begged.

Rob stepped out of the hangar and ran across the tarmac for them with both their bags. He stopped alongside Jasmine, slightly out of breath from the short run. "I'm so glad we were able to catch you."

"I already explained to the young lady that I can't take you with me," he casually replied. "Much too risky. It's not about money."

"This is extremely important," Rob interjected without hesitation.

"Someone need a kidney?"

"Please, just name your price," Rob insisted.

There was a long moment of silence while Max tapped his fingers on the control panel and appeared deep in thought. "One hundred dollars," he announced then cast a nod at Jasmine, "and an evening with the lady."

Rob appeared surprised then delighted. "Deal!"

Jasmine looked at her boss, horrified by his response. Rob didn't even notice the look she'd given him as he tossed their wet bags into the craft. He attempted to pull her toward the sliding side door, but she refused to budge. When she didn't move from her spot, he looked back at her and appeared surprised by the look she was giving him.

"What's wrong?" he demanded.

She stared at him with surprise while folding her arms across her wet blazer. "Don't I have a say in this?"

Rob leaned closer to her and muttered while grinning. "We're getting off cheap."

"Who's getting off cheap?" she snapped hotly.

"Come on kids," Max announced from the pilot seat. "Bus leaves in one minute."

Rob glared at her and raised his brows almost demandingly. "Say yes to the nice man and let's go."

"Tick, tick, tick," Max chimed in from the helicopter.

Without warning, he started the helicopter, startling both. The sound was nearly deafening. Rob stared Jasmine down. He pointed his finger at her, leaned closer to her ear, and practically had to shout.

"You got us into this--"

Jasmine held her head high and kept her arms folded across her chest. "No, absolutely not."

Max groaned and threw his head back against the pilot's seat. "It's just dinner," he informed her then offered a charming smile. "I promise."

Max directed Rob to the sliding side door and motioned Jasmine to the seat beside him. They continued their staring match for a moment longer. Jasmine finally groaned and hurried around the helicopter. She climbed into the front passenger seat as Rob buckled himself into the back. Max shut his door and strapped himself in then assisted Jasmine with her seat harness and headset.

Max looked at her and grinned with a humored look. "I hope you don't get airsick," he announced playfully. "It's going to be one hell of a rough ride."

She shut her eyes and attempted to remove herself from the entire situation. The helicopter lifted off and maneuvered swiftly across the airfield through the developing storm. They weren't even in the air ten minutes before Jasmine and Rob started feeling nauseous. Max hummed "Singing in the Rain" while skillfully flying through the dark skies.

"Must be something very important to go through all this trouble," Max remarked then eyed Jasmine and grinned slyly. "And hostility."

Rob clung to the back seat and appeared pale. "It's an important business deal with William Kensington," he informed him. "We've been trying to find him for months. I need to get out to that ship to fix a problem."

"William Kensington? Isn't he that eccentric millionaire who avoids business like the plague?" Max laughed and shook his head. "Must be worth quite a bit of money for you to risk flying with someone like me." He grinned deviously while looking at Jasmine and raised his brows. "I'm considered high risk."

Rob shut his eyes and rested his head against the back seat. The conversation wasn't improving his airsickness. "How long until we get there?"

"About an hour," Max announced with little concern. "Relax. Enjoy the ride."

After several minutes of turbulence, the flight became smoother. Max looked at Jasmine as she relaxed and no longer held onto the straps with a death grip.

"We haven't been properly introduced. I'm Max. Just Max."

She attempted to be polite after everything they'd been through, including the rough turbulence. "I'm Jasmine," she responded then indicated Rob. "And the ill man in the back is my boss, Rob Stiller, President of Avec, Incorporated."

"Isn't that some high profile investment company?" Max asked.

Rob replied while nauseous, "Yes."

Max glanced at the pale man in the back seat. "There's a little bag back there. Use it if you must woof woof." He again focused his attention on Jasmine. "So what do you do for Mr. President?"

"I'm his personal assistant," she replied then shifted uncomfortably. "At least I think I still am."

Max glanced at Rob in the back. "You still with us, Rob?"

"Yeah," he groaned while keeping his eyes closed. "Don't talk to me."

Max chuckled in his throat. "I did warn you."

Rob grumbled something but didn't open his eyes.

# Chapter Two

The mid-sized cruise ship, *Queen Ariel*, was adrift in the middle of the ocean and possibly off course. The helicopter circled the ship in the pouring rain. There wasn't any sign of activity on deck, which was to be expected considering the weather conditions. Jasmine was uneasy at the sight of the stalled cruise ship. It had a chilling, ghostly presence. If Max was concerned, he didn't give any indication. The helicopter landed on a special, elevated pad marked clearly with an 'H'. The chopper barely shut down when Rob sprang from the back, ran to the railing, and threw up over the side. Max and Jasmine stepped out into the pouring rain and watched him while making identical faces.

"Hope he has better luck with boats," Max retorted.

"Thanks for the lift, Max." She handed him her business card. "You can reach us at the number on the card for our, uh, arrangement."

Max accepted the card and chuckled softly. "I've never heard a date referred to as 'an arrangement'. Sounds so sinister," he teased. "Good luck with the business deal."

Jasmine smiled but had nothing to offer. She approached Rob, who still appeared sick. When they turned, Max was already heading down the steps and out of sight. Once they claimed their briefcases, they approached the steps as the rain poured down upon them, once again soaking them.

"Odd that the crew hasn't come to greet us," Jasmine remarked as they headed for an interior door. "Must have their hands full with whatever caused the ship to stop."

"Probably don't want to get wet," Rob muttered.

"Still," she remarked while looking around despite the rain. "This is creepy."

§

Rob and Jasmine, both soaking wet, entered the massive Neptune Lounge and stopped in the doorway, sharing the same look of surprise. The lounge was chillingly empty. There weren't any crewmembers or passengers.

"This isn't right," Jasmine remarked, now shivering for several reasons.

"Where is everyone?" Rob gasped and looked around. "A ship's bar is never empty."

They heard the faint sound of a helicopter then exchanged concerned looks, dropped their briefcases, and hurried from the lounge. Rob and Jasmine ran the entire way to the deck and stopped just before the railing in time to see the helicopter flying away from the boat.

Rob slammed his hands on the wet railing. "Damn it. What's going on around here? He must've noticed something was wrong. Why would he just leave us?"

"They must be somewhere," Jasmine announced with less enthusiasm. "Let's go to the main lobby. There has to be someone there."

They watched the helicopter as they walked toward the doors, shaking their heads in disgust. The helicopter suddenly rocked then crashed into the water. Rob and Jasmine stopped and stood by the railing in the pouring rain with a look of horror on their faces. The helicopter exploded moments after impact.

Jasmine jerked having witnessed the explosion. Her shoulders sagged as she groaned softly. "Oh, Max--" she gasped.

"What on earth would've caused him to crash?" Rob cried out with surprise. "That can't be a coincidence."

§

The soaking wet couple hurried down the staircase and slowed as they neared the bottom, reaching the lobby. The massive lobby was empty, void of life. No one was minding the desk, leaving everything exposed. They walked across the multi-level, elegant lobby while looking around. Even the gift shop remained open and unattended. Anyone could enter and take anything they wanted, although nothing was touched or out of place. They approached the front desk and looked around with increasing concern. Rob looked behind the desk for any signs of life, appeared puzzled, and shook his head.

"This is definitely not right," Jasmine muttered softly, feeling her fear rising.

"Where the hell did they all go?" he demanded.

"Abandoned ship?" she asked while casting a concerned look at him.

"That's ridiculous," he practically exploded. "The ship's not sinking." He looked around, considered his comment, and then muttered, "I hope."

§

As Rob and Jasmine made their way through the ship, they discovered all the lifeboats were missing, indicating that the crew and passengers had in fact abandoned ship. But why? As they continued on their journey, they ended up on the bridge. The bridge was abandoned as well. Not even the captain had remained onboard, which had to be bad. Rob and Jasmine stared at several demolished controls and noted some bloodstains on the floor. They looked at each other with horror. It was the first sign of something more sinister.

"The ship's controls and radio have been destroyed," Rob informed her while indicating the crushed panel. "This is bad, Jasmine."

"What should we do?"

§

Rob sat at the massive bar in the elegant, empty lounge and poured himself a drink while Jasmine paced the length of the lounge. She was anxious, soaked to the bone, and concerned for their situation. Rob's ability to drink away his concerns was almost more troubling.

She finally turned and stared at his profile while he drank. "What about your cell phone?"

Rob finished another glass of scotch and immediately refilled the glass. "No reception this far out. Whatever knocked out the radio and controls took any satellite with it." He took a large gulp from the glass. "Someone has to come along eventually. We'll just wait here until they do."

She groaned softly and ran her fingers through her wet hair. She was so cold despite the warmer outside temperature. "I need to find some dry clothes," Jasmine finally informed him. "Will you come with me to the gift shop in the lobby?"

Rob downed the entire glass of scotch. "Why? You know where the lobby is," he remarked without care. "You'll be okay. Just go."

Jasmine frowned, remembering why she hated her job, and left the lounge.

§

Jasmine wandered through the gift shop within the lobby and looked at shirts with the ship logo on them. She found a white button shirt and a pair of jean shorts in her size. She bit the tags off with her teeth while approaching the changing room. Being the ship was abandoned, she could just as easily have changed right there on the gift shop floor, but the thought didn't settle well. Jasmine changed into the dry clothes, feeling relief for the first time, and hung her wet dress and jacket over the changing room door. She slipped into a pair of tennis shoes and had just tied them when she heard a clunk from the gift shop. Jasmine tensed and stared at the changing room door as if expecting someone to charge in and attack her with a chainsaw.

She was being ridiculous. The ship was abandoned. She probably heard Rob. Her unsympathetic boss probably thought changing into dry clothes was a good idea after all. Despite convincing herself there was nothing to fear, she was hesitant while opening the door and looked across the gift shop. A statue lay on the floor near one of the shelves and rolled slightly. Jasmine wasn't sure what caused the statue to fall, but it had to be a coincidence. She released a sigh of relief, left the changing room, and headed across the gift shop to the lobby.

As she approached the desk, she heard a thump from one of the offices in the back. Jasmine darted behind the desk, snatched a paperweight shaped like a cruise ship, and nervously approached the office. She definitely heard movement from within the office. For a moment, she thought about running away, but it soon became too late. The door opened. Jasmine coiled back with the paperweight and stood frozen while staring at the door. As someone stepped into the doorway, Jasmine lunged forward prepared to strike with the marble paperweight. Max caught her arm before she could crush his skull and swiftly tossed her over his hip and onto the lower portion of the desk. The paperweight flew from her hand and struck the floor with a loud thud. As he held her pinned to the desk, they stared at one another with shared looks of surprise. Max was quick to release her and helped her to her feet, stabilizing her by her elbows.

"Jasmine, I'm so sorry," he gasped. "Are you all right?"

She painfully rubbed her shoulder and lower back then gave him a stunned look. "What are you doing here? I thought you'd left," she announced. "Didn't you crash into the ocean?"

"I'd thought the same about you and Rob," Max replied then looked around. "Where is he?"

"Probably passed out in the lounge by now," she muttered. "He's nursing a bottle of expensive scotch." She again eyed him with concern. "Who took the helicopter?"

"Damned if I know," he remarked while sighing as he looked around. "I wish I knew what was going on around here. We should collect Rob."

"We should let him rot," she muttered under her breath while continuing to rub her shoulder.

Max eyed her with a sympathetic smile. "Again, I'm sorry about that."

"I'll live."

"I'm surprised your boss let you wander around the ship on your own," Max remarked. "I don't know what's going on, but this place is seriously creepy."

"Chivalry has died, Max," she informed him. "In the world of business, those in charge are perfectly willing to sacrifice those of us beneath them."

"You may want to consider a career change," Max informed her while raising a brow.

"If I had a pen and paper, I'd write my resignation here and now."

"We'll leave that for another time," he informed her. "Chivalry isn't dead. You can be the Watson to my Sherlock. We'll look out for each other."

"I appreciate that," Jasmine replied and smiled for the first time.

Max led her from the lobby and toward the main staircase. The lounge was just beyond the stairs. They entered the lounge and discovered it was empty. Rob was gone! Jasmine looked around with surprise. Where would he have gone? Did he actually leave her without even telling her where he was going? Or did something more sinister occur?

"Are you sure this is the right bar?"

"He was here just twenty minutes ago," she announced while shaking her head in disbelief.

Max walked across the lounge and looked over the bar. When he didn't find anyone behind the bar, he turned back to face her and shrugged. They leaned against the bar and sank into thought, attempting to figure out their next move.

"The control room and the radio have been destroyed," Jasmine informed him. "I doubt either can be repaired."

"So was the one in the lobby office," Max replied.

"So what do we do now?"

"I'm open to suggestions," he replied.

"I think we should lock ourselves in a room somewhere," she muttered while rubbing her chilled shoulders despite having changed into dry clothes.

"Should we look for Rob first?"

She glared at him, giving her silent answer.

"Why don't we check out the galley, gather something to eat, and lock ourselves in the Presidential Suite for the night?"

"How do we get in?"

Max flashed a master key card then extended his hand to her. She managed a smile, grabbed the bottle of scotch from the bar, and left the lounge with him.

# Chapter Three

Jasmine remained tense as she stood in the large kitchen while Max sifted through the refrigerator, loading items into a basket he'd found. She didn't like being exposed in the kitchen with so many hidden corners. Without knowing why an entire cruise ship would abandon ship, she was concerned for their safety. She watched Max approach a large refrigerator with a glass door. It contained dozens of bottles of wine for the dinner menu. Max opened the sliding glass door and selected a bottle. As he read the label, he smiled with satisfaction.

"Not bad."

He placed the bottle into the basket along with the rest of the items. A pot suddenly crashed to the floor. Jasmine cried out and jumped into Max's arms. Max appeared startled by her actions more than the sound. He held her securely against him and looked around the kitchen to locate the source of the sound. A fat rat scurried across the floor.

He laughed at her expense and offered a humored grin. "Just a rat."

Jasmine groaned softly and met his gaze, looking into his blue eyes for the first time. She marveled at his eyes only a moment then looked away, ashamed she even had a lustful thought in their current situation.

"You must think I'm feeble and helpless," she remarked and considered pulling away, but when he didn't release her, she stayed where she was. "I'm not usually this pathetic."

"Perhaps if I wasn't so tense and uneasy, I might consider how feeble and helpless you are," he teased while grinning.

Max finally released her and collected his filled basket. They headed across the massive kitchen toward the dining room door. Jasmine opened the door and nearly collided with Rob. Both screamed to see the other. Jasmine jumped backward and collided into Max.

"Jesus," Rob cried out. "You scared me!"

"Serves you right," she lashed out, her startled state turning into an angry one. "Where the hell were you?"

"Looking for you." He then seemed to notice Max and was surprised to see him. "Where did you come from?"

"It's a long story," Jasmine informed him. "Max suggested staying in one of the rooms tonight as a safety precaution."

"One?" Rob almost demanded and eyed Max suspiciously. "What are you up to?"

Max frowned with annoyance. "A few hours ago, you were willing to trade her body for passage to this ship, and now you're worried about her virtue? You're a piece of work, Rob."

"He's a piece all right," Jasmine muttered.

"Oh, now *I'm* the bad guy," Rob demanded.

Jasmine examined the Presidential Suite while carrying her glass of wine and insecurely clinging to her arm. She nodded her approval at the luxurious, two-bedroom suite. Max and Rob sat on the chair and sofa across from each other and attempted to stare the other down.

"This is very classy," Jasmine announced, barely even paying attention to the looks the men gave each other. "I've always wondered how the other half lived."

Max casually sipped his wine and eyed her. "It's a nice place to visit, but you wouldn't want to live there."

"Those who have not are the first to criticize those who have," Rob announced while glaring at Max. "I'll have you know; I work very hard for what I have."

"I never said you didn't, Rob," Max remarked. "Don't be so defensive."

"Why not?" Rob snarled. "You're quick to cut down my lifestyle."

"You're right, Rob," Max muttered without looking at him. "Have another drink."

Max sat back in his chair and sipped his wine. Rob finished his drink and stood with some difficulty. It was clear he was drunk, although it could be argued he'd been drunk since his stint in the lounge.

Rob pointed to the room on the left. "I'm taking that room," he announced matter-of-factly. "The two of you can fight over the other room."

Rob staggered to the second bedroom and slammed the door shut. Jasmine approached the sofa and cast herself onto it.

Max eyed her and shook his head. "He has some serious issues."

"He's one of those men who doesn't know how to relax," she informed him. "He likes control and being the center of attention."

"Probably pays women to spank him too," Max teased while hiding his smile.

"I don't recall scheduling those appointments," Jasmine teased back.

Max finished his wine, set the glass down, and stood. "If you don't mind, I'd like to borrow your bathroom and steal a pillow for my sofa."

"I doubt I'll get much sleep anyway," she announced. "You can have the bedroom."

"Unlike your boss," Max began, "I wouldn't feel right letting you sleep on the sofa while I took the bed. Remember? I promised you chivalry wasn't dead."

§

Jasmine tossed restlessly beneath the covers and whined softly in her sleep. A shadow passed outside the deck window. Jasmine woke abruptly and looked around the dimly lit room feeling slightly disoriented. She saw light coming from the living area, shining through the partially open doorway. She looked across the room once more and climbed out of bed, remaining fully dressed, under the circumstances. She approached the bedroom doorway and looked into the living room. Max lay on the sofa with a blanket over him and appeared to be sleeping peacefully. Jasmine approached the sofa and kneeled on the floor near him.

"Max--?"

Max jerked awake with a startled gasp. He looked at her, rolled onto his back, and groaned while running fingers through his dark hair. "Don't do that."

"I had a terrible dream," she announced gently. "Everyone was dead."

Max shut his eyes. "You can relax," he announced. "The lifeboats were launched. No one died. I promise."

His remark didn't make her feel any better. "Will you stay with me in the bedroom?"

Max cast a look at her through partially opened eyes. He twitched slightly but acted casual toward her request. He sighed and sat up. "Don't let me catch you snoring."

Jasmine stood and returned to the bedroom with Max following while carrying his pillow. A sly smirk crossed his face, although she couldn't see it.

"Now I know why guys take girls to horror movies," he muttered to himself.

Max entered the room after her and shut the door behind him. Jasmine climbed under the covers into a sitting position and hugged her knees. Max cast his pillow on the bed and practically fell on top of it. Jasmine watched Max as he seemingly fell back to sleep. Jasmine pulled the covers over him.

"Thanks, Max."

Max turned from his stomach onto his side facing her and smiled gently. "As long as you feel safe."

Jasmine slipped beneath the covers and lay on her side facing him as well. She stared at the handsome man while he slept for at least ten minutes while listening to the wind from the storm outside. She thought she heard something other than the wind, but it could have been almost anything. She finally shut her eyes and attempted to sleep.

Two A.M. Max slept nestled against Jasmine from behind with his arms securely around her. She held Max's hand to her chest while sleeping peacefully. A shadow moved past the bedroom window, followed by a faint wheezing sound. Jasmine slowly woke, lifted her head, and looked around. She then realized Max was spooned against her and the secure way she cuddled his arm. She actually liked the way it felt having a man clinging to her, pressed against her the way he was. She returned her head to the pillow without changing positions, not wanting to disturb him and ruin the mood. She then heard a faint scratching that also woke Max. He kept his arm securely around her but seemed to listen for the sound again, curious about it.

"What was that?" Jasmine asked softly.

"Mice, I think," he replied but didn't seem convinced.

"Must be big mice," she remarked.

Max repositioned himself against Jasmine, keeping his body snug against hers, and returned his head to the pillow. "Nothing to worry about. Go back to sleep."

With the way he pressed against her, she wasn't sure it was possible to return to sleep. Her mind seemed fixated on his body against hers. She couldn't deny the arousal she felt. She then heard a low thud. Both jumped up and apart while looking around the room. They knew that wasn't a mouse. Max sprang from the bed and looked around the dark room. They heard the thud again. Max ran from the bedroom. Jasmine hurried after him not wanting to be alone in the room. Max entered the dimly lit suite with Jasmine on his heels. The thud was louder. They saw the door vibrate as something pounded against it. Jasmine gasped with surprise. Rob appeared from his room, looking hungover and exhausted.

"What's going on out--?"

The door vibrated again with a loud thud. They heard a low wheezing and a possible snarl from within the corridor. Max ran to the door and placed the dead bolt across it. The door violently vibrated several times. Max jumped back with surprise.

"The sofa," Rob cried out.

Max helped Rob push the heavy sofa across the room and in front of the door. Both men backed away and stared at the door as it continued to vibrate.

"My God! What's out there?" Jasmine gasped.

Max backed away from the door and pulled Jasmine into his arms while keeping a close watch. The doorknob lock cracked and the sturdy bolt caught. They heard a loud snarl through the sliver of an opening. Something moved past the door. Rob appeared horrified and moved closer to them without looking away from the door. The vibration and snarling stopped. The light was once more seen from the hallway.

"What the fuck was that?" Rob softly cried out.

Max clung to Jasmine a little tighter than she found comfortable. "I'm not sure I want to know," he replied.

"What about the window?" Jasmine gasped.

"It can't break the windows," Max informed her. "They're too thick. It would've gotten through the door first." He shook his head. "It doesn't make any sense. We were running around the ship all day and never ran into anything like what we heard outside that door."

"Maybe it's nocturnal," Jasmine remarked.

"I think I've slept enough for one night," Max announced.

"Yeah, me too," Rob muttered.

# Chapter Four

Early the following morning, Max and Rob sat in front of the coffee table with a small map of the ship before them. The remainder of the night had gone without incident, although none got much sleep after their scare.

Max pointed with enthusiasm to a location on the map. "This is the quickest route to the galley," he informed Rob. "We'll grab a duffel bag, fill it with non-perishable foods, and be back within twenty minutes."

Jasmine came out of the nearby bedroom wearing expensive shorts and a designer blouse, compliments of the previous occupant. She dried her damp hair with a towel then eyed the conspiring men with increasing suspicion. Whatever they were plotting, she hadn't been included.

"What are you two doing?" she asked while tossing her towel aside.

"Stocking up for a long hibernation," Rob casually informed her then gave her a curious look. "How can you shower at a time like this?"

Jasmine glared at Rob, dumbfounded by the question. "What else is there to do? If we're going to be stuck here together, I'd rather not stink." She then smirked. "Besides, I'm going to take advantage of the rich people's clothing they left behind. I may as well be comfortable."

Max subconsciously eyed his tacky ship's logo clothing and considered the comment. "She has a point," he remarked. "I could use a little freshening myself."

"So could I," Rob remarked, "but I don't want that thing coming back, busting in here, and cornering me in the shower either."

§

Max, now showered and changed into an expensive, casual outfit, peered into the empty kitchen. When nothing moved, he glanced back at Jasmine and Rob, who was still in his clothes from yesterday.

"Looks clear," he announced softly.

All three entered the kitchen with some anxiety, casting looks around them as they hurried for the pantry. Max carried an empty duffel bag they'd found along the way. While Max and Jasmine scanned the kitchen, keeping watch, Rob opened the pantry door. Two women stood within the food storage room and screamed as they struck Rob with bags of rice. Rob dove away from the pantry doorway while shielding his head. The women stopped their assault and looked at the three newcomers.

"Oh, thank God," Shelly cried out with relief.

"We didn't know there were others still onboard," Rita informed them.

Both women were in their late twenties to early thirties. They wore fashionable gym wear with their hair pulled up into ponytails, suggesting they may have been in the gym working out when they were left stranded.

"The guys will be thrilled," Shelly announced.

Max appeared curious. "How many of you are there?"

"There's Rita and me," Shelly announced while indicating her friend. "Davis, Braddon, and Collin."

"Didn't you hear the helicopter when we arrived?" Max practically demanded. "Why didn't you come and warn us? We could've left."

"Anderson went nuts. He locked us in the gym and took off," Rita announced as she vigorously shook her head. "When we finally made it to deck, we saw the helicopter crash into the water. We didn't know what had happened."

"It must have been Anderson who took the helicopter," Jasmine remarked.

"Let's talk about it back in the gym," Shelly informed them. "I still don't feel safe out here."

Max looked at Rob and Jasmine. "Well?"

"What have we got to lose?" Rob reluctantly replied then muttered, "Except our lives."

Jasmine removed a butcher knife from a set of knives on the wall and sighed. "I suppose we should have a look."

§

The ship's gym was three connecting rooms. The first room contained the weight machines and exercise equipment. The second room contained the steam room, whirlpool, and sauna. There were men and women's locker rooms attached to the second room. The third room was the spa, which had its own entrance from a different corridor. They had a second way out, in case they were trapped. There were three men waiting within the gym for their companions to return. Collin was a mousy looking guy in his late thirties with a nervous look about him. He was also the only one who hadn't been dressed in gym wear. His casual cruise wear was worn and dirty, as if he'd seen more action than the others had.

Davis was a tall, fairly muscular man, who'd obviously spent a lot of time in gyms and not just onboard the ship. His excessively bronzed skin indicated he'd spent a lot of time at the poolside during the cruise as well. Braddon was a fairly attractive man, although he didn't exactly fit into the gym scene. He resembled an executive attempting to fit in with the fitness crowd in order to make business deals. His workout clothes were more fashionable and less functional, dressing to impress.

Once the women, their three new friends, and the supplies they'd collected were safely inside, Davis and Braddon pushed heavy equipment in front of the gym door to keep anything from getting inside. Max, Rob, and Jasmine looked around the large exercise room with some concern. The entire front wall was a large glass window overlooking the pool one deck below. It didn't contain a walkway, but the idea of a glass wall was still concerning.

Jasmine clutched her butcher knife while fidgeting then muttered, "Not exactly the Presidential Suite."

If Max were uncomfortable, he didn't show it. He eyed the three unfamiliar men. "So who'd like to tell me what came after us last night?"

"*That* was a vampire," Braddon bluntly informed him while resting his foot on an exercise machine.

They stared at Braddon without expression, seemingly sharing the same thought. He'd obviously lost his mind.

"A what?" Rob questioned, apparently thinking he hadn't heard him correctly.

"A vampire," Davis reiterated. "At least that's what best describes it." He frowned while sinking into his own thoughts. "First, the crew started to disappear, then some of the passengers went missing. Then, the night before last, the captain and first mate were attacked in the control room." He drew a deep breath. "The ship stopped and we'd heard a barely human man was seen hovering over the captain. The others swore it was drinking his blood. The bridge was destroyed in the attack, and the crew couldn't radio out, so they just started evacuating passengers. Several men got together to try to kill it. None were seen again."

Collin fidgeted and seemed unable to stand still. He was clearly traumatized by something. "Except me," he remarked while darting looks around the gym. "I was with those who went to hunt it down. We were separated in the cargo area, and I never saw anyone after that. I returned to deck, but all the boats were gone. I can only hope the other passengers made it safely off the ship. There was a lot of blood on deck."

"And there's just one of these vampires?" Rob asked.

"We think so, but we're not sure," Davis replied. "Whatever it is, we're pretty sure it only comes out at night."

"So, we're stuck onboard with some sort of vampire?" Max asked, sounding as if he didn't believe a word of it. "How long until the Coast Guard comes looking for us?"

"One of the crew thought two days," Collin informed them. "That's a day overdue for our next port. We should have been there today."

"So by tomorrow afternoon, someone should come looking for us," Max asked then eyed the others. "What sort of weapons do we have?"

"The purser had a gun, but he must've taken it with him," Davis replied. "We have two flare guns and two antique pirate swords. Relatively dull."

Shelly produced a knife sharpener from the bag she carried. "I found this in the kitchen."

Collin eagerly snatched it with trembling hands. "I'll start sharpening the swords." He disappeared into the sauna area without further comment.

"Are you sure this place is safe?" Jasmine asked, again looking at the wall of windows.

"It tried to get in last night, but couldn't even move the doors," Braddon replied. "It can't get to the windows, and even if it could, they're made from shatterproof glass, so it's safe."

"We have enough food to last us a week, if necessary," Rita informed them.

"Sounds like a pretty sound set up," Rob remarked.

Max exchanged curious looks with Rob and Jasmine. "Any objections?"

Rob was quick to agree. Jasmine reluctantly shook her head. Davis led Rob and Max from the gym. Shelly approached the large windows overlooking the swimming pool below.

"I can't believe we were having so much fun just the other day," Shelly muttered softly. "When things started getting a little crazy, the five of us, including Anderson, decided to hang out in the gym while the crew investigated. When everything went to hell, we barricaded ourselves in here."

"We knew they were loading the lifeboats," Rita continued, "but there was so much chaos and the screaming--"

"We decided to wait it out here rather than attempt to reach the lifeboats," Shelly remarked. "Collin showed up after the screaming stopped. His stories were a bit alarming."

Jasmine approached one of the weight benches near the window and sat on it. Braddon joined the three women and leaned against the glass.

"We're perfectly safe in here," he informed Jasmine. "The creature tried to jump up to the window from the deck below, but it never got anywhere near the window."

"You saw it?" Jasmine gasped. "The vampire?"

"Well, from a distance," Shelly replied. "The pool deck was dimly lit."

"It's human looking," Rita informed her. "We couldn't see much, but we heard Collin describe it. He had a closer look, however brief."

Shelly and Rita started talking between themselves. Whatever was said, both women stood and walked away while talking softly. Braddon sat on the press near Jasmine, who stared out the window a moment longer.

"I can't believe there's no way off this ship," Jasmine muttered softly.

"Trust me, we've checked," Braddon replied. "All the lifeboats and rafts are gone. Every form of communication has been destroyed. Our best chance is to remain here." He indicated the window. "We can see help arriving. We have flares, weapons, food, water, and even entertainment. We're pretty much set for a few weeks." He offered a mildly comforting smile. "Nothing to worry about. Collin will try to upset you with his horror stories, but you'll see there's little to fear during the day. At night, he can't get to us."

"I hope you're right about the glass."

"You couldn't even shoot a bullet through that stuff," Braddon teased.

# Chapter Five

Later that afternoon, Rob joined Davis and Braddon by one of the elliptical trainers, where the two men were attempting to show off their strength while competing against each other. Rob wasn't interested in joining their pissing match, but since he was moderately bored and mostly drunk, he was easily amused. Max sat alongside Collin at the bar toward the back of the gym. Collin was attempting to get drunk, but Max seemed to have other ideas and kept him from achieving his goal.

"Why were you and the others down in the cargo area?" Max asked, fishing for information, possibly not buying any of his story. "Did you follow the creature?"

"We followed the blood." He then whispered as his eyes widened, "They're down there."

"Who?"

"The dead people," Collin softly replied with horror filling his eyes. "He collected them. We saw the bodies. By the time we realized what we were actually hunting, he already had us trapped. I was the only one who escaped." He removed a wooden cross from his pocket. "I found this. It kept him away from me. Stake through the heart. That's the only way to kill a vampire. That and sunlight. Cutting off their head seems to help. I've seen all the movies."

Max was becoming frustrated with Collin's delusions, but he continued to press him for more information. "Does he have a coffin or something in cargo?"

"I don't know. We never got that close, and there's not a lot of light down there," Collin informed him. "But that's where he is until it gets dark." He stared into Max's eyes. "Then he'll be coming back for us. We're not safe here. We're not safe anywhere."

§

Max joined Jasmine near the windows in the gym. She'd spent most of her day staring out the large windows, scouring the deck below, looking for any signs of life or the creature. She kept her butcher knife from the kitchen close at hand just to be safe. The sun had finally set, leaving the ship's deck only dimly lit. She glanced at Max as he sat alongside her.

"Did you get anything useful out of the others?" she asked, although his look gave her all the information she needed.

"Davis and Braddon took my line of questioning as a challenge to their authority," he informed her with a bored sigh. "Apparently, I'm a threat. Collin is borderline psychotic, but I think he's onto something. He thinks the creature may be injured."

"That's good, right?" she asked with some enthusiasm and straightened. "It may just die on its own."

Max made a face. "Unfortunately, that might also mean it's recovering and could become stronger."

Her smile faded. "That's not so good."

"He's convinced the creature is living in the cargo hold somewhere."

"Could we seal off the cargo exits?"

"Perhaps, but I don't know how many exits there are," Max replied in a defeated tone. "We'll need to find another map. There may be too many other escape routes." He sighed and looked out the window at the dimly lit deck below. "We're not doing anything tonight. Tomorrow we'll take advantage of the daylight and collect some supplies."

"Like what?"

"Axes, wooden stakes, crosses from the chapel. Anything that myth says works," Max informed her. "If he does get in here, I'd like to be prepared."

There was a loud thump against the glass. Max and Jasmine turned to see the frightening looking creature resembling a man clinging to the glass while staring in at them. It looked almost like a man but with some animalistic features. They could clearly see the fangs stained with blood in its mouth. It had sharp, cat-like claws on its left hand, but the fingertips on the right had been severed and healed, leaving nubs without claws. Jasmine let out a startled cry as they jumped away from the window. The others ran across the room and stopped several feet away, staring with horror. It was the first time any of them had seen it up close. Rob appeared completely horrified and backed further away from the window. The others just stared with horror.

Braddon approached the glass with a mocking smile on his face, amused by their fear. "There's no reason to be alarmed. He can't get through."

"Famous last words," Rob muttered.

The creature struck the glass several times with a loud, terrifying thump. The glass suddenly cracked causing everyone to scream and jump, including Braddon.

"Into the lounge," Davis cried out.

As they turned to run for the connecting room, the glass shattered with the next strike. Max pulled Jasmine away from the window. Braddon ran for the connecting doorway as the vampire creature crashed through the glass. Despite Max and Jasmine being closer, the creature ran after Braddon, tackling him to the ground. The vampire plunged his claws into Braddon's back then went for his neck. Jasmine could only stare in horror, wondering if there was anything they could do to save Braddon. Max pulled Jasmine toward the others and the connecting door. Davis suddenly closed and bolted the door before they reached it. The creature jumped off Braddon, who still twitched, and turned toward Max and Jasmine. Max pushed Jasmine toward the broken window.

"The ledge," he cried out.

They climbed through the opening in the thick glass and teetered on the small ledge. The vampire jumped into the opening behind them. They moved along the small ledge as fast as they could without falling. The vampire jumped through the opening, clung to the glass, and ran for them. Both saw the creature and were horrified that it could cling to the glass. The creature lunged for Max. He attempted to defend himself against the creature, lost his footing in the battle, and plummeted into the pool below with a loud splash. As the creature turned toward her, Jasmine reached the railing and plunged a butcher knife into its shoulder. The creature was momentarily stunned by the pain. Jasmine looked over the railing and saw Max climbing out of the pool. She saw some blood tinging the water, but he was alive.

"Run, Jasmine!"

He motioned for her to run then ran from the pool area. Jasmine climbed the railing and landed on the deck. The creature wheezed and hissed at her. Jasmine cried out and ran along deck. She could hear the wheezing and hissing behind her, but she didn't dare look back. She bolted through a doorway without knowing where it led and ran along the unfamiliar corridor with the creature running behind her. It had a severe limp that kept it from catching her, but it still managed to remain only a few feet behind. Jasmine turned the corner and skidded, nearly falling, losing her bloodied knife. To her horror, there was only one set of doors at the end of the corridor. She was trapped! She had no choice but to run through those doors. She bolted through the open doors, past the church pews, and toward the altar. She saw the large, gold cross on the wall in the front. She jumped onto the altar, snatched the cross, and turned while standing on top of the table, prepared to strike the creature. The vampire creature squealed from the doorway and looked around with agitation and fear. Jasmine looked back at her surroundings.

"He can't cross into the church," she gasped.

Jasmine slowly climbed down from the altar and walked toward the back doors and the creature. She carried the three-foot cross in her hands. The creature squealed with panic and ran away. She paused halfway down the aisle and fell to her knees while breathing heavily then sobbed.

"Oh, Max, please be okay."

The others remained quietly within the spa after the attack occurred. They didn't move and barely said a word in the twenty minutes since they barricaded the connecting door. Rita and Shelly clung to each other in an attempt to keep the other from panicking.

The men were equally shaken by what had just happened, most having witnessed the carnage involving Braddon. Most just concentrated on breathing and controlling their elevated heart rate.

"Do you think Jasmine and Max got away?" Rob asked softly while eying the others.

Although the connecting room had been quiet for nearly twenty minutes, they now heard the creature's faint wheezing from the other side of their barricade. Everyone quickly backed away from the bolted and barricaded door. There was a tremendous vibration as the creature struck the door. Shelly cried out, no longer able to control her hysteria.

"It's going to break down the door," Rob gasped.

Davis retrieved the two sharpened swords and handed one to Rob, who uncertainly accepted it and stared at the weapon with horror.

"We'll kill it if we have to," Davis announced.

"Those won't work against a vampire," Collin insisted while frantically running his fingers through his hair with one hand and clutching his cross in the other. He darted looks around the room. "We need to get out of here."

"And go where?" Davis demanded, his stress levels climaxing. "If it gets through this door, it'll get through all the doors."

"We're not safe here," Collin continued to chant. "We should go to the chapel. It may not be able to enter."

"The chapel is down a level and clear on the other side of the ship," Rita cried out. "It's at the end of the hall. What if it doesn't work? We'll be trapped."

"We're going to die if we stay here!"

"Shut up," Davis shouted at Collin.

The door vibrated with a crash and dented, frightening everyone.

"He's stronger than yesterday," Collin announced as he frantically paced. "He's going to come through that door."

Shelly began to wail hysterically, feeding off Collin's fears.

Davis turned and grabbed Collin by the shirt. "Sit down and shut up!"

The door vibrated and puckered away from the frame. The next hit would tear down the door.

Collin backed up to their only remaining exit barricaded with a spa sofa. "We have to go now!"

Rob looked from the nearly busted door to Collin. He ran after Collin, motioning the others to follow. Rob helped Collin and Shelly move the sofa away from the door. The three ran out the doorway into the ship's corridor. As the door flew open, tossing the heavy sofa aside, Davis and Rita bolted into the women's locker room. They locked the door and blocked it with a heavy bench. Both backed away from the door and braced their backs against the lockers. Davis clutched his sword as they stared at the door. They didn't hear anything.

"It's gone," Rita gasped then eyed Davis.

"I think it went after the others," he informed her, almost sounding relieved. "Let's place another bench in front of the door in case it comes back."

# Chapter Six

Rob and Shelly ran along the corridor trailing behind Collin. When they realized they weren't being chased, they paused by a map of the ship located on the wall. Collin realized they stopped and ran back to them. He pointed down the corridor.

"The chapel is this way," Collin cried out while attempting to catch his breath.

Rob pointed to the map. "These are flood doors."

"So?" Collin demanded.

"If we can get the flood doors to close in this section, the creature will be locked out," Rob informed him.

"Engage them now, and he'll be trapped in here with us," Collin snarled. "Let's go!"

They watched Collin run for the stairs. Rob reluctantly pulled Shelly behind him in the direction Collin headed.

"He's going to get us killed, I know it," Rob muttered while looking around.

"The chapel's on a dead end," Shelly insisted and stopped him in the corridor. "If he's wrong about this whole vampire thing, we're trapped."

"What other choice do we have?" Rob asked.

"The purser's office on main deck," she insisted. "It's like a fortress. They keep all the records there. The door is solid steel. Even flood proof, I was told."

"That's only one deck down," Rob announced with enthusiasm. "We'll go after Collin and tell him."

They heard a faint wheezing behind them, causing both to look down the corridor. Rob became alarmed even though they didn't see the creature.

"He's coming," Shelly cried out.

They ran down the stairs and across the main lobby. The vampire chased after them only a few yards behind and gaining on them. Shelly pointed out the purser's office. They bolted inside and slammed the door. The vampire struck the door roughly, but it didn't budge. It struck it again. It still didn't move. Rob and Shelly leaned against the door while panting heavily.

§

Rita paced the women's locker room while Davis sat on a bench and nervously tapped his fingers on the sword that lie across his lap.

"If a rescue comes, they'll never find us in here," Rita informed him.

"We don't have any other choice," Davis remarked. "At least it gave up on us."

"For now," she added. "It came back once. If it knows we're here, it could return."

"It's been almost an hour," he informed her. "I think we're safe for tonight. We can work on a plan for tomorrow when we can move around the ship freely."

"There is no safe place on this ship," she muttered and continued to pace. She finally stopped and groaned. "I need to use the bathroom."

Rita headed for the bathroom in the back, leaving Davis to tap his sword nervously. Once Rita finished in the bathroom, she washed her hands then placed her wet hands to her face, feeling her flushed cheeks. She looked at herself in the mirror and frowned at how ragged she looked. She removed some paper towels and dried her hands and face. A hollow, metallic thump caught her attention. Rita looked around with confusion and attempted to locate the source of the sound. The panel in the ceiling opened. As she turned, the vampire dropped to the floor practically on top of her and hissed, exposing bloodstained teeth. Rita attempted to scream, but his teeth sank into her throat, cutting off any sound.

Within the locker room, Davis finally stood and approached the bathroom door. He twirled the sword with boredom and paused before the door.

"Come on, Rita," he announced. "Some of us have to go too." There was no response. Davis tapped on the door. "Rita, come on."

When there was still no response, Davis opened the bathroom door and peered inside. There was a large pool of blood on the floor. He then saw the vampire kneeling over Rita's blood covered body where a large portion of her throat had been torn out. The vampire turned with blood running down his chin and a killer look in his eyes. Davis gasped with horror and slammed the door shut. He wasted no time running for the barricaded door and shoved the benches out of the way then darted into the corridor while clutching his sword.

§

Jasmine paced the altar near the front of the church while carrying her large cross. She heard movement from the hall, alarming her. She cautiously approached the back door while holding the cross close to her chest. Collin suddenly collided with her and both fell to the carpeted floor. Collin picked himself up with some unsteadiness then helped the dazed Jasmine to her feet.

"Are you okay?" he gasped then appeared relieved. "Am I ever glad to see you."

"What happened?" she asked with concern.

"He got through the second door," Collin informed her. "The others wouldn't follow me to the chapel."

"It wouldn't come inside the room," she announced. "You were right. I think it's not allowed."

"I knew I was right," he announced excitedly then frowned after realizing the cost of being right. He saw the large, gold cross and picked it up from the floor. "That's one big cross to bear."

Jasmine took the cross from him and held it to her chest. "It makes me feel safe."

Collin looked past her then ran to the front of the church. She watched him run with purpose and wondered what was possibly going through his mind. He opened a wooden baptismal font and exposed the holy water then glanced at her as she approached.

"We can use this," he announced with enthusiasm. "All we need is a container."

Collin walked around the church in search of a container and disappeared into a back room. He returned a moment later with a bottle of wine. He emptied the wine into a large, gold goblet on the altar then approached the baptismal font and filled the bottle with the holy water.

§

Morning finally came, although it seemed to take forever. Light shined into the chapel through the stained glass window in front of the altar. Jasmine woke from her light sleep where she lay on the wooden church pew and looked around. Collin lay beneath the altar, clinging to the three-foot, gold cross. Jasmine sat up with some stiffness.

"Collin, it's morning," she announced barely loud enough for him to hear.

Collin jerked awake with a soft gasp then looked around and sat up as well.

"Is it safe?" she asked him.

"I hope so," he muttered while seeming groggy. Judging by the empty wine goblet alongside him, he'd single-handedly finished the entire bottle of wine himself.

Jasmine ran toward the door.

Collin saw her heading for the door, bolted after her, and stopped her just before the entrance. "Whoa, whoa," he cried out. "Where are you going?"

"I have to find Max."

"We only assume it can't stand sunlight," Collin informed her. "I could be wrong."

Jasmine looked around the church and saw a wooden staff near the altar with a cross on top of it. "Fine. I'll take that, just in case."

She approached the altar and removed the large staff. Collin followed and again stopped her. He took the staff from her, surprising her, propped it over the pew, and stepped on it. The stick snapped. The staff with the cross on top was now only three feet with a jagged, wooden edge.

"You daze him with the cross," he informed her then thrust the jagged edge in the air. "And stab him through the heart with the wooden end." He handed Jasmine the staff and collected his bottle of holy water. "Let's go."

As they cautiously left the church, Jasmine was relieved he more or less volunteered to go with her. For a mousy guy who appeared to be losing it just yesterday, his newly found aggression was surprising and welcomed.

§

Jasmine and Collin entered the spa through the open door and looked from the busted connecting door to the women's locker room. They checked the locker room then looked around and exchanged looks. There was no one around. Once inside the women's locker room, Collin approached the bathroom. He paused within the doorway and turned pale.

"Jasmine--?"

She joined him by the bathroom door and looked past him. She saw the large amount of blood on the floor and walls. Both looked around the room.

"I don't see signs of another attack," Jasmine remarked. "You said Davis and Rita weren't with you, Rob, and Shelly. Maybe either Davis or Rita got away."

They heard someone clearing their throat, catching their attention. Both looked around, but there was no one there. They then heard Rob's voice over the intercom.

"May I have your attention please," Rob announced from hidden speakers. "Would all live passengers please report to the main lobby? Thank you."

Jasmine slapped Collin's arm and motioned.

He clutched his arm and glared at her with discomfort. "That hurt."

§

Rob sat on the desk in the lobby with an ax across his lap while Shelly ate a candy bar and paced just before the desk. As Jasmine and Collin ran across the lobby, Shelly jumped with surprise. Rob jumped off the desk, met Jasmine halfway, and hugged her with relief, surprising her.

"Oh, Jasmine," he gasped overjoyed. "I thought you were dead."

She uncertainly returned the embrace, although she found his sudden concern for her out of character. "For a moment there, so did I."

Collin looked at Rob and Shelly. "Are we it?"

Davis appeared on the stairs and casually walked down them. "I'm still here," he announced with little enthusiasm. "It got Rita. Fucker came down through a vent in the ceiling."

"Has anyone seen Max?" Jasmine asked with concern.

They all shook their heads. Jasmine lowered her head and rubbed her arms insecurely.

Rob placed an arm around Jasmine's shoulder and pulled her to his side. "I'm sorry, Jasmine."

"Maybe we should hunt the bastard down and take care of him first," Davis announced.

"Bad plan," Collin remarked. "We tried that once and it ended in disaster."

"This time will be different," Davis informed him. "You guys went down there at night. We know what we're dealing with now. He's resting during the day."

"Resting, maybe, but we don't know that he's incapacitated," Collin lashed out. "He may be able to function just fine in the darkness of the cargo area."

"What's our plan?" Rob asked.

"You have to drive a stake through his heart and cut off his head," Collin informed them.

"Doesn't sound too difficult," Rob muttered while making a face.

"I'll help you sharpen some wooden poles, but I'm not going back down there," Collin insisted. "I'll wait with Shelly and Jasmine in the chapel."

41

"We'll need someplace secure for tonight," Davis announced. "I don't know that I trust the chapel."

"I do," Collin informed him without hesitation. "That's where we're going."

"We'll meet you there before dark," Rob replied.

# Chapter Seven

That evening, Jasmine and Shelly paced the chapel while Collin sharpened the cross staff pole, creating the perfect weapon. Both women were growing concerned as it got later and later. Soon it would be dark. Rob and Davis were gone the entire afternoon, and the women were convinced something went wrong. If the guys had gotten themselves killed, those within the chapel would have no way of knowing. Jasmine's thoughts again strayed to Max. If he survived, he should have responded to the lobby call Rob put out that morning. He'd been gone nearly twenty-four hours, and her heart sank with the realization that he wasn't coming back.

"It's going to be dark soon," Shelly spoke what was on their minds. "They should've been back by now."

"We can't go after them," Collin informed her without even looking up from his work.

Jasmine leaned against the chapel doorway and stared at Collin several feet away. She wanted to argue with him, but they wouldn't even make it to the cargo hold before dark let alone have any time to search for the missing men. She reluctantly turned back toward the doorway and nearly collided with Max. Jasmine let out a startled scream then felt relief sweep over her. She threw her arms around him and hugged him gratefully.

"Oh, Max," she cried out. "I was so worried."

Max half-heartedly returned the hug. Jasmine pulled back and looked at him for the first time. He was pale and weak. She gently touched his cold and clammy face and immediately became concerned by his condition.

"Are you okay?"

Max attempted a weak smile. "Not really."

Jasmine led him into the chapel and helped him onto the back pew. He'd managed to change clothes again, indicating he'd been hiding in one of the guestrooms.

Jasmine fussed over him as she sat alongside him. "Can I get you anything?"

Max pulled her to his side and studied her. "No, I'm just glad you're okay," he announced in a voice that conveyed his weakened state. "That's all that matters."

Collin slowly approached and eyed Max with a strange look. "Did it injure you?"

"Just a scratch on my shoulder," he replied. "I doped myself up in the doctor's office."

"Maybe I should have a look at the scratches," Jasmine announced and reached for his shoulder.

"Later," he insisted. "I just changed the dressing on it. I gave myself a shot of something not so friendly. Knocked me out most of the day."

Collin and Shelly exchanged concerned looks.

Max noticed their looks and turned defensive. "The scratches are healing," he firmly remarked. "I'm tired, but I'm fine."

Jasmine clung to Max's neck. He held her against him, smiled, and shut his eyes. Davis and Rob entered the chapel with disgusted looks on their faces.

"That place is a fucking maze down there," Davis announced with frustration.

Both eyed Max, surprised to see him. Jasmine pulled away from Max and looked at both men, glad they'd made it back in one piece.

"Max," Rob announced. "You're alive."

"Just barely," Max teased. "Where were you?"

"In the cargo hold," Rob replied. "There's no way we'll ever find him in there. Dark, congested, and disorganized." He stared at Max suspiciously. "You look like hell."

"Thanks."

"You weren't bit, were you?" Davis demanded.

Jasmine uncertainly eyed Max and waited for his response along with the others.

"He scratched me on the shoulder," Max again insisted then stood, becoming hostile. "We're lucky to be alive, no thanks to you, you bastard!"

"What are you talking about?" Davis demanded.

"You know damned well what I'm talking about," Max snarled. "You locked us in the gym with that thing to save your own ass." He then looked at Jasmine. "I have to go. I'm not feeling well enough to deal with him."

Jasmine followed Max to the doorway. "There's no place else to go, Max."

"I'll be fine," Max informed her. "The captain's cabin is pretty secure. I just wanted to make sure you were all right."

Max touched her face and stared at her a moment. He leaned closer and gently kissed her on the lips. As he pulled away, Jasmine stared at him a long moment and fidgeted.

"I'm going with you."

"Jasmine--" Rob warned.

Jasmine clung to Max's arm and stared into his blue eyes. "I want to stay with you, Max. I need to know that you're okay."

He offered a warm smile and gently patted her hand on his arm.

§

Max sat on the sofa in the captain's cabin with his left sleeve rolled up and injected a dose of Morphine into his arm. He grimaced then set down the needle. Jasmine sat alongside him and helped roll down his sleeve. She cast a timid look at him.

"Can I look at your injury?"

Max forced a tiny, knowing smile. "It's bad, Jasmine," he informed her. "I don't think I'm going to make it, but I think you already knew that."

Jasmine stared at him with a horrified look in her eyes. "What? No, you're going to be fine. Don't talk so--"

"Please, Jasmine," he replied timidly. "My arm is tingling, and the wound won't stop bleeding. I just wanted to see you one last time." He touched her face while staring into her eyes. "I love you, Jasmine. I just wanted you to know that. Please, go back to the chapel before it gets dark."

"No, Max," she announced firmly. "You won't die. You can't." Jasmine placed her arms around his neck and buried her face into his chest. She sobbed softly as Max held her against him. "I love you, Max. Please don't leave me. You promised."

45

Max removed an envelope from his jacket and extended it to her. She refused to accept it.

"I want you to give this to my friend, Benson," he insisted. "His name is on the envelope. He'll take care of you for me. I promise."

"No, you won't die."

"Jasmine, please," he announced gently. "Don't do this." He set the envelope down on the coffee table and looked into her eyes. "Don't make it harder than it already is."

Jasmine leaned toward him and kissed him gently on the lips. He responded without hesitation. Despite her tears, she kissed him more passionately and with added aggression.

Max responded eagerly then pulled away. "I'll walk you back to the chapel."

Jasmine once more leaned against him and kissed him, this time with more aggression. Max clung to her and helplessly returned the passionate kiss.

§

Max and Jasmine were naked and united beneath the sheets on the bed within the captain's quarters. As Max kissed her neck and pressed against her, Jasmine gasped softly and held back her tears of sorrow, fearing she'd lose him. She warmly kissed his neck and attempted to push the thought of him dying from her mind. Max moaned softly and shut his eyes to the sensation of her lips on his neck. His lips parting slightly as he gasped, exposing sharpened fangs. He lowered his mouth to her shoulder, his fangs close to her skin, then closed his lips and warmly kissed her neck.

After their intense lovemaking, Jasmine rested her head on Max's chest while he securely held her in his arms. He stiffly flexed his wrapped right arm and shoulder.

Jasmine eyed his movement and became concerned. "Are you okay?"

Max smiled warmly and gently kissed her forehead. "I'm wonderful."

"You're feeling better?" she asked with some surprise.

"Actually, I'm feeling much better," he announced. "That last Morphine shot must have done the trick."

Max suddenly rolled on top of her and kissed her warmly. She returned the kiss with a pleased smile.

"Oh, Max--"

She kissed his neck as his hands disappeared beneath the covers. Max groaned softly. Jasmine pulled back, opened her eyes, and saw the fangs in his mouth. Before she had time to express her alarm, he kissed her passionately on the mouth and pressed against her beneath the covers. Jasmine jumped with surprise and anxiety. Max met her gaze and grinned timidly while partially exposing the fangs.

"Sorry," he replied. "I was trying to be gentle."

Jasmine forced a tiny smile despite her concern. "It's okay."

As he lowered his mouth to her neck, Jasmine suddenly tensed and let out a soft gasp. She felt him gently kiss her neck and throat, grateful he hadn't bitten her.

"I love you so much," he whispered.

Jasmine shut her eyes and clung to him, not wanting to let go as he moved against her. "I love you too," she whispered and fought her tears at the thought of his fate.

# Chapter Eight

Max stood in the chapel doorway while holding Jasmine's hand in his. The remaining survivors stood near the altar and talked quietly among themselves while casting stray looks at the couple by the doorway. Jasmine was almost certain they were keeping their distance from Max because they didn't trust him. She didn't care how they felt. She didn't want to leave him.

"Max, please change your mind and stay," she begged, feeling concern for his safety.

Max lowered his head and fidgeted uncomfortably. He then lifted his eyes and met her gaze with a serious look. "You saw, didn't you?"

She fidgeted slightly. "Yes."

Max ran his tongue over the sharp fangs then smiled, appearing tense. "Do they make me look more intelligent?"

"You knew you were converting, didn't you?"

"Not until after," he announced defensively. "I truly thought I was dying. I wouldn't have subjected you to that, had I known." He drew a deep breath then sighed. "The scratches are almost completely healed now, but an hour ago, they were black. I swear I wouldn't have taken advantage of you if I'd known. This is my last chance to protect you. I'd like you to remember me that way and not as a half-crazed bloodsucker. I'm afraid something will happen. I'm afraid I'll become like that creature and try to hurt you." He touched her face. "I'll always love you. That's how I want to be remembered."

Max quickly kissed her, turned, and walked away before she could protest. Jasmine held back her tears.

Collin slowly approached her and stood only a few feet away. "He was bitten, wasn't he?"

Jasmine broke down and cried.

Collin uncertainly placed his arms around her. "I'm really sorry, Jasmine," he announced gently. "I wish there was something I could say, but there isn't. Anything short of killing the master--" Collin suddenly became silent as if realizing he'd said something inappropriate.

Jasmine pulled away, vigorously wiped her eyes, and stared at him. "What was that?"

He stared back at her with concern and shook his head. "Nothing. There's nothing anyone can do."

"No," she protested. "You said something about killing the master. Are you suggesting that if the one that bit him dies, he might return to normal?"

"That is so much a myth, even I can't believe it could be real," he attempted to explain.

"But if Max kills the vampire--?"

"He becomes the master," Collin informed her. "That's also a myth."

Her eyes widened with realization. "If I kill the master, I can save him."

"I know I didn't say that," Collin immediately protested. "What you're considering is suicide."

§

Ten minutes to sundown. Jasmine hurried through the cargo hold, clutching the ax and the sharpened cross staff in her hands while keeping alert to everything around her. She looked at her watch several times and knew it was possible the vampire was already up and about. She could be setting herself up for slaughter, but she had to risk it. The cargo hold was a maze of crates and aisles. She didn't know where she was going or the fastest way to get there. She looked around with concern and anger in her eyes. A foul odor caused her to stop. She turned to her right and walked down another aisle. Jasmine made a disgusted face and held her hand over her nose and mouth.

"What's that smell--?"

As she approached, she saw piles of dead, decaying bodies of those killed over the last few days. She was more alarmed by what she saw beyond those bodies. Jasmine grimaced while keeping her nose and mouth covered as she walked across several bodies and severed limbs. As she got closer, she saw an antique coffin on top of several crates in the center of the bloodbath. Jasmine nearly stepped on Rita's body. She suddenly gasped with surprise and horror at the sight of the familiar woman. She composed herself and approached the coffin with determination. Jasmine climbed on top of the crates and pulled open the coffin lid. She saw the hideous vampire creature in his coffin with its eyes closed.

Jasmine set the ax on one of the crates she teetered upon and raised the cross staff above her head. The creature's eyes suddenly open and it leaped up, knocking her off balance. Jasmine cried out and fell onto the pile of decaying bodies. Several rats scurried away with loud, annoyed squeaks. Jasmine recovered the staff and scrambled to her feet, stumbling over the decomposing bodies. The vampire glided down from his coffin and nearly landed on top of her. Jasmine cried out and bolted away from him, having reached a solid footing beyond the piled bodies. She spun with the cross raised, but he was gone. Jasmine looked around the dimly lit cargo area. Shadows were alongside crates, on the ceiling, and within the bodies. He could be lurking anywhere! Jasmine clutched the staff, keeping the cross exposed.

A shadow moved behind her, but she didn't see it. Jasmine nervously scanned the area before her. The shadow moved closer to her from behind. Jasmine suddenly whirled around with the staff positioned, cross up. Max stood before her. He turned and lowered his head to avoid looking at the cross, as if in pain. Max attempted to look at her but was unable.

"What are you doing down here, Jasmine?" he demanded. "You have to go back with the others."

"I can save you, Max."

Max placed his hand over his eyes to shield them. "Do something with that. It's giving me a terrible headache."

Jasmine nervously looked around then lowered the staff, allowing Max to lift his head and meet her gaze.

"If I can kill the vampire, you'll be restored to normal," she informed him. "If *you* kill him, you're stuck."

"And if he kills you, then what?" He touched her face. "I appreciate what you're doing for me, Jasmine, but I can't stand the thought of you dying because of me."

Max followed through with a gentle kiss to her lips. He pulled back, met her gaze, and then returned for a more passionate kiss. Jasmine attempted to hold him back. In one swift movement, he knocked the staff from her hand and pushed her on top of a nearby crate. Jasmine managed to break off the kiss.

"Max, stop!"

Max kissed her despite her protest then pulled back just far enough to meet her gaze and smiled charmingly through his fangs.

"What's wrong, Jasmine?" he asked in a mocking tone. "Don't you want me?"

Jasmine was now nervous. "Of course I do, but there's a killer vampire nearby."

Max released Jasmine and turned toward the area covered with piled bodies. He casually folded his arms across his chest. "This is cozy. Not much of a housekeeper."

Jasmine recovered her staff then indicated the crates. "Can you get that ax?"

Max approached the crates, playfully skipping between the bodies with a lively step. He balanced on one foot and snatched the ax. Max turned and skipped back through the bodies while eyeing them as he hummed a lively tune.

"Hmm, suddenly I'm very hungry."

Jasmine made a face and held her stomach. The vampire suddenly dropped down behind her. She felt a slight gust of air and spun around. The vampire struck her across the face with his right, clawless hand. She hit the crates and fell to the floor slightly dazed. The staff flew several feet away from her. Max hissed and charged for the vampire, dropping the ax to the floor and nearly striking Jasmine. He tackled the vampire into several crates. Despite being excessively heavy, the crates crashed to the floor beneath them. Max hovered over the now stronger vampire. Both held each other's throat in their hands. The vampire pulled Max closer to him then cast him off and across the room. Max was propelled backward into the crates and the coffin. All three crashed to the floor. The vampire easily sprang to his feet. Jasmine and the ax were gone.

The vampire looked around and smelled the air then approached some nearby crates. Jasmine jumped around the crates behind him with the ax coiled back. As the vampire spun, Jasmine swung the ax and severed his right, clawless hand. She was surprised that she had missed and attempted to swing again. The vampire knocked the ax from her hands and lunged for her throat. Max suddenly leaped gracefully through the air and tackled the vampire into another stack of crates.

They flung each other around while hissing and growling like wild animals. Max bit the vampire at the base of the neck. The vampire squealed and attempted to force Max off him, but he refused to take his teeth from the creature. Max suddenly kneed the vampire in the groin, causing him tremendous pain and pulled his teeth free, giving the vampire just enough time to slash him across the chest. Max leaped back with surprise and pain. The vampire caught Max by the throat, sinking his claws into his neck. Max cried out and struggled against the claws in his flesh. Without releasing him, the vampire shoved Max backward and against several crates while keeping his claws tight on his throat.

Jasmine grabbed the ax, ran alongside them, and cried out with anger and fury. "No!"

She swung the ax and severed the vampire's head. The head flew across the cargo bay and landed near the dead bodies. The vampire frantically clutched at his stump giving Max the opportunity to shove him away. The eyes on the severed head looked at Max, allowing the body to follow through and lunge for him. Max dove out of his path and grabbed Jasmine by the arm, pulling her several feet away. The vampire's head continued to watch. The body charged for them as the head cried out with a hideous, animal like sound.

Collin suddenly sprang out from an aisle with the cross staff in his hands. He lunged forward and plunged the sharpened end into the vampire's chest. The head cried out in agony as the body was tackled to the ground with the cross sticking out on top of the pole. Collin grabbed either side of the cross and pushed down with his entire body. The spear made a distinct crunching sound just before striking the floor on the bottom. The creature's head wailed. The headless body's limbs flailed several times then became motionless. The head gasped and the eyes rolled back. Collin panted and slowly backed away from the body.

Jasmine looked at Max as he clutched the deep scratches on his chest. The scratches slowly faded along with his fangs. Max sank to his knees and clutched his head in agony. Jasmine fell to her knees alongside him and attempted to look at him.

"Max! Max, are you all right?"

He groaned while clutching his head with both hands. "One hell of a hangover."

Collin approached them and studied the tormented man. "He'll probably be weak for a day or two," he remarked. "Let's get him upstairs so he can rest."

Collin and Jasmine pulled Max to his feet and half carried him from the cargo hold.

# Chapter Nine

Max slowly woke to sunlight flooding into the bedroom of the Presidential Suite. He uncertainly looked around then saw Jasmine sitting on the edge of the bed alongside him. She touched his face and smiled warmly.

"How are you feeling?"

"Sore," he replied with a groan. "Where am I?"

"The Presidential Suite," she proudly announced. "On our way home. You've been out for two days."

Max touched his teeth and appeared relieved. "Oh, thank God," he gasped. "I had some pretty nasty dreams." He eyed her with concern. "The others?"

"They're around."

"Oh, so it's just us alone in the Presidential Suite?"

Before she could answer, Max pulled her over him and onto the bed alongside him. Jasmine cried out playfully. Max rolled on top of her and kissed her passionately.

Max and Jasmine walked along the main deck in the bright sunshine of the gorgeous, warm morning. Jasmine clung to Max's arm with a contented smile. Collin approached them with a young, female Coast Guard officer attached to his arm.

"And I killed the vampire single-handed with my staff," Collin announced with vigor.

The woman smiled lustfully while clinging to him. "I'd like to see that staff."

Collin grinned and laughed softly. He then seemed to realize they had company. They paused before Max and Jasmine. "This cruise is finally starting to get exciting."

"I've had enough excitement, thanks," Jasmine replied.

Collin laughed then continued onward with his attractive Coast Guard officer. Max and Jasmine continued on their stroll in the opposite direction.

"Before reality returns us home, I have a small confession to make," Max announced.

Jasmine eyed him and immediately became concerned. "You're not married, are you?"

Max suddenly stopped, completely ignoring her comment, and stared with surprise at the helicopter on the landing pad. He immediately frowned.

"Oh, great."

Rob approached them from behind and slapped Max on the back. "Max, good to see you up and about," he announced. "We were worried."

Max looked back at Rob and offered a humored but distracted smirk. "I'm a tough bastard." He then looked back at the helicopter with the same concerned expression.

"You're a bastard all right," a man suddenly announced from behind him.

Max turned and came face-to-face with Benson, a well-dressed, distinguished looking man in his late forties. Despite his expensive, worn casual wear, he looked as if he'd be more at home in jeans and sneakers.

Max smiled almost meekly. "Benson, what are you--?"

"You crazy son-of-a-bitch," Benson lashed out. "You know you're not licensed to fly, and my insurance won't cover whatever it is you did to my helicopter."

"Not me," Max protested. "Someone stole it."

"Oh, right," Benson scoffed. "Someone stole it *after* you stole it."

"I had to come out and get you," Max insisted. "No one else would fly."

"You're absolutely crazy," Benson muttered. He then shook his head with disgust. "Some cruise that was. Sat in a lifeboat, filled with men I might add, for several days until the Coast Guard found us."

Max grinned timidly then indicated Jasmine. "Benson, this is Jasmine," he announced. "I'm taking her home with me."

Benson stared at Jasmine with surprise. His mood immediately improved. "Thank you, Lord," he cried out then grinned. "Back to sleeping in late."

Jasmine looked at both men with an odd stare. "What's going on?"

"You seemed to like me as a flyboy," Max replied while attempting to hide his embarrassed smile. "I didn't want to ruin that image. All my life, I've been told how to act, who to like, who to date, what to wear. I realized, one day, that I never had *real* friends. Three years ago, I walked away from my life. I wanted to find people who liked me for me, not for status and wealth."

Jasmine stared at him with a strange look. "So who are you then?"

"William Maxwell Kensington."

Rob suddenly bolted forward and nearly knocked Jasmine over. "You knew I was coming out here to see you! Why didn't you say something?"

"Because I didn't want to be bothered with business deals," Max informed him.

"I'd have a bit of fun playing him," Benson confessed. "He booked this trip for me because he knew I needed to get away from him for a while. That's before other passengers started hounding me about business." He glared at Max. "Still no reason to steal my helicopter."

"Benson's my pilot and driver," Max confessed.

"Listen, Max," Rob announced, turning all buddy buddy on him. "We really need to talk."

"I'm not interested, Rob," Max replied then turned to Jasmine. "Let's just go home." He then looked at Benson and grinned. "I'll fly."

Benson glared at him. "Like hell you will," he scoffed. "Get your pampered, rich boy ass into that chopper! I want my ass home in one piece!"

Max laughed as they approached the helicopter on the landing pad. Benson climbed into the pilot's seat while Max opened the back door for Jasmine.

Jasmine looked at him and smiled. "Tell me something, Max. Down in the cargo hold, did you really intend to bite me?"

He chuckled softly and grinned. "I still might."

Jasmine laughed and climbed into the helicopter. Rob waved them off then frowned with disgust and walked away. Max looked back at the ship and smiled, revealing small fangs. He ran his tongue over the pointed fangs, smirked, and then climbed into the back alongside Jasmine. As he shut the door behind them, the helicopter lifted off from the landing pad.

# The End

# Ravenous

# Chapter One

The dark, wooded back road in the middle of nowhere was barely passable as the rain continued to pour down on the dreary night. A black car cautiously traveled the treacherous road. Kate Harford strained to see out the windshield as the wipers rapidly passed over the glass. Kate was an attractive woman with long, copper colored hair. She'd been dressed for a casual evening out with some friends at the movie theater in the nearest city, which was quite a distance from her small hometown. Getting home in the storm at night was becoming a bit of a challenge, making her regret the decision to go out on such a night. She passed an old car parked alongside the road with a flat tire. Kate stared at the license plate on the car and noted the two passengers seeking refuge inside.

"Oh, my God, that's Judy's car," Kate said aloud to herself.

She pulled over to the side of the road just before the parked car. A man in his mid to late twenties got out of the disabled vehicle and ran up to her driver's side window in the pouring rain. Kate lowered her window and looked at the unfamiliar, already drenched man.

"We got a flat tire and ran into that ditch," the man informed her above the loud rain.

"I work with Judy," Kate announced, nearly getting soaked from her open window. "Would you guys like a lift to town?"

"That'd be great," the man replied then motioned toward the passenger in the car behind her.

A woman in her early to mid-twenties got out of the car and ran through the pouring rain to join him. Judy jumped into the back as the man rounded the car and hopped into the front passenger side. Both were completely soaked from just those few minutes in the pouring rain.

"Kate," Judy gasped with relief while breathing heavily from her short dash, "I'm so glad you happened along."

"You're lucky--on a night like tonight," Kate informed her.

Kate pulled onto the road and continued her slow journey in the bad weather.

"Have you met my boyfriend?" Judy asked while leaning forward from the back seat.

"No, I don't believe I have," Kate replied and looked briefly at the wet man in the passenger seat.

"Randy, this is Kate, a friend from work," Judy announced cheerfully.

Kate and Randy exchanged pleasantries. Randy wasn't what Kate would consider attractive by any means, although he was obviously Judy's type. He was built fairly muscular, had several visible tattoos, and wore a leather jacket. She often went for the bad boy type, and Randy fit the bill. Judging by the scowl on his face, he wasn't the most pleasant of men either. Judy, on the other hand, always maintained such an innocent look. She was a petite blonde woman with innocent, trusting eyes. Always friendly and polite, it seemed odd she chose men with extremely dominating personalities and the occasional anger issues.

"Is there someplace in town I could take you?" Kate asked. "I don't think there'll be any garages open this time of night."

"My brother has a garage on the corner of Main Street," Judy replied. "He lives upstairs. He can tow my car back to town tonight."

"Great," Kate said and offered a tiny smile. "At least things are looking up considering all that's happened to you tonight."

"It's been one hell of a night," Judy said and collapsed against the back seat. "I got into a fight with my mother, and she threw me out."

Kate appeared surprised and briefly eyed her co-worker through the rearview mirror. "Oh, that's terrible. Will you be able to stay with your brother?"

"Randy and I decided it was a good time to look for a place of our own," Judy announced simply. "We were actually on our way to Montana. Randy has some friends who live out there."

"Looks like our plans were ruined by that piece of shit car of yours," he remarked lowly.

"My brother will have it up and running by tomorrow afternoon," Judy informed him simply. "Montana's not going anywhere."

"I don't want to stay another night in this area," Randy snapped as his agitation increased. "If I have to hear from your mother one more time, I'll kill her."

Judy looked out the side window and ignored the comment. Kate continued to concentrate on the barely visible road ahead, but she glanced at Randy after the comment. They rode in silence for several minutes. Kate was feeling uneasy with the silence, particularly knowing the foul mood of the man alongside her. His silence made her uncomfortable. Randy stared out the side window and watched the darkness of the woods without saying a word. He finally straightened in the passenger seat and looked sharply at Kate.

"Stop here," he announced in a gruff tone.

Kate glanced at him with a puzzled look and didn't particularly care for his tone. "What? Why?" she asked with surprise.

He pulled a gun from his pocket and aimed it at her. Kate looked from the gun to Randy with near shock. His expression was hard and cold.

"Because I said so," he growled lowly.

Judy quickly sat up in the back seat and stared at her boyfriend with a look of horror. "Randy, what are you doing?" she gasped.

"We're getting out of here tonight," he snapped without looking back at her. "And we're taking this car." His eyes burned through Kate. "Now stop the car!"

Kate stared at the barely visible road ahead of her. Her body trembled. What did he intend to do with her? She knew who they were and where they were going. Judy sat forward from the back seat and smacked Randy on the shoulder.

"Put that thing away! I know her!" Judy cried out in anger, although Kate could feel her fear. Even Judy didn't know what he intended to do with Kate.

Kate shifted looks from the man and woman to the road before her. Randy began yelling at Judy and a shouting match commenced. Kate saw the winding road up ahead and allowed several scenarios play out in her mind while the couple remained preoccupied with their arguing.

"Your mother will have the police on us before we can even get back to the car," Randy lashed out. "Don't think she wouldn't hesitate pressing charges against you as well!"

"Kate," Judy announced in a timid but concerned tone. "He won't hurt you. Pull over. I promise he won't hurt you."

Kate glanced back at Judy through the rearview mirror. She no longer saw the young girl she worked with; she saw a desperate woman who'd done something irreversible. It occurred to Kate at that moment, despite what Judy said Randy was going to kill her. Kate pressed her foot down on the accelerator as she approached the sharp, steep curve.

"Pull over!" Randy shouted in anger while waving the gun. "Pull over or I'll shoot you right now!"

Now as opposed to later? By his comment, her fears were verified. The car took the sharp turn at fifty miles an hour and slid around the curve on the wet road, barely keeping the tires on the pavement. Both Randy and Judy were tossed around the seat.

"What the hell do you think you're doing?" Randy yelled in anger.

Kate looked sharply at Randy with no emotion in her eyes. "Driver's side airbag," she replied curtly.

She didn't take her eyes off him as the tree became clearer before them. Randy saw the tree and screamed as the car slammed head on into it. There was a tremendous crack. Kate was thrown back against the seat as the airbag exploded in a cloud of white dust. Randy flew forward and struck the windshield then was thrown back, appearing dazed. Judy was thrown forward into the back of the passenger seat then across the back seat. Kate gasped after the initial shock. Her ears rang and her body tingled. Despite the hard crash and his bleeding head, Randy managed to keep the gun in his hand. He looked at her with a slightly dazed expression, realized what had happened, and aimed the gun at her. Kate gasped while releasing her seatbelt and opened the door. She fell from the driver's seat and onto the muddy ground near the woods. A gunshot echoed directly behind her. Despite her mild disorientation, Kate scrambled to her feet and ran into the woods.

"You bitch," Randy could be heard screaming from the car as he struggled to get out. "I'll kill you!"

Kate ran through the darkened woods, sliding on the muddy ground, and tripping over rocks. Randy's yelling became faint. She slowed down to a fast walk and looked behind her. The rain continued to pour down. Thankfully, she wasn't being followed. She continued further into the woods, attempting to figure out where she was and the best way to return to the road. She had to avoid the man who would most certainly kill her the next time he saw her. The ground suddenly gave out beneath her feet. Kate slipped down the three-foot bank and splashed into a heavily flowing stream. She sprang to her feet in the waist deep water and looked around while removing her wet hair from her face. Although she had no idea where she was or which way to go, downstream seemed the most logical direction. It had to lead somewhere. She crossed the stream and crawled up the muddy bank to the opposite side.

# Chapter Two

Kate walked for nearly half an hour along the bank of the stream. The cold, wet rain washed most of the mud from her hands, face, and clothes. She hadn't seen any sign of life and was just about ready to give up hope when she saw a distant light up ahead. Kate briskly walked in the direction of the light. She no longer cared what sort of light source she followed; she was just happy to see any sign of life. She approached an open field and paused at the woods' edge. A rather large, impressive mansion sat nestled in the middle of the large clearing. The interior, as well as the exterior, were well lit. Music could be heard coming from within the mansion walls. It was sweet relief. Kate jogged across the estate grounds toward the back of the mansion. As she got closer, she realized she heard the sounds of a party. She approached the back door and promptly knocked on it. Within a few minutes, the door was opened by an older man in a butler's uniform. He studied her a moment then raised his gray brows with surprise.

"Do come in, madam," the butler announced with some show of concern.

Kate stepped into the back mudroom and shivered from her soaked clothes. The butler closed the door behind her and again studied her.

"I need to call the police," she gasped while attempting to warm herself. "It's urgent."

The butler stared at her a moment as if unable to comprehend her statement. "Can I get you a drink? You look as though you could use one." He gave her a quick once over. "Perhaps some dry clothes?"

Kate slowly nodded while continuing to shiver.

"If you'd follow me," the butler announced, "I'll take you to one of the back rooms where you can change out of those wet things."

The butler turned and left the mudroom. Kate hesitantly followed him then looked down at the white marble floor and the trail of mud she was leaving.

He noted her look and offered a tiny smile. "Don't worry," he announced. "It's easily cleaned."

The butler, Parker, seemed so proper despite her appearance and mysterious arrival at his back door. Parker was a thin, older man, although he appeared sturdy beneath his expensive, black butler attire. He was rather attractive for a man in his sixties. They walked halfway across the kitchen when a handsome man, possibly in his thirties, wearing a hand tailored tuxedo entered through a set of swinging doors.

"Parker," the handsome man announced as he entered without even looking. "Where's that champagne?" The man saw Kate and stopped abruptly in his tracks. His surprised look was quickly replaced with a warm, pleasant smile. "Sorry, Parker. I hadn't realized you were taking care of another guest." The man approached Kate and looked her over through pale blue eyes. "Ralin Brucker," he announced and extended his hand.

Kate extended a trembling, dirty hand. She looked at her hand then pulled it back with embarrassment. "Kate Harford," she replied timidly.

Ralin was possibly the most handsome man she'd seen in a long time. He was nearly six foot tall, and although not excessively muscular, he was built sturdy. He had dark brown almost black hair trimmed business short and a bronze complexion. His cologne was mild but almost intoxicating. For a moment, Kate almost forgot her traumatic evening and thought about how frightful she looked. She then remembered her near death experience and forgot about the handsome man standing before her.

Ralin looked at Parker while maintaining his cheerful demeanor. "Draw the young lady a bath and find her something suitable to change into." Ralin looked back at Kate and tilted his head in question. "What exactly happened to you?" he asked with a tiny smile. "And how on Earth did you end up on my doorstep?"

"It's a long story," Kate replied gently. "I need to contact the police. I crashed my car, and there's a dangerous man following me."

Ralin appeared intrigued then turned protective. "You'll be safe here," he announced then laughed in his throat, finding something funny in his comment. "I promise you that."

"Can I use your phone?" she asked with a little more insistence. "I don't have my cell phone. I left it in the car."

Ralin stared at her in the same manner as Parker had. A tiny smile then crossed his face. "Actually, I don't believe in phones," he replied simply. "I doubt you'd get cell service this far out anyway. Parker will see that you're made comfortable, find you something appropriate to wear, and give you a room for the night. Tomorrow morning, we'll see you safely to town or where ever it is you wish to go."

"Isn't there some way to contact town?" Kate asked with a look of concern. "I really need to notify the police. That man--"

"As long as you're here, you don't need to worry about *that man*," Ralin stated simply. "The best thing for you is to stay here until morning."

"There was another woman in the car who might be hurt," Kate attempted to explain. "She may need an ambulance."

"Who's the other woman?" Ralin asked while raising a curious brow.

Kate hesitated. "A co-worker of mine."

"A friend of the man who's chasing you?" he asked simply.

Kate nodded.

Ralin forced a tiny smile. "I don't think she requires your concern. Helping her may bring further harm to you."

As callus as his comment sounded, he was right. Judy didn't deserve her concern.

"I suggest a nice, hot bath and a change of clothing," Ralin announced cheerfully as if a bubble bath would solve all the world's problems. "I'll be back to check on you in an hour."

Parker approached with a bottle of champagne. Ralin took the bottle and left the kitchen. Parker turned to Kate and extended his hand toward the staff wing.

"This way, madam."

Despite the oddly concerned feeling tingling through her body, Kate didn't seem to have much choice at the moment. She reluctantly gave in and followed the butler. A hot bath did sound inviting.

§

Kate dried her hair as she left the bathroom and entered the bedroom portion of the servant's room while wearing a borrowed robe. A black evening dress lay across the bed along with a pair of high heels. Kate eyed the dress with concern then looked around the bland room.

"What sort of place is this?" she asked softly to herself. There was a gentle tap on the door. Kate quickly approached the door and opened it. An older woman in a maid's uniform stood in the doorway with a pleasant smile on her plump face.

"Lord Brucker sent me to assist you, madam," the maid said in a husky voice.

"Lord Brucker?" Kate muttered with surprise. She allowed the woman to enter the room and closed the door behind her. "I don't understand what's going on around here. Why did you bring an evening dress?"

"His Lordship thought you'd feel better if you attended the party," the maid replied cheerfully and approached the gown. She turned to face Kate and eyed her sympathetically. "I do hope you're feeling better after your ordeal--poor child."

Kate's head was swimming. She shook her head and looked back at the woman. "I'd feel better if I could notify the police. It's been a long night already."

"You're perfectly safe here," the maid replied simply and picked up the gown. She turned to face Kate while collecting the gown to slip over Kate's head. "Save those unpleasant matters for the morning."

Kate stared at the pleasant woman and marveled at her sincerity. It was possible the older woman had never been unhappy a day in her life.

"*His Lordship* would be disappointed if I didn't attend, wouldn't he?" Kate questioned while raising a curious brow.

"Oh, very," the maid replied dramatically.

Kate nodded then rubbed her temple. "This is a bad sign," she muttered softly but then considered something. A party meant many people. Someone would have a cell phone she could borrow. They couldn't all feel the same way about phones as *Lord* Brucker. "What *sort* of party is he hosting?"

The maid became giddy with glee. "His sister just married. We're all very excited, even if she did marry an outsider."

It was an odd comment, but Kate brushed it aside. Apparently, she was attending a wedding reception whether she wanted to or not.

# Chapter Three

Kate sat before the vanity while the maid, Helana, fixed her hair in a French twist. Kate applied some makeup and watched the older woman behind her applying bobby pin after bobby pin to hold her hair in place.

"Plenty of single men downstairs," Helana chirped pleasantly. "I noticed you weren't wearing a ring."

"After the night I've had, I'm not really in the mood to manhunt," Kate said simply.

"You'll change your mind, I promise," Helana said with a giggle. "Very refined, prominent men. All well-off, if I may say so."

"Tell me about Lord Brucker," Kate said and eyed the woman through the mirror for a reaction.

Helana's expression didn't change. She cheerfully continued to apply bobby pins to Kate's hair. "Oh, His Lordship is a fine catch, indeed! He's so handsome, don't you think? Of course you do, or you wouldn't have enquired about him."

Kate shook her head, giving up. Helana had romance on the brain, and she wasn't about to change gears. There was a gentle knock on the door. Helana bounced excitedly.

"Oh, that's his Lordship now to escort you to the party," Helana announced and hurried toward the door. "It's so exciting!"

"Confusing would be the more appropriate term," Kate muttered under her breath then stood and turned toward the door as Helana opened it.

Ralin stood before the door and smiled when he saw Kate. "I'm glad you've decided to join the party," he announced cheerfully and extended his hand to her.

Kate walked toward him and wondered if she really had a choice. She smiled despite her reluctance and accepted his hand. Ralin linked her hand onto his arm and escorted her down the hall, through the kitchen, and toward the ballroom. Two servants, bowing politely, opened the massive, double doors. The reception was filled with well-dressed men and women dancing to a live orchestra. The room was decorated to the highest standard for an elegant wedding reception. The area was filled with flowers and round tables lining the walls. The orchestra played on a stage at the far end of the ballroom before a wall of glass. In the center of the amazing room, the bride and groom danced. They were an attractive, lovely, young couple. She looked like a fairy tale princess in her expensive dress, and him, her prince charming. Kate and Ralin received several stares as they entered the ballroom. Parker approached them with two champagne glasses. Kate accepted the glass and attempted a smile. Two men approached them. One man laughed softly and slapped Ralin on the shoulder.

"Couldn't get a date, so you had to kidnap one, eh?" the man announced cheerfully.

The second man laughed. Kate didn't find it funny. It was almost close to the truth. She suddenly felt very uncomfortable.

"Stop; you're frightening her," Ralin remarked while hiding his tiny grin then led her across the ballroom toward the couple, who now stopped dancing. "I'll introduce you to my sister." They paused before the couple.

The fairy tale princess eyed Kate and appeared jovial. "Hardly looks like someone who trekked miles in the mud and rain," Falice remarked.

Ralin laughed softly and turned to Kate. "Kate, this is my sister, Falice. Falice, this is Kate Harford." They politely shook hands.

Her prince finished his conversation with an older woman and turned toward his bride and Kate. He smiled charmingly. "You must be Kate Harford," he announced and shook her hand. "I'm Britton Chase." He released her hand.

Kate studied him, looking for any sign of normalcy. It was odd how everyone already knew her. Had his Lordship announced it to the entire reception hall?

"Have you tried the buffet? These people really know how to throw a party," Britton informed her.

"I haven't," Kate replied gently.

Britton took Kate by the arm, excused himself to Falice, and stole her away from Ralin. "I'll tell you what's best," he announced and led her toward the long buffet table. More than the buffet, Britton seemed to have an agenda, wanting to get her alone. "Ralin said you were in a car accident and walked all the way here. Dumb luck that you actually found this place. Not many people happen by here."

Kate quickly looked at Britton and stopped him halfway to the table. "Where is here? What sort of place is this?" she found herself practically demanding. "How does a man live in the middle of nowhere and not have a phone?"

Britton chuckled in his throat and herded her back in the direction of the buffet table. "Let's just say, it's best not to ask too many questions," he teased. "Ralin Brucker is just *one* of those people you can't describe in a night."

"I've had a long night already, and I'm really not up for the mystery," Kate informed him bluntly. "I have an uneasy feeling about this place."

"They're different, Kate," Britton explained simply and handed her a small, china plate. He then proceeded to place small appetizers on her plate. He considered his comment then laughed in his throat. "Very different but completely harmless."

"Are you sure?" Kate asked nervously.

"I promise," Britton replied and placed more treats on her plate.

There was that phrase again; *I promise.* There was something unsettling about that phrase tonight. Kate looked down at her plate. Britton had filled it with tasty treats, more than she would ever eat.

"Ralin is a recluse in every sense of the word," Britton informed her. "I know exactly how you must have felt stumbling into this place. Everyone is so friendly yet so odd. As an outsider once myself, I just felt it my duty to put your mind at ease. Trust me; you're in the safest place imaginable. Embrace the weird world of Lord Ralin Brucker."

Britton led her back to Falice and Ralin for some pleasant conversation that almost seemed normal. Kate drank most of her champagne and nibbled on one or two of the treats on her plate. Britton helped by picking at several himself. Kate was actually grateful for Britton. He made an uncomfortable situation a little less uncomfortable. Britton and Falice finally made their way through the crowd and continued to socialize, leaving Kate once again alone with Ralin.

He remained attentive and studied her a moment while smiling cheerfully. "Are you feeling better now?" Ralin asked.

"A little, though I think it may just be the champagne," Kate replied and fidgeted nervously.

Ralin studied her a moment longer. "Are you uncomfortable around so many people?"

Kate set her plate down on one of the small tables and finished her champagne. "No, not at all. I'm just a little shaken with everything that's happened. I feel a little helpless."

"Your trauma is over. Everything that you're feeling is phantom," Ralin replied, acting as if nothing bad could touch her in his world. "The car will be fixed, the rain will stop, and life will continue as it always has." A tiny smile crossed his face. "As it is-- if that's how you wish it."

Kate laughed at the comment. "A boring evening at home sounds good to me."

"Care to dance?" he asked warmly while removing her empty champagne glass. Parker breezed past to collect the glass as if perfectly timed.

Kate looked around with some apprehension at the slow dancing couples. She then looked at Ralin. He was possibly the most charming, attractive man she'd seen in a long time. After the night passed and she had time to think about everything, she'd probably kick herself for not taking advantage of the perfect situation. Perhaps she needed to listen to Britton's advice.

"I'd love to," she replied, deciding to make the best of her bad situation.

The evening passed quickly. Ralin and Kate danced most of the night, and she was surprised how much time she'd spent in his company. He told her stories of his sister and Britton and gossiped about his guests. After the first few dances, she felt at home in his arms, almost as if they'd been lifelong lovers. The night was almost like a fairytale evening in an enchanted castle. When the clock struck two in the morning, the music stopped. It was obviously the end of the night for the orchestra. The guests applauded the talented men and women. Parker passed by with two glasses of champagne on a silver platter. Ralin claimed the flutes of champagne. Kate swore Parker could read Ralin's mind.

Ralin handed her one of the glasses and smiled charmingly. "Would you like to take a little walk to unwind?"

Kate nodded with more enthusiasm than she had shown earlier in the evening. She was surprised at the good time she was having with this strange man. All suspicions and concerns seemed to have flowed away with the music. She found herself 'embracing the weird world of Ralin Brucker'.

# Chapter Four

Kate and Ralin walked hand-in-hand through the dimly lit, grand hallway. Ralin indicated the countless suits of armor that lined the hall and explained what time period they were from and what country they originated. Kate wasn't sure if he was just a fascinating man, or if it was just the champagne making it seem that way. She was starting to believe she could listen to his soothing voice for hours.

"So what possesses a man to live in the middle of nowhere without as much as a phone?" Kate asked with a tiny, curious smile. "Just that private, or do you like the seclusion?"

Ralin shrugged slightly and looked along the hallway. "More of preserving a way of life, I suppose."

Kate eyed Ralin with a curious look. "Preserving a way of life? What do you mean?"

Ralin seemed uncomfortable with the conversation. He grinned at the comment. "Sometimes, a little mystery is a good thing."

"You're a strange man, Ralin Brucker," Kate informed him simply. "You're good at avoiding telling me anything personal about yourself."

"That's not true," Ralin replied with a sly grin. "I sleep in silk boxers. What could be more personal than that?" His smile mocked her.

"It's not your boxers that I'm interested in." She looked around the extravagant hallway then looked back at him. "What are you a Lord over? Why no phones? Why the big secret about living in total seclusion?"

Ralin turned to face her while maintaining his grin. He looked into her eyes. "I'll be completely honest with you, Kate," he began gently. "I like you; I like you a lot. But if I were to tell you everything you wanted to know about me, you would be immediately turned off." His smile faded to a smirk. "You'd no doubt turn and run from this house."

Kate stared back at him, her curiosity suddenly piqued. "You barely know me, but you presume to judge my character. What could you possibly be hiding that would be such a turn off? Are you the leader of some underground cult?" she asked with a hint of mockery.

Ralin stared at her with little emotion. Kate searched his eyes and immediately became concerned by his lack of response. She pulled her hand from his.

"That *was* a joke," she announced gently.

"The only way I could possibly explain myself to you, Kate, is if you'd agree to spend several weeks adjusting to my way of life. Once you've gotten to know me, my lifestyle wouldn't shock you nearly as much as it would right now."

Kate backed up a step and slowly shook her head with a nervous look in her eyes. "I'm familiar with cults, Ralin," she informed him firmly. "I'm also aware that remaining here wouldn't be a very good idea."

Ralin took a step toward her. Kate immediately took another step back to keep distance between them.

"You've got the wrong idea," he informed her. "Cult is a strong word."

"What would you call it?" she snapped lowly.

Ralin ran his fingers through his hair and exhaled deeply. "The more I say, the worse you'll think of me," he replied and looked at her with sympathetic eyes. "I just have to hope that you'll decide to take a chance and return after you're gone." Ralin backed away from her with a defeated look upon his face. "I'll have Parker show you to your room and make arrangements for your safe return to town in the morning."

Ralin placed his hands in his pockets, appeared defeated, and walked away from her down the long hall. She watched him until he disappeared around the far corner. Kate released her shaken breath and hurried back to the ballroom. She needed to find someone with a cell phone she could borrow, and she needed to do it fast. She cursed herself for not following through with that plan from the start. Kate practically ran into the ballroom and suddenly froze in the doorway. The entire ballroom was empty! Not just the guests. The buffet tables, reception decorations, band, and the guests were all gone. The room was completely cleaned without a trace of the party having taken place just twenty minutes ago. Kate took several steps into the ballroom and looked around with surprise and possible horror. She then felt a presence behind her. Kate spun with a startled gasp and came face-to-face with Parker. She sighed and relaxed slightly.

"Sorry, madam," he announced simply while remaining pleasant. "I didn't mean to startle you. Would you like to be shown to your room?"

"Where did everyone go?" she asked firmly.

"They went home, madam," Parker casually replied.

"Everyone?" she asked with confusion. "We were only gone a few minutes."

"I'm sorry, madam. Was there someone in particular with whom you'd wished to speak?" Parker asked.

Kate looked around the room once more with that same bewildered look. She slowly shook her head, feeling moderately dumbfounded. "No, I suppose not."

Parker then smiled gently. "In that case, I'll show you to your room."

Kate paced the elegant upstairs bedroom wearing an oversized shirt with the sleeves rolled up. She paused every few minutes to look out the large window into the darkness of the woods. There were no signs of life as far as the eye could see. She looked at the king-sized, canopy bed with the satin comforter neatly folded down for her. She hadn't considered sleeping. She paced the length of the room again. There was movement in the hallway. Kate hurried quietly to the bedroom door and listened. Someone walked down the hall. Kate looked at the clock on the wall. It was three in the morning. Who was wandering around at that hour? She looked back at the door and slowly turned the knob. The door opened with a slight creak. Kate held her breath a moment then looked into the dimly lit hallway.

In her bare feet, Kate left the safety of her room and quietly crept along the upstairs hall. She looked around with some concern then walked down the broad, wood carved staircase. The downstairs was also dimly lit. The entire house had an elegant but eerie feel about it. Kate paused at the bottom of the stairs and listened a moment. She could hear someone further down the hall, perhaps in the adjoining hallway with the many suits of armor. Kate quickly and quietly hurried toward the connecting hallway and looked down it. The many suits of armor lent a creepy series of shadows. At the very back of the hallway, Kate could see someone turn the corner. Ralin had gone the same direction earlier that night. Kate waited a moment then walked along the broad hallway. She eyed each suit of armor as she passed. They looked like soldiers on guard, waiting to pounce on her with every step. She paused at the end of the hall and looked in the direction the unknown person had traveled.

There was a beautifully carved door at the end of the short hallway. Kate hesitated then slowly approached the door. She paused before the door and listened a moment. There was no sound. A cool draft brushed past her feet from the space at the bottom of the door. The cool air convinced her this might be an entrance to a basement of some sort. Kate contemplated a moment longer then nervously opened the door. It creaked slightly, causing her to hold her breath and stop pulling. She then pulled it open far enough to peek inside. The lighting beyond the door was worse than the rest of the house. She could barely see the narrow, stone steps spiraling downward. The walls contained the same, old stone. A damp, musty smell filled the stairwell.

Kate stared at the spiral stone stairs a long moment then pulled the door open further and stood on the small landing before the steps. She listened a moment from her position at the top of the steps and remained by the security of the partially opened door. The sound of dripping water could be heard echoing deep within the basement. Something about the sound caused Kate to shiver. Soft voices could be heard echoing faintly somewhere beyond the bottom of the stairs. Kate held her breath a moment and considered returning to the safety of her room. She would then have to hope that Ralin kept his word and took her to town in the morning. Still, she stood at the top of the basement steps staring down them. Something piqued her curiosity, despite having had enough excitement for one night. She wanted to know what Ralin was into. What if they were doing some sort of sick human sacrifice? What if she was to be that human sacrifice? She ran her fingers through her hair and looked from the door to the steps. Was she being a little paranoid? What sort of cult was Ralin into?

The door creaked and closed behind her. Kate turned with a soft gasp and attempted to open the door, but it wouldn't open. She hesitated then looked back to the basement steps. She released a nervous breath and cautiously proceeded down them, taking each step with great caution. The steps were cold and damp beneath her bare feet. There was no railing along the wall, so she ran her hand along the damp stone to keep her balance and sense of direction. The sound of dripping water and voices seemed to get louder as she approached the bottom of the spiraling, stone steps.

There was a small room at the bottom. It was nearly dark and very cold. Kate could hear the voices coming from the next room over which contained a glowing light. The voices were heard more clearly now. Kate slowly approached the partially opened door within the dark room. She paused and peeked through the opening. The room was large, dimly lit, and filled with the nearly one hundred guests from upstairs. They all faced the opposite end of the room, with their backs to Kate. Toward the front of the room was an ancient altar covered with fresh flowers. Falice and Britton stood toward the front of the room holding hands while Ralin stood in front of them facing the group. He held a champagne glass filled with a dark substance and raised it. Everyone raised their own glasses filled with dark liquid.

"Tonight, we not only celebrate the unity between Falice and Britton, but Britton's commitment to join us and become one of us," Ralin announced cheerfully. "Let us toast the newlywed couple and Britton, for the new path he has chosen." Ralin turned and joined the group facing Falice and Britton. Ralin held his glass toward the couple. "To you, Britton, and your step into immortality."

Everyone chanted in response and drank from their champagne glasses. Falice leaned toward Britton while slipping her hands inside the opening of his shirt and kissed him warmly on the lips. When she broke off the kiss, her fangs were clearly visible. Kate watched in horror as Falice slipped his shirt beyond his shoulder, exposing his neck. She then lowered her mouth to his neck and sank her teeth into his flesh. Britton flinched then relaxed as his bride feasted upon his blood. Kate gasped softly and jumped away from the door with a horrified expression. The light in the small room suddenly came on. Kate whirled around and stared at Parker standing near the spiral stairs. The room was filled with wine racks, which were filled with bottled blood.

"Is there something I could help you with, madam?" Parker asked while cleverly raising his brow.

Kate moved swiftly toward him and the stairs behind him. He didn't take his eyes off her. "No," Kate replied while trembling. "I'm fine, thanks."

"Perhaps you'd care to join the others?" Parker questioned and indicated the ritual room.

Kate then noticed the tiny fangs in his mouth. Her eyes widened with concern. "Thanks, no," she replied and ran past him and up the stairs.

# Chapter Five

Kate pulled open the door now slightly ajar at the top of the spiral stairs and ran along the grand hallway past the many suits of armor. She could hear the echo of faint voices. Although they were coming from downstairs, it almost sounded as if they were coming from the armor themselves. Kate ran even faster along the hall in her bare feet. She spun the corner and nearly fell to the floor from her speed. She turned and ran for the front door at the opposite end of the main hallway.

"Kate!" came Ralin's voice from behind her.

Kate ran up the foyer steps and pulled on the door. It wouldn't open. She looked back while pulling roughly on the door. Ralin slowly walked along the hallway toward her.

"Kate, please, let me explain," Ralin announced in a pleading tone.

"Explain!" she cried out while yanking on the doorknob. "Explain what? That you're a vampire! I don't need further explanation!"

"You don't understand," he said gently. "It's not what it seems. Just give me five minutes."

The door suddenly opened, startling Kate. She ran out of the house and into the pouring rain. She ran only a few yards through the wet grass and mud before colliding with someone. Kate cried out and looked at the man before her. To her horror, she stared at Randy. He was soaked and angry from spending hours in the rain possibly searching for her. He raised the gun and pointed it at her face.

"You've caused me a lot of trouble tonight," Randy growled. "The police are crawling all over your wreck of a car. Judy rolled over me the first opportunity she got." He pulled the hammer back on the gun while aimed at her face. "I'm going to enjoy this."

Kate stared at Randy with horror. She couldn't believe this was happening to her. Vampire on one side and a crazed killer on the other.

"At least let me give you a ride back to town," Ralin called from the porch. "You can't walk to town in this mess." He was oddly silent while staring across the dimly lit estate grounds through the pouring rain. "Who's out there with you?"

Kate continued to stare at Randy and could almost see the idea forming in his mind. He was desperate for a way out and needed money and a getaway car. Randy grabbed her arm and pulled her closer to him, keeping the gun aimed at her.

"Accept his offer," Randy growled lowly. "I get his car; you live. Got it?"

Kate slowly nodded, although she knew he would never keep his part of the bargain. He turned her to face Ralin and kept the gun aimed at her back.

"Tell him we're friends," Randy growled lowly.

Kate stared at Ralin, who walked across the porch toward the steps while staring at them. Despite his calm demeanor, he appeared to be pacing, awaiting their approach.

"Okay, I'll let you give me a ride to town." Kate then hesitated with a fixed expression on her face. "This is Randy, a friend of mine."

"Very well," Ralin replied simply then moved back to the house and stood near the doorway. "Come inside and at least get a change of clothing. You can't go to town looking like that."

Randy forced Kate toward the house. She nervously walked up the porch steps and looked at Ralin as she passed.

Randy smiled and gave Ralin a polite nod. "Much obliged to you."

Kate and Randy entered the mansion foyer. Ralin entered behind them and shut the door. Randy turned Kate to face Ralin and aimed the gun at him.

"Take me to your car," Randy growled lowly.

Ralin appeared unaffected. "And if I don't?"

Randy seemed slightly surprised by Ralin's calm attitude then his hostility returned. He pointed the gun at Kate's temple. "Then she dies."

Ralin slowly walked down the foyer steps and glared at the man with the gun with little expression. "I'll take you to my car, and then you let her go," he replied simply then walked past them and down the hall.

Randy forced Kate to follow. They approached the back hallway beyond the grand hall. Kate watched each suit of armor as they passed then looked at Ralin ahead of her. His attitude displayed little concern for their situation. He had nothing to fear. He wore the vampire shield of invincibility. Kate was the only one with something to fear from both ends. They passed through the door to the stone spiral stairs and proceeded down them. Kate became tense. She watched as Ralin passed through the darkened wine cellar and into the large, dimly lit room before him. Kate and Randy entered the empty room behind him. Ralin stopped near the front of the room before the altar and turned to face them. Kate looked around the empty room with some concern and confusion. Where had everyone gone? How did such a large group disappear so quickly? Randy also looked around with some confusion then looked back at Ralin and pressed the gun harshly against Kate's temple, causing her to gasp.

"Is this some sort of trick?" Randy demanded.

Ralin leaned his backside against the altar and folded his arms across his chest. "No, it's no trick," he replied simply then smiled, revealing tiny fangs in his mouth. "You just picked the wrong family to screw with."

"I'll kill her, I swear!" Randy shouted in anger, possibly not even noticing Ralin's fangs.

Kate could hear movement in the shadows all around them. Randy nervously looked around. Kate became tense and did the same. She looked back at Ralin. He didn't move nor comment. There was a deafening squeaking sound coming from the ceiling. Both Kate and Randy looked up to the dark ceiling. The ceiling appeared to drop as a hundred king-sized bats dove down upon them. Kate screamed. Randy released her and cried out while firing his gun at the swooping bats. The sound of their wings and their squealing was almost deafening, echoing off the stone walls. Ralin dove for Kate and pulled her away from Randy. Randy dropped the gun as the bats attached themselves to him. He swatted at them then fell to his knees while screaming and covering his face and head.

The bats swooped back up to the ceiling as quickly as they had appeared. Kate clung to Ralin's arm and cowered behind him. She looked from the ceiling back to Randy, who slowly lowered his arms and jumped with nervous fright. Ralin extended his hand outward. The gun slid along the floor and flew into his hand. He casually crushed the gun and dropped the twisted metal to the floor. Randy sprang to his feet and batted feverishly at his body as if fighting off some invisible creature. Ralin released Kate and approached Randy, who backed away with a look of fear on his face. Ralin exposed his fangs and sighed a low hiss.

"We'll be watching you very closely," Ralin hissed softly. "The next time you consider harming another, you won't survive long enough to tell about it."

Randy stared at Ralin and his fangs. He cried out and ran from the room. The door slammed behind him.

Ralin turned toward Kate and folded his arms across his chest. His fangs were once again gone. "Will you give me five minutes to explain now?" he asked gently.

Kate nodded and lowered her exhausted body to the step before the altar. Ralin approached and sat on the step alongside her while she watched him with some apprehension.

"I know most people's perception of vampires," Ralin began. "It's true some vampires were the *undead*, drinking human blood to sustain life, and killing mercilessly. That's not true of us. We're an evolved civilization. We drink blood on occasion, but none of us has killed a human. We work closely with blood banks across the country. None of us are *dead*, but we have crossed into immortality, so we may not be killed. We don't sleep in coffins, and we may walk in daylight." Ralin studied her as she sat quietly and without comment. "We're actually rather shy people."

Kate glanced at Ralin and stared for several minutes. "How do I know you're not lying?"

"Have you been harmed?" he asked while cocking his head. "Randy, of all people, didn't he deserve to have the life sucked out of him? Was he even harmed apart from a few traumatic, emotional scars? What possible motive would I have for lying to you?" He studied her a long moment in silence. "If it were a matter of forcing you to stay, I would have done that, had it been my intention. Why bother explaining things to you, if I could simply bite you and make you stay?"

Kate continued to stare at him. "I believe you," she replied gently. "Will you still return me to town?"

"Of course, I will, as had been my intention all along," Ralin replied simply. "Everything that's happened here tonight has been a tremendous shock to you. I can understand if you never want to see me again, but I can hope that, with time, you can see beyond our differences." Ralin stood and extended his hand to her.

Kate accepted his hand and allowed him to pull her to her feet. They were only inches apart. Kate stared into his eyes as a tiny smile crossed her face. "I'm not doing anything tomorrow night."

Ralin allowed a soft laugh to escape along with a slight sigh of relief. "Tomorrow would be perfect." Ralin led her down the steps and toward the wine cellar. "Could I interest you in the sunrise? There's a spectacular view from my roof."

Kate smiled and laughed softly. She released his hand and clung to his arm. "That sounds nice--" They continued into the wine cellar. "--as long as you promise not to incinerate." They walked up the spiral, stone steps. Kate's voice trailed behind. "Can you do that fang thing again?"

Ralin chuckled softly.

# The End

# The Feast

# Chapter One

The quiet little town was reminiscing of an earlier day and age. Kinder Corners had clean streets lined with small homes surrounded by white, picket fences. The town seemed almost perfect. The church was over one hundred years old and doubled as a gathering place for most of the town activities. It was a pleasant fall afternoon for the annual Labor Day picnic sponsored by the church. In the clearing behind the church, townspeople enjoyed the bonfire and outdoor games, while children chased one another around. Older men played horseshoes while their wives gossiped at the picnic tables. The younger generation was heard just beyond the small wooded area where they swam in the lake.

Despite all the activity on either side of the tree line, one man in his mid to late twenties sat beneath a tree and read a book. Brodric Hawthorne was the handsome newcomer to Kinder Corners. His nearly black hair and bronzed skin were second only to his dark, dreamy eyes. If not for his quiet intellect and inability to socialize, most of the younger women in town would have found him irresistible. Fortunately for the young women, his older brother was equally handsome and open to all temptation. There was enough of Haven Hawthorne to go around, and judging by the group of women surrounding him by the beer keg, he would have little trouble securing overnight company.

Two eighteen-year-old girls sat at one of the picnic tables and watched the bonfire where the older generation now square-danced around it. Sable Renshaw and Shauna Decker watched their parents embarrass themselves with their country bumpkin dancing.

"Frightening, isn't it?" Sable muttered in disbelief.

"If I ever square dance, shoot me," Shauna remarked in a low, bored tone.

Sable laughed at her friend's comment. Sable had a certain girl-next-door appeal. Her golden-brown hair hung down to her shoulders when it wasn't pulled back into a ponytail. She blended in with the town more than her attractive friend did. Shauna was Sable's polar opposite. She dressed flashy, allowing sneak peeks at her cleavage, and wore her shorts as short as acceptable within the small town. She allowed her blonde hair to flow wild and wavy with the perfect windblown look. Despite her fair complexion, she wore dark eyeliner and bright red lipstick. Shauna returned to her earlier preoccupation and watched Haven and his girl collection.

"He's such a fox," Shauna announced while sighing almost dreamily.

Sable eyed Haven, unable to understand the attraction to the flirty man, and shrugged with disinterest. "Not my type."

"You don't have a type," Shauna remarked without taking her eyes off Haven. "I hope college at least teaches you how to properly lust."

Sable glared at her friend, offended by the comment. "I lust."

She snorted a laugh. "Sure you do," Shauna scoffed. "If I were going to college, I'd have all those college guys lining up at my door."

"And you'd flunk out too," Sable informed her. "I hope you grow out of this sexual phase you're going through. You don't want a reputation."

"Too late," Shauna chirped cheerfully and finally looked at her friend. "I can't help it. I just can't choose one." She gave Sable a quick, disapproving once over. "At least I've been out there. Can't imagine you in college and never been kissed."

"I'll survive somehow," Sable snapped back. Her eyes strayed to Brodric beneath the tree with his book. She attempted to keep from staring, but it was difficult. She'd never seen a man so handsome before.

"Don't stare too long," Shauna remarked, breaking her from her trance. "Your mother will have a fit."

Sable glared at her friend. "She wouldn't if you didn't mention that I liked him."

"As if she'd ever have to worry about you chasing an older man," Shauna remarked then reconsidered the comment. "Or any man, for that matter."

"Will you stop?"

Shauna leaned forward while grinning slyly. "Your parents are busy dancing around the bonfire. Just go talk to him."

Sable stared at Brodric a moment longer and actually considered it. Pastor Milo and his wife, Loren, approached their table and collected some of the discarded paper plates and cups. Sable was suddenly self-conscious and avoided looking at the handsome man reading his book beneath the tree.

"When do you leave for college, Sable?" Milo asked cheerfully.

"I'm leaving tonight," Sable informed him while shifting uncomfortably as if she'd been caught staring at a handsome older man. "I agreed to stay for the picnic since I know how much these gatherings mean to my parents. They'll drive me to the campus afterward."

"That's wonderful," Loren chirped. "Don't forget to stop back and see us over your breaks."

Sable nodded and shifted slightly on her picnic bench. Milo and Loren continued through on garbage patrol.

Shauna watched them leave then immediately leaned closer to Sable. "Go over there and talk to him."

Sable's parents arrived at their table as if mysteriously summoned to intervene. Both were in a great mood after their lengthy hoedown.

"That was fun," Mrs. Renshaw announced then smiled at her daughter. "Are you ready to go home and get your things?"

"We could leave tomorrow if you'd prefer," her father added.

"No, we'll stick to the original plan," Sable replied, now fidgeting. "I'll meet you at the car. I just want to say goodbye to my friends."

Her mother and father nodded then headed toward the parking lot. Sable and Shauna exchanged looks.

Shauna raised her brows and smiled slyly. "Go on," she groaned. "You know you want too. He'll probably be married before you come back from college." Shauna had to keep from laughing. "What do you have to lose?"

Sable hesitated, grinned, and then sprang up from the table. Shauna giggled and watched her friend approach Brodric beneath his tree. Sable paused before the handsome man engrossed in his book. There was no denying his sex appeal even if he was six or seven years older than she was. She knew she stared a moment too long, but she felt compelled to take in his unintentional sexy pose; his legs stretched out and crossed at the ankles. His intellectual appearance made him even sexier in her mind. When he noticed her, she again fidgeted. She considered walking away but forced herself to sit down alongside him. As Shauna said, what did she have to lose? If she embarrassed herself, she was gone after tonight anyway.

"Not much for picnics?" she asked in a tone more confident than she actually felt.

Brodric shut his book and smiled almost timidly. "I'm not great with crowds," he replied in possibly the sexiest voice she'd ever heard. "Even less for crowds I don't know."

"I know what you mean," she immediately replied for lack of anything better to say. "This is a strange bunch. Lived here all my life and I still don't understand them."

Sable looked back at Shauna, who encouraged her with a firm look, her eyes nearly bulging out of her head while silently commanding her. Sable looked back at Brodric, who appeared slightly uncomfortable but willing to give her his undivided attention. Sable fidgeted while staring into his dark eyes. She was almost rendered speechless by his hypnotic gaze.

Sable forced herself to speak. "I'm leaving for college tonight, but I'd wanted to say hello for a week now." She felt her heart pounding as she extended her hand. "I'm Sable Renshaw."

Brodric accepted her hand and smiled. She could feel her heart beat faster as they finally touched.

"Brodric Hawthorne," he announced pleasantly. "It's a pleasure to meet you."

As he released her hand, she was disappointed their touch had ended. Sable fidgeted while staring at him, wishing her heart would stop beating so fast.

"I hope you don't think me too forward--"

There was an odd silence as Brodric waited for her to finish her comment. Sable tensed, hesitated only a moment, and then kissed him passionately on the mouth. She'd never kissed a man before, that wasn't just playful banter, so she didn't even know if she was doing it right. The way his lips felt against hers was indescribable, causing an ache to shoot through her entire body. Shauna was heard clapping her hands and giggling as she nearly fell off the bench. Sable pulled away just as quickly and met Brodric's stunned gaze.

Sable smiled with embarrassment. "See you around."

She stood despite the weakness in her legs and immediately headed for the parking lot without looking back. Brodric stared after her a moment in silence, pondered what had happened, and then returned to his book. Haven approached Brodric while watching Sable disappear around the church toward the parking lot. Haven cast himself to the ground alongside his brother.

"Hmm. You got a real hot one there," Haven snickered.

Brodric eyed his brother while shutting his book. "A little on the young side, don't you think?"

"Oh, please. Put morality on the back burner," Haven announced boldly. "Half these women would be thrilled to marry outside their own family."

Brodric stared at Haven with a displeased look. "What did that bastard Stuart give you this time?" he demanded. "It's not helping your personality any."

Haven groaned while grinning, revealing his drugged state. "Lighten up and have some fun."

"Seems to me you're over indulging enough for both of us," Brodric muttered. "Are you ready to go?"

"The night's still young," Haven announced while grinning. "I couldn't possibly disappoint all the love-starved farmer's daughters just begging to get laid."

Brodric frowned and returned to his book. "Excuse me while I vomit."

Haven chuckled lowly and casually looked around. "You make a fine martyr, Brodric."

Haven stared at Shauna, who remained at the picnic table by herself. She caught his look and smiled seductively. Haven returned the smile and slapped Brodric's leg. Brodric jumped slightly and glared at his brother.

"I think I've found my next conquest," Haven announced. "Give me an hour to bang that one."

Brodric didn't bother looking and rolled his eyes behind the pages of his book. Haven sprang to his feet and approached Shauna at the table.

# Chapter Two

The bonfire continued to burn into the evening as night fell. There was more dancing, although many of the forty and over crowd had gone home. Milo and Loren remained throughout the festivities and danced to the younger crowds' music. Since it became too dark to read, Brodric was forced out from behind his book. He spent the next hour attempting to avoid an attractive, young schoolteacher, Erica Stradford. Erica was considered a blonde bombshell with cleavage to match and had the attention of plenty of men around town, but since their arrival, she had her sights set on the handsome and shy Brodric. She continued to follow him around despite his attempts to evade her.

In a darker area near the woods, a seemingly ordinary man in his mid to late twenties slipped something to Haven. Stuart was viewed as a respected young man, who worked at the local pharmacy with his uncle, but many in the younger crowd were aware of his side job in the illegal drug trade industry. Judging by his slightly uptight and energetic behavior, he sampled a little too much of his own product. Haven slipped the wiry man some money, completing their transaction, and then took two cups of beer and joined Shauna, who was halfway to the lake waiting for him.

The local law, Deputy Dwight, had a heated debate with a young woman. She argued back, which was never wise when dealing with Deputy Dwight. The young deputy was riding a power trip, which he believed entitled him to get his way in every situation. Although not considered unattractive, his personality made him less attractive, particularly to single women. Despite being off duty, he insisted on wearing his uniform as a symbol of his status. The young woman didn't share his entitled ego and eventually walked away. She would undoubtedly pay for her lack of interest in the deputy at some later date in the form of a traffic ticket. She obviously didn't care and wasn't playing his game.

Wally, the town bartender, had watched the entire scene unfold and glared his disapproval at the deputy's overreach of authority. Wally was closing in on thirty, so his chances with most of the younger women remaining at the picnic were bleak. His interest in the situation seemed more protective than jealous. Perhaps his position as bartender allowed him to connect with the younger drinking crowd on a different level. He glared at Dwight as he passed him on his way to a few snacks remaining on the buffet table. Dwight glared back at him. Dwight obviously saw Wally as a threat to his aggressive moves when it came to young women.

Brodric joined Wally at the buffet table with Erica still following him. Wally eyed the interaction between the handsome newcomer and the coveted blonde schoolteacher. Brodric helped himself to a handful of pretzels then sat down at one of the nearby picnic tables. Erica sat alongside Brodric, taking up all available space between them. She appeared puzzled by his behavior.

"Why are you avoiding me?" Erica asked.

"I'm not interested, Erica," Brodric announced without bothering to look at her.

Wally eased his way closer to the table with his own plate of leftovers and kept a close ear on the conversation. He sat several feet away at the opposite end of the table.

"Is it because I was involved with Haven?" Erica asked while cocking her head to the side. "You don't have to worry about that. He won't care. That's been over for a while."

"That was over before it started," Wally muttered then grinned smugly at his comment.

Erica glared at him on the opposite end of the table in an attempt to silence him without words.

He chuckled softly at the look he'd received. "Your reputation precedes you, darling," Wally continued. "Take the hint. He's not interested."

Erica was obviously searching for some snide remark to silence the nosy bartender, but she fell flat. She sneered at Wally then stood and walked away.

Brodric watched her leave then shook his head in disbelief. "What's with this town?" he asked as Wally slid closer to him with his plateful of food. "Women turn into animals after sundown? I thought small town life would be more, well, secluded."

Wally laughed between mouthfuls of food. "You want seclusion? You have to stay on that out-of-the-way piece of land you and your brother bought," he casually informed him. "Here in town, everyone knows everyone's business. Somewhere someone has a running tab on everyone. Who they dated; whose car is parked overnight in whose driveway. It's a living hell."

"So why do you live here?"

"I'm the town bartender. It's my job to listen to gossip and help spread it. I thrive on it," Wally teased. "Don't worry about Erica. She's just drunk as usual. By tomorrow, she'll be her usual bitchy self."

Brodric didn't seem convinced. He groaned softly and fidgeted. "I think I'd better collect Haven and get him home," he muttered. "I'm sure he's beyond drunk himself by now."

"I suggest you do that," Wally remarked in a serious tone. "Dwight was looking for him. Seemed real pissed."

"Why?"

"Apparently Haven's been making moves on his would-be girlfriends. Your brother has already slept with half the women who've turned Dwight down."

"Great," he muttered. "That's all I need." Brodric stood with a disgusted groan and headed toward the lake.

Stuart and a young woman made out within the dark lake, as did other couples. The lake was notorious for skinny-dippers and after dark water sports. The moon provided just enough light to see the few couples making out within the lake. Brodric paused near the lake's edge and eyed the passionate couples within the water. From the soft gasping and grunting, at least two of the three couples were doing more than just making out. Brodric glanced at Stuart and his latest conquest. They appeared to be in the blissful foreplay stage of their 'swim'.

"Has anyone seen Haven?" Brodric almost demanded with limited patience.

Stuart enjoyed the woman's kisses along his neck and shoulder. He barely glanced at Brodric and gave a slight nod.

"He's in the woods behind you," Stuart replied with a soft moan of pleasure.

Brodric turned and nearly collided with Deputy Dwight. Deputy Dwight stood rigid with his thumbs resting in his gun holster and gave Brodric an arrogant look.

"I was wondering the same thing myself," the deputy announced in anger.

The deputy turned and headed for the woods in a bit of a hurry. Brodric walked briskly alongside Dwight, keeping pace with his long, determined strides.

"Just remember your position, Deputy," Brodric lectured, hoping to avoid a confrontation involving the law and his brother. "I know you're upset by Haven's indiscretions--"

Dwight pushed Brodric aside, not caring to hear his lecture. Brodric sneered his disgust for the man and hurried after him into the mostly dark woods. Dwight and Brodric stepped into the clearing partially brightened by moonlight and stopped when they heard the distinctive sound of male moans. Although still fully dressed, Haven was on top of Shauna with his hands firmly caressing her body. Deputy Dwight took a step closer with Brodric directly on his heels. Both men stopped with the same look on their faces. There was blood covering Shauna as she lay motionless with her eyes open. Haven's head suddenly turned, noticing them. A large amount of fresh blood ran down his chin and he had a mouthful of her flesh between his teeth.

Dwight's trembling hand reached for his gun. Brodric could only stare at his brother with horror. Haven leaped off Shauna and took off across the woods. Despite his trembling hand, Dwight shot several times then ran after him. Brodric took a step toward Shauna's motionless body and stared at her partially eaten flesh. He slowly backed away without taking his eyes from her. Dwight was heard yelling followed by more gunshots. Brodric twitched, came back to life, and ran after him.

The modern music continued to play from the back of the church grounds, although it wasn't nearly as loud on the playground directly alongside the church. A young couple in their early twenties sat on the swings and stole romantic kisses. Obviously a couple in love, Tina and Oscar couldn't take their eyes off each other. They heard movement coming from the wooded area not far from the playground and looked around. They could hear the echoing sound of gunshots.

"They really went all out this year," Tina announced with a hint of a smile. "Fireworks and everything."

Oscar wasn't convinced that was what they heard. "Sounded more like gunshots," he remarked and appeared concerned while standing. "Maybe we should check it out."

Tina stood from her swing and stopped him. "Don't trouble yourself," she announced with a dreary sigh. "You know Stuart. He's always setting off those M-80s. He's a real jerk when he snorts that homemade stuff of his."

While standing near the swings, they heard a faint snarl like a wild animal. Both looked around attempting to locate the source of the sound.

"What was that?" Oscar asked as his eyes dramatically widened, clearly concerned.

Dwight was now heard yelling from the bonfire area just behind the church. The music stopped, concerning both.

Oscar took a few steps toward the back of the church. "Maybe we'd better--"

He turned to look at Tina, who was standing just behind him. Haven leaped from the jungle gym and onto Oscar, knocking him to the ground. Tina screamed when she saw them. Haven and Oscar struggled while rolling around in the dirt

Milo, who had been just inside the church kitchen, hurried toward the fighting men. "Stop this! Stop at once!"

He reached down to pull the two men apart when blood suddenly sprayed onto his face. Milo jumped back with surprise and horror as Tina screamed. Despite his surprise, Milo lunged back in and pulled Haven off Oscar. Oscar twitched from the large gash across his throat. Milo saw the blood flowing from Oscar's throat and barely had time to look at Haven. Haven slashed Milo across the face with claws protruding from his fingertips. Milo cried out while clutching his bleeding face as he fell to the ground. Tina screamed and ran for the parking lot. Haven ran after her like a crazed maniac. Loren ran from the kitchen, saw the blood covered young man, and screamed hysterically. Dwight ran toward them from the bonfire area.

Milo clutched a bloodied handkerchief to his face and pointed toward the parking lot. "He's after Tina," he cried out. "Help my daughter!"

Dwight clutched his gun and ran for the parking lot. Loren frantically pulled her husband to his feet and away from the now dead young man.

§

Tina ran across the parking lot with Haven only a few yards behind her and gaining fast. She pulled her car keys from her pocket without missing a stride and jumped into her SUV. Tina frantically hit the electronic door locks and started the car with a little added vigor, revving the engine. Within the headlights, Haven could be seen running toward her vehicle. She threw the car into drive while gasping and sobbing hysterically. A determined, hateful look suddenly crossed her face at the sight of Haven in her headlights. She stepped on the gas. The SUV burned out in the stone parking lot and jetted toward him. She was determined to hit him. As she was about to make contact, he leaped onto the hood and crashed headfirst through the windshield. Tina screamed as he collided with her in the driver's seat.

There was mass movement within the SUV as it swerved out of control. Dwight ran around the side of the church just in time to see the SUV plow into the church with a loud crash. Dwight skidded to a stop and stared with horror and possible disbelief. There was a moment of eerie silence as he stared at the crash. The vehicle's horn suddenly sounded, jolting Dwight from his trance-like state. He ran toward the church and the wrecked vehicle sticking partway out the wall. There was a tremendous explosion, as the force of it knocked him backward. Milo stumbled around the corner and saw the massive fire and the tail end of his daughter's SUV. Horror flooded his blood covered face.

"Tina!"

Hawthorne's farmhouse and barn were nestled on a large plot of secluded farmland. Despite their age, both appeared to have been recently remodeled and someone had been working on landscaping. A shadow moved along the porch within the darkness and entered the house. Only a few seconds passed when a black SUV flew up the long driveway to the farmhouse and came to a grinding stop. Brodric jumped out of the SUV, ran for the house, and hurried inside. As the front door slammed shut, a snarl was heard followed by a male cry and several crashes.

# Chapter Three

Five years later. Hawthorne's farmhouse was in complete disrepair. Every window was boarded, there were burn marks on the siding, and derogatory words were spray-painted on nearly every corner. The landscaped yard was dead and decayed. Oddly enough, the barn appeared untouched. It was apparent the town had taken out their anger on the old farmhouse. Two teenage boys approached the barn and looked around to make sure they weren't seen. They entered the barn, shutting the door behind them. Izzy was athletically built, and rightly so since he was the star quarterback on the school's football team. His dirty blonde hair was moderately spiky, giving him a fun appearance. Fuller was a jock wannabe. He had the build but lacked the talent it took to be part of that world. He seemed more of the rich boy type attempting to pull off the bad boy look. His dark hair was perfectly styled and his clothing suggested wealth. Both looked around the interior of the barn. Izzy tossed his duffel bag from his shoulder and allowed it to fall to the dry ground, creating a small cloud of dirt.

"Are you sure this is a good idea?" Fuller asked, remaining tense and skeptical.

"Stop your whining," Izzy snarled. "You sound like my mother."

They walked through the large, well-kept barn filled with cobwebs hanging just above head level. A black hawk suddenly flew past them, startling both. Fuller let out a startled cry then attempted to turn and walk out. Izzy grabbed his shirt and forced him to follow.

"Ms. Renshaw wants a story for class," Izzy informed his less adventurous friend. "This is the story."

"You know, everyone says this place is haunted."

Izzy glared at his designer friend while knitting his brows. "Dude, what ghost haunts a barn?"

Fuller continued to look around, causing his own chills. "You know they never found him."

"That's why it's the perfect story," Izzy boldly announced then grinned. "Scare the pants right off Ms. Renshaw."

Fuller considered the comment then hinted at a smile. "Wouldn't mind seeing that myself."

They paused near the wooden loft ladder. Both looked up the ladder to the cobwebs above.

Fuller vigorously shook his head and appeared alarmed. "No way," he practically cried out. "I'm not going up there."

"Wuss."

Izzy climbed the tall ladder, his spiky hair collecting the cobwebs as he vanished into the dark loft. Fuller watched him disappear and fidgeted. Izzy suddenly cried out in the darkness, alarming Fuller.

"What? What?" Fuller cried out.

"Damned spiders!" came Izzy's hostile voice from the second-story loft.

Fuller groaned with relief and placed his hand on his chest. A shadow moved past one of the dingy, dirty windows. Fuller caught only a glimpse of someone outside and looked at the remaining windows.

"Someone's coming."

"Hide, man," Izzy cried out from above him.

Fuller jumped around in place several times, looking for anywhere to hide. He spun several times with anxiety before running into the end stall and huddling in the corner. The barn door was heard opening with its familiar creak. Fuller hugged his knees to his chest and held his breath. Black boots and a trench coat were seen as someone slowly made their way through the barn. A sling blade swung casually back and forth past the boots. The intruder suddenly stopped and allowed the sling blade to tap against the wooden floor beneath the coating of dirt. He continued toward the end stall. Fuller remained perfectly still and pinched his eyes shut.

The stall door creaked opened. Fuller tensed while opening his eyes and stared at the doorway, but there was no one there. Fuller held his breath and maintained a look of concern. A man wearing a black trench coat suddenly jumped into the doorway with the sling blade raised, prepared to swing. Fuller saw the grotesque mask worn beneath the black cowboy hat. As his attacker snarled, Fuller cried out and scrambled against the corner of the stall while shielding his face. He then heard a muffled laugh. The mask was raised to reveal another teenage boy. Jamie laughed while Fuller continued to stare with shock on his pale face. Izzy was heard laughing from the loft above.

Fuller's expression suddenly hardened as he stared at the boy beneath the trench coat. "Very funny, Jamie!"

"Bet you shit your pants," Jamie teased.

Jamie shed his trench coat and hat to reveal his lanky frame. The classic prankster, Jamie had the face of a comedian and the soul of the devil. He was less attractive yet funny to behold.

Izzy climbed down the ladder while grinning deviously. "Sorry, man. I couldn't resist."

"Not funny," Fuller cried out. "Not funny at all."

"Was from where I was standing," Jamie teased then turned to Izzy. "Is the camera in place?"

"Ready to go," Izzy announced cheerfully. "Are you sure it'll work?"

"Of course, I'm a genius," Jamie announced while grinning proudly.

Fuller muttered, "That's debatable."

"Motion detector activated," Jamie informed him. "We'll be able to record everything that moves."

"Plenty of hawk footage," Fuller remarked.

"Let's go," Izzy announced then looked around and grimaced, "before someone really does find us here."

They left the stall and entered the aisle. The partially open barn door swayed slightly. All three looked at one another with curious expressions.

"Hmm," Jamie teased. "Interesting."

Jamie raised his rusted sling blade and approached the door. As he reached for the partially open door, it suddenly slammed and latched from the outside. A hawk cried out and flew across the barn, startling the three boys. The lights flashed on and off. Several more hawks joined the flight while making horrific sounds and lunging for scurrying rats. As the hawks swooped past their faces for their fleeing meals, all three boys screamed.

Fuller lunged for the door and pulled on it, but it wouldn't budge. "Son-of-a-bitch! It won't open!"

Jamie and Izzy hurried to help him. All three struggled to open the door. It suddenly unlatched and all three fell through the open doorway. Izzy, Jamie, and Fuller scrambled to their feet just outside the barn and ran across the field toward the back road. The barn door slammed shut. The motion sensor camera panned across the barn and zoomed in on a man on ground level in a black hat and matching trench coat. He raised a shotgun and pulled the trigger. The video feedback went black.

§

Kinder Corners High School was in surprisingly good shape for its age. It was a smaller, old building consisting of only two floors since the population of the town didn't call for a larger building. Many buildings within the small town were original, giving Kinder Corners that nostalgic feel. Kids milled around outside the building on the beautiful spring morning and socialized with their friends before classes began. The bell rang, signaling it was time to make their way to homeroom. The kids hurried for the front doors to avoid being late.

Izzy, Jamie, and Fuller collected in their first class together and talked about things only important to teenagers. They were joined by five other teens, which completed their circle of close friends. Ally had the appearance of the daughter of Satan in her black outfit. Her once blonde hair dyed black further lent to the paleness of her skin tone. Black makeup gave the final touches to her daughter-of-the-dead ensemble. Tonya was the cheerleader obsessed with her hair and makeup. She groomed her strawberry blonde hair while checking out her flawless makeup through her tiny compact mirror.

Darrin was the scrawny computer nerd complete with glasses that tended to slide down his nose. He kept his face buried in his computer programming book, although he was obviously paying attention to the conversation being had as well. Cara was the artist of the group with a preppy sort of appeal. She sketched scenes of horror within her sketchpad and periodically added her two cents. The last one in their group was Elana, who flirted with Izzy. Far from the cheerleader, princess type like Tonya, Elana was their sexually uninhibited friend.

The bell rang, alerting the students to the beginning of another class. As if on command, all the students turned around and gave their full attention to their teacher. Sable Renshaw entered the classroom and closed the door behind her. She was now a young woman of twenty-three and was teaching in the same school she'd gone to as a kid. Several boys grinned and exchange comments about their beautiful teacher. Although she still maintained her girl-next-door appeal, she'd lost some of her innocence. After the death of her best friend, she was forced to reevaluate her life. Sable wore a simple dress with the hem just below her knees, although when she sat on her desk, it repositioned itself above her knees, allowing the boys to gawk at her legs. She glanced over several papers then looked at her students and smiled with a slight grimace.

"While most of your stories were rather entertaining, I doubt the credibility of some of them." She looked at Izzy sitting with his friends near the back of the class. "Izzy, your article is riddled with defamation of character and speculation."

Izzy straightened in his seat and stared at her with surprise. "But that's what really happened," he insisted. "Jamie and Fuller were my witnesses."

"I somehow doubt your version of a haunted barn is accurate," she informed him. "The assignment was supposed to be news, not fiction."

"But it's true," he protested. "We all saw it."

"It's the ghosts of the people they found hanging from the rafters," Fuller added, attempting to prove Izzy's story.

Sable groaned although refraining from rolling her eyes at the young men. "I think we'd better have a little discussion on urban legends," she informed them. "This is a case of truth being distorted and twisted into a tale meant to frighten and entertain."

Ally raised her hand and gave Sable a stern, serious look. "My sister was one of the victims that night, Ms. Renshaw."

Sable lowered her head sadly in a moment of silence. She gently rubbed her arms with some insecurity, looked up, and attempted a smile. "Okay. Let's discuss that night."

"Six people were brutally murdered by some creature at the lake," Ally announced without being asked.

Jamie raised his hand and practically jumped out of his seat with enthusiasm. "Then the police found all these bodies hanging from the rafters in Hawthorne's barn," he announced excitedly. "Haven and Brodric were Satan worshipers. They killed those people as human sacrifice."

Tonya made a face and wrinkled her nose. "I hear they were all naked."

Darrin played with his pen but didn't look up from his computer-programming book. "They never caught Haven," he added with little emotion. "Some claim he's still out there."

Sable looked around the classroom and sharply raised her brow. "Anyone else?"

"I heard Brodric was released due to lack of evidence against him," Cara remarked. "I never heard they'd found bodies in the barn."

Another student attempted to chime in on the debate. "I heard these teens were killed while parked--"

Sable stood while groaning. "All right," she announced as she shook her head. "Enough fabrication for a while. Haven Hawthorne was high on cocaine and alcohol at the church picnic and murdered three people." She eyed the students. "There were no other bodies and nothing was ever found in that barn."

"But that girl said she saw--" Ally began, but Sable cut her off.

"What girl?" Sable asked while making her point.

Ally appeared unable to answer.

Sable looked around the classroom. "The reason no one has names is because there was no girl who saw something. This is our very own urban legend. A story surrounding a real life tragedy was altered as it was passed around."

"But Brodric Hawthorne--" Tonya protested. "He's, like, evil or something."

"Brodric Hawthorne is a victim of paranoia," Sable insisted. "He didn't have any part in what his brother did that night. Some very cruel things happened to him because people were afraid. Afraid of something they didn't understand. To them, taking it out on Brodric justified their fears and made them feel they had control over the situation."

Izzy muttered, "He's still a major prick."

Sable eyed Izzy and frowned. "Next week, we're reading "To Kill a Mockingbird"."

There were several groans from around the room.

"Circumstances and the way people deal with them can emotionally scar," Sable informed them.

"I understand what you're getting at, Ms. Renshaw," Izzy announced, "but what I wrote really happened."

"That place is haunted," Elana gasped.

"I wouldn't go out there," Darrin muttered without looking up from his book.

"You couldn't get me to talk to Brodric let alone go anywhere near his place," Tonya insisted.

"He freaks me out," Ally muttered.

Jamie snorted a soft laugh and muttered, "Imagine--a freak being freaked."

"Okay enough," Sable announced then huffed softly.

Ally politely raised her middle finger to Jamie. He snickered at her annoyance.

"It's very important only to write the truth and not use distorted facts," Sable informed them then casually leaned against her desk. "That being said, I'm going to ask Mr. Hawthorne to be our guest speaker."

There were several gasps around the room.

"I want everyone to write questions to ask our guest speaker," Sable informed them then made a face. "I want to make certain they're appropriate."

"Cool," Jamie exclaimed then wrote on his tablet. "How many people have you disemboweled?"

Sable glared at him. "No funny business, understand?"

Izzy leaned back to Fuller and muttered, "Damn. She's got balls bigger than mine."

# Chapter Four

After a long morning, Sable entered the faculty lounge and collapsed on the old, worn sofa. She was only there a moment when she realized the other teachers were staring at her. She glanced at them with moderate suspicion. Why were they all staring? She thought they were beyond the whole 'talking behind the new teacher's back' drama.

"What's going on?" she finally asked, unwilling to play games with those who had taught her now turned co-workers.

Among the faculty was Erica, who was now in her late twenties. Five years hadn't changed the attractive woman any. Despite her position as a high school teacher, she dressed moderately inappropriate and a little provocative. She shut the lounge door and approached Sable on the sofa with a look of dread.

"It's all around school that you intend to have Brodric Hawthorne as a guest speaker," Erica remarked.

Sable sat up, eyed those within the faculty room, and then looked back at Erica. "Yeah, so?"

Several teachers shook their heads and finally looked away. Several moans were heard around the room.

Erica folded her arms over her chest and sharpened her glare. "So? I dated the guy before his brother went psycho," she announced boldly. "He's as demented as they come. You can't bring him into a school full of children. That's worse than a loaded gun."

Sable stared at her, briefly stunned, and then grinned while looking around the lounge. "Let's have a show of hands," she announced boldly. "How many of your ancestors burned witches?"

None were humored but most of the teachers minded their own business now. Erica sat on the coffee table before Sable and crossed a dainty leg over the other, exposing plenty of thigh in her short skirt. Erica had no issue wearing dresses with short hemlines and moderately high heels. How she wore those shoes the entire day was a mystery to most.

"Believe me, Sable," Erica announced in a tone almost resembling concern. "I'm only telling you this for your own good. The man's a lunatic. You haven't been back here that long." She shifted uncomfortably, but that may have been due to her dress creeping up to an unhealthy level. "Have you spoken to him? He's pure evil."

An older teacher leaned back in his chair at the table. His expression appeared to go blank as he drifted back into another time. "A man can only take so much," the older teacher began. "He either fights back or snaps. I saw what they did to him after the funeral--"

§

Five years earlier. The older teacher's story began back at Hawthorne's farmhouse. Several townspeople stood outside Brodric's house holding torches in the dark, brightening the area. A group of men forcibly pulled a struggling Brodric from his house and onto the lawn. They began to beat him while the others threw rocks at the farmhouse windows. Others headed onto the porch with gasoline cans, prepared to douse the place. Police sirens wailed and lights flashed red and blue. As the police cars pulled up, everyone dispersed and fled the scene. The officers got out of their squad cars and watched men and women running away with their torches. Wally's pick-up truck flew up the driveway and stopped behind the police cars. Wally jumped out of the truck, ran past Deputy Dwight, and approached the moderately beaten Brodric as he slowly pulled himself to his knees.

"Are you okay?" Wally asked while helping steady him. "Do you need an ambulance?"

Brodric shook his head with exhaustion. "No."

Deputy Dwight watched the quickly dispersing crowd with little emotion. He casually placed his thumbs in his holster and sighed while shaking his head. "We'll stick around a few minutes, so they get the point."

Wally stared at the deputy with his mouth hanging open.

Brodric slowly stood and glared at the deputy with surprise. "Aren't you going to arrest them?"

Deputy Dwight appeared almost offended by the question. "What? Half the town?" he remarked while holding back a laugh. "What purpose would that serve?" He shook his head and waved off Brodric. "I'll talk to them in the morning when they've had a chance to cool off."

Brodric stared at him with surprise then became enraged. Wally attempted to help steady Brodric, but he pulled away and staggered back to his house.

§

Present day. The teachers within the faculty lounge stared in silence at the older teacher while he remained deep in thought. They listened intently to his story.

"Our own police wouldn't arrest any of them," the teacher announced then snorted a soft laugh. "Thought it would create more tension and hostility." There was a long pause, causing the others to wait with anticipation. "Over the next few months, his home was vandalized and people would attempt to physically harm him if he came to town. No one did a damned thing to stop them."

Sable stared at the older teacher with surprise as her mouth hung open. "I'd never heard those stories."

The older teacher finally came back to life and looked at her. "Of course not," he remarked. "No one would ever admit to it. I wasn't there, but I've heard things. I know some of the people behind the attacks. Some of them my own neighbors. Those good, God-fearing folks silently judging from their front porches."

"Let's not feel sorry for the psychopath," Erica suddenly interrupted his story. "He could have moved. I think there's more to those stories."

"Yeah, the fact that all the vandalism and attacks occurred while Deputy Dwight was on duty," the old teacher remarked. "Never happened on nights Sheriff Conrad was working. He would've stopped it."

"If Dwight was such a bad influence, he never would've been appointed sheriff," Erica informed the older teacher.

Sable groaned and stood while glaring at those within the teacher's lounge. "This is where the kids get it," she announced with disgust. "Adults like you. You people are afraid of an urban legend."

"Your best friend was butchered, Sable," Erica snarled while bolting up from where she sat on the coffee table. "Or did you forget?"

"No, I haven't forgotten," she snapped, "but by Haven not Brodric."

"Suit yourself, but you'll need permission from Principal Dithers," Erica countered and raised a mocking brow. "I don't think you have enough clout to get him to agree to it."

Sable sneered at Erica then left the lounge. They watched her leave then began to talk softly among themselves.

§

It was just a few minutes before the end of last period. Sable stood in the hallway near her classroom with a man in his late forties. Principal Dithers wasn't exactly unattractive, but his naturally creepy nature made him unappealing to most. He wore his dark hair slicked back like an old-fashioned mobster, and despite his height, he stood slightly hunched, making him seem shorter than he was. Principal Dithers stood unusually close to Sable and appeared to undress her with his eyes. He tended to make most women uncomfortable with his sexual overtone.

"I don't think it's a good idea, Sable," he announced while practically breathing down her shirt.

"He didn't kill anyone," she protested. She was still in disbelief by the way people in town reacted to an innocent man. "Why are you so uptight about him speaking to my class?"

"Have you seen him since you've been back?"

"I haven't had the opportunity," she remarked and wondered why everyone kept asking her that. "He doesn't come to town much."

"Very rarely. He's not the man you remember," Dithers informed her. "Anyone setting foot on his property is greeted with a shotgun." Principal Dithers' eyes once more strayed to Sable's bosom. He returned her gaze and thoughtfully touched her shoulder. Sable eyed him with scrutiny. "Even if you could get close enough to talk to him, he'd never speak to your class."

Sable pulled away from him with increased agitation. Some of that had to do with his traveling hands. "That's my problem," she scoffed while folding her arms across her chest, mostly so he couldn't stare down her shirt. "Do I have your permission or not?"

Principal Dithers straightened for once and attempted a smile. "You can give it a shot, but I doubt you'll get anywhere."

Sable returned to her class just before the bell rang, ending the day. Students flooded the hallway from every classroom, leaving the once quiet hallway filled with commotion. Cara walked along the hallway toward her locker with Darrin filing in behind her.

"Hey, Cara," he announced in an attempt to sound casual but came off somewhat shy.

"Hi, Darrin," she replied in a neutral tone.

When she stopped by her locker to deposit some books, he stopped alongside her.

"I was wondering if you'd like to--?"

Izzy slammed himself harshly into the locker on the other side of Cara, causing her to jump with surprise. Jamie caught Darrin around the neck and rubbed the top of his head with his fist. Darrin protested and attempted to pull away.

"Hey, Cara," Izzy announced in a lively tone. "We're going back out to Hawthorne's barn to collect our camera. Wanna come along?"

Cara appeared horrified while staring at both boys. "You're going back out there?"

Jamie cast Darrin aside, almost knocking him to the floor, and smiled wickedly at her. "Not me," he announced cheerfully. "I have a date."

"Fuller's going along," Izzy informed her. "We're hoping we caught some spooks on film."

"But after what happened, why would you--?"

"All for the sake of journalism," Izzy announced with a grin on his face. A frown soon replaced it. "That and I need an 'A' to remain on the football team." His cheap smile returned. "So are you in?"

"Well, I--"

Jamie mocked her with his grin. "You aren't afraid, are you?"

"Maybe a little," she muttered. "When are you going?"

"Tomorrow after school," Izzy replied. "Hawthorne goes to Wally's on a Friday afternoon. Doesn't get home until dark."

"Well," she reluctantly replied. "I'll think about it."

"Cool."

Both boys left, leaving her once again alone with Darrin, who approached while staring at her.

"You'd be crazy to go anywhere with Izzy and his friends," Darrin announced.

Cara sank into thought while leaning against her locker. "Maybe, but I'd love to see that place for myself."

# Chapter Five

The town hadn't changed much in the five years Sable had been away. It was still the quiet, cozy town it always was, except Sable's opinion of those within it had rapidly changed during the course of one afternoon. She didn't know how seemingly charming people could be as bad as what she'd heard. She didn't know how they could seek revenge on Brodric Hawthorne for his brother's crimes. She hated that she was seeing them differently now. Sable approached an old building, which was now the bookstore. Brodric Hawthorne exited with a small bag of books. She was almost stunned she'd actually seen him in town.

Something about Brodric looked different. He no longer looked innocent and harmless. He wore a long, black trench coat and received several stares from the *nice* people around town. Although he held his head high, he didn't acknowledge anyone. His expression appeared harsh and almost dark. Sable stopped and watched him, along with the others in town, as he approached his black Jeep. She convinced herself to take advantage of the perfect opportunity and hurried after him.

"Mr. Hawthorne," she called after him, almost startling a few elderly women.

He didn't look back, although he must have heard her. Sable jogged to catch up to him and ignored the looks she was receiving from those who had stopped to stare at the recluse. As Brodric walked down the center of the sidewalk, people parted and moved out of his path, each of them staring at him.

"Mr. Hawthorne!"

He didn't stop until he reached his Jeep then flung the door open as if suddenly annoyed and tossed his bag into the vehicle. Sable approached him and immediately slowed. Brodric whirled around to face her, causing her to jump back with surprise.

"What?" he demanded with a frightening look in his once compassionate eyes.

Sable fidgeted a moment and stared at the dark and sinister man standing before her. Everyone had been right! She immediately shamed herself for falling for their stories without finding out for herself.

"I'm Sable--"

"I *know* who you are," he snarled while leaning his forearm against his door and allowing his eyes to pierce through hers.

Sable suddenly fidgeted and almost forgot everything she'd intended to say. "I, uh, was wondering if I could have a word with you--"

"No."

Sheriff Dwight stood just near the corner in the distance and appeared to be watching them closely. Brodric turned to get into his Jeep.

Sable reached for his arm to stop him. "Please, just--"

Brodric turned and grabbed her wrist before she could barely touch him. She was stunned by his amazing reflexes and his firm grip. Dwight bolted across the sidewalk toward them.

"*Don't* touch me," he snarled while glaring into her eyes.

Sable was stunned by the chilling look in his eyes as they cut through her. Dwight stood before them as Brodric released her wrist. He glared at Dwight and sneered his disapproval.

Dwight eyed Brodric then looked at Sable. "Is this man bothering you?"

Brodric appeared annoyed while casually placing his hands in his pockets.

Dwight saw him, jumped, and pointed a warning finger. "Remove those hands and keep them where I can see them."

Brodric frowned and placed both of his hand on his car door. His annoyance with the sheriff was evident. Dwight looked back at Sable.

"Do you mind, Sheriff?" she scoffed while folding her arms across her chest. "We were having a private conversation."

"It didn't look that way from where I was standing," Dwight announced boldly.

"Your concern is unwarranted and unappreciated," Sable informed him. "If you'll excuse us--"

Dwight appeared surprised then annoyed as well. "You brought quite an attitude home from college with you," he announced and pointed a warning finger at her. "I suggest you lose it." He then turned to Brodric and glared at him. "I'll be watching you."

Both watched Dwight walk a few feet away then pause near the curb to continue watching them. Sable turned back to Brodric, who still glared at Sheriff Dwight.

"Please," Sable softly protested. "Just five minutes."

Brodric finally returned his attention to her. "Sorry, darling. I don't have time to indulge in your little girl fantasies."

He climbed into his Jeep then slammed the door and started the engine. She watched as his Jeep burned out onto the main street.

Dwight approached her while watching Brodric fly down the road then eyed her. "You're just asking for trouble," he informed her. "Take my advice. Stay away from Brodric Hawthorne."

Sable glared at him then turned and walked away.

§

Later that evening, Sable's car pulled up to the farmhouse and stopped alongside Brodric's Jeep. She slowly got out of her car and stared at the vandalized house with a look of horror. It was worse than she imagined.

"Jesus--"

She then looked at the surprising preserved barn and marveled at its untouched condition. She turned while shutting her car door and came face-to-face with Brodric. Sable gasped with surprise, took a step back, and struck her car. Brodric took a step forward, putting no distance between them. Thankfully, he wasn't carrying his shotgun.

"You certainly don't value your life much."

She attempted to compose herself, although it was difficult while plastered against her car door with fear. "Please, I just need a minute of your time."

His harsh and cold eyes stared into hers. "Talk fast."

"I'd like for you to speak to my class," she announced, coming right to the point for her visit. "I want them to see you're not some monster."

A strange smile crept across his face. "But I am."

Sable attempted to move past him to put some distance between them. He placed a hand on either side of her door near her head to keep her from moving. She held her breath and attempted a calm tone.

"I'm serious, Mr. Hawthorne."

"So am I, Miss Renshaw."

She fidgeted at the mere fact that he knew her name. "This is your chance to tell people how you feel."

"No one cares how I feel," he snarled while eying her. "Neither do I anymore."

Sable stared into his eyes and saw only a tiny spark of the handsome man she desired all those years ago. That man was almost completely gone. She nervously looked away.

"Okay, you've made your point," she remarked while feeling her tension rise. "I'll leave you alone."

"What's wrong?" he announced while scanning her eyes, attempting to get her to look into his. "Can't look me in the eyes? Suddenly frightened by my closeness?" A slightly twisted smile crossed his face. "You didn't seem to mind it much at the church picnic."

Sable met his gaze with a firm glare. "You're not the same man I knew five years ago."

He stared into her eyes and showed no expression. "Five years ago, people didn't loathe me."

They stared into each other's eyes in silence for what seemed a lifetime, although it was only a few seconds.

"I don't loathe you," she remarked softly.

"Really?" he scoffed. "You along with everyone else in town wouldn't even look at me at your friend's funeral. This town made me into the monster they believed me to be."

"I know you're bitter about the way you've been treated, and you have every right to be," she began, "but don't you think it's time you and the town forgave each other?"

"No," he snapped without hesitation. "This town can rot in hell for all I care." His eyes narrowed while staring into hers. "As well as everyone within it."

"I'm sorry you feel that way, but at least I'm willing to make amends," she replied and drew a deep breath. "If you change your mind, you can contact me at the school."

Brodric didn't move nor allow her to move. His closeness and the way his hands kept her trapped against the car made her nervous. She couldn't let him know he succeeded in frightening her. She eyed his hands on either side of her head.

"Do you want me to leave or not?"

Brodric stared into her eyes without emotion. For a moment, she wasn't sure what he intended to do. He then removed his hands from the car, opened the door for her, and stepped out of her way. Despite her weak legs, Sable got into her car with some dignity. Brodric shut the door for her, placed his hands in his pockets, and watched her leave. She watched him watching her through the rearview mirror until he was out of sight.

# Chapter Six

The following evening, Cara, Elana, Izzy, and Fuller hurried toward Hawthorne's barn to avoid being seen. All four looked around before slipping through the large door. Once inside, both girls looked around the interior with nervous expressions. Izzy swiftly climbed up to the loft while Fuller looked around. He seemed particularly uneasy as well. They heard Izzy cry out from the second floor loft.

"Fuck!"

All three jumped with surprise and looked up.

Izzy peered over the edge. "The camera's been smashed into a million pieces!"

"What?" Fuller cried out.

Izzy climbed down the ladder and jumped the last few feet. He turned toward them with a concerning look. "Someone found it," he announced while fidgeting. "We'd better get out of here."

As they turned to leave, Elana stumbled over something embedded in the floor. She looked down and saw a large metal ring had been uncovered beneath the dirt and old hay.

"What's this?" she asked.

She pulled on the metal ring, causing the floor to move. The boys immediately recognized it to be a trapdoor in the floor. Izzy and Fuller pulled open the compartment door to reveal rickety old steps leading down to a basement or possibly a fruit cellar. All four looked at one another in silent question.

Fuller suddenly appeared horrified and shook his head. "Oh, no," he proclaimed. "I'm not going down there. We should just leave."

"We will," Izzy replied. "Just as soon as I see what's down there."

Izzy walked down the rickety steps into darkness, lighting his lighter along the way. The others watched in silence. The entire compartment suddenly brightened. They heard Izzy gasp then laugh nervously.

"You guys have *got* to see this."

Fuller uncertainly walked down the steps, since it wouldn't be the first time Izzy tried to scare him. He stopped and stared with his mouth hanging open. "Oh--shit!"

The compartment was only a ten by ten-foot room. Along the back wall was a strange, large tube lying on the floor. It had a layer of ice covering it, creating a thin film of fog against the warmer air above it. Strange colored buttons lined a small panel in front. Izzy approached the tube as both girls appeared at the bottom of the rickety stairs. Izzy brushed away some of the surface ice. A faint shadow was seen within the tube.

"My God," Cara cried out. "What is it?"

Both boys shook their heads.

Izzy continued to examine the tube then grinned deviously. "I say we find out."

"Let's not," Fuller muttered.

Elana looked around the tube and appeared curious. She suddenly gasped then smiled with delight. "You guys know what this is?"

"That's what we're trying to figure out," Izzy announced with limited patience.

"This is one of those cryogenic tubes," she cried out excitedly. "Where you freeze your body when you have a funky disease."

"Okay, I'll buy that," Izzy remarked while eying her, "but what's it doing in Hawthorne's barn?" He checked over the colored buttons and noticed the unlit green one alongside the lit red one. He indicated the button and grinned. "Ten to one says this is the button."

"I think we should call Sheriff Dwight," Cara announced while insecurely rubbing her chilled arms.

"What for?" Izzy demanded and straightened while looking at her.

Cara stared back at him with a horrified expression on her face. "Because it's obvious to me *who* he has in that tube."

Elana eyed her with surprise and gasped, "His brother?"

"Of course it's his brother," Cara practically cried out. "Am I the only one paying attention here?"

Elana clung to Izzy's arm, practically bounced around, and grinned with delight. "I've got to see him."

"I'm with Cara," Fuller interjected while standing firm. "We should call Dwight."

"Dwight will come in here with his guns blazing," Izzy remarked. "He's been itching to try his new gun. We'll never know who's in there."

"Come on, guys. Don't--" Cara pleaded.

Elana pointed to the button while bouncing around excitedly. Izzy pushed the button. Cara and Fuller immediately groaned. The red light went out as the green one lit. They heard the loud sound of a vacuum seal being broken. Cara backed up to the steps. The other three jumped back as cold air formed a large cloud over the tube and them. All three fanned the cold air in order to see what was in the tube. As the cold vapors dissipated, they saw Haven lying in the tube perfectly preserved.

Elana slowly reached out and touched Haven's frozen arm. "He's cold," she gasped softly. "I think he's dead."

"Thank God," Cara muttered from her position near the steps. "Close him up and let's get out of here."

"We're going to be heroes," Elana proclaimed. "We found Haven Hawthorne's body!"

"Imagine what Dwight will do to Brodric for trying to hide him," Izzy remarked.

"Hide him? Bullshit," Elana exclaimed. "He was trying to keep him alive!"

They heard movement from upstairs followed by the distinctive sound of someone walking around.

Cara looked up the steps then back at the others. "You guys," she gasped with alarm. "I think there's someone upstairs."

"Probably Jamie again," Fuller muttered.

"No, Jamie went to the drive-in with Tonya," Izzy informed him while staring at the low ceiling directly above their heads.

"I'm serious. Someone's up there," Cara informed them while staring up the steps. "What are we going to do?"

"Guys?" Darrin called from upstairs. "Where are you? I know you're here."

"It's just Darrin," Fuller moaned.

Izzy suddenly grinned deviously. "Oh, have I got a top-notch scare for him."

"Forget it," Cara snapped hotly. "Darrin's a nice guy."

Izzy frowned and watched as Cara climbed up the steps, leaving the compartment.

Elana smirked her disapproval. "Someone's got the hots for that geek."

"I say we scare him," Izzy casually announced.

Both boys searched the room for something useful, but they didn't find much.

Elana approached the tube and looked inside at the motionless man. Despite his frozen stasis, he was still handsome. "Damn," she muttered softly. "He was good-looking." She kneeled alongside the tube and leaned closer to examine the dead man.

Fuller picked up a stick and a hammer and indicated them to Izzy. "Will this do?"

Izzy looked at Fuller holding the items then caught a glimpse of Elana alongside the freezer tube. She was bent over the open tube with her head inside.

Izzy suddenly grimaced. "Jesus, girl! What are you doing?" he cried out. "Kissing a corpse?"

Within the main barn, Darrin nervously looked around while listening to the faint sound of voices coming from somewhere. Cara suddenly appeared behind him, startling him.

"Damn," he cried out while clutching his chest. "Don't do that!" He then looked around with concern. "Where are the others hiding?"

"We found a compartment beneath the floor," she informed him, still seeming tense from the encounter.

Izzy and Fuller were heard screaming from the underground room. Darrin looked toward the back and noticed the open compartment door. He took a step toward it, but Cara stopped him from going closer.

"They're just trying to scare you." Cara looked back at the opening in the floor. "Give it up! It's not going to work," she called behind her. "I'm leaving with Darrin!"

Cara motioned him toward the outer barn door. Fuller and Izzy suddenly appeared from the compartment and slammed the heavy trapdoor shut. Cara and Darrin turned around with some surprise to the loud thump of the door crashing into place. Fuller and Izzy tossed an old bale of hay over the door and ran for them.

Fuller grabbed Cara's shoulders and wildly jerked her. "It killed Elana!"

Cara frowned with distaste while brushing his hands from her shoulders. "Very funny, Fuller."

Izzy joined them and hurried them toward the door. The trap door vibrated beneath the bale of hay.

"We have to get out of here," Izzy cried out.

"No one's buying it, Izzy," Cara remarked while casually folding her arms across her chest. "Now leave Elana out."

Izzy pulled Cara to the door without further comment. He clutched her arm so tight; she cried out in pain. Before she could protest, the compartment door vibrated harshly. The bale of hay suddenly propelled upward and the door splintered. All four jumped with surprise.

Darrin grabbed Cara's arm. "Let's do as he says," he announced and pulled Cara out the door.

Cara and Darrin hurried out the barn door and waited for Izzy and Fuller, who were just behind them. Izzy ran out the open barn door with Fuller directly behind him. Fuller was suddenly projected through the air and pulled back into the barn like a rag doll. He was heard screaming hysterically just inside the barn.

Izzy ran back inside, let out a scream, and reappeared through the doorway now holding his bleeding arm. "Let's get the fuck out of here!"

"Fuller--" Cara gasped.

Izzy clutched her arm with his bloodied hand and forced her to run away from the barn. All three ran from the clearing and into the nearby field.

# Chapter Seven

The black Jeep drove up the driveway to the farm and slowed near the old, renovated barn. Brodric looked out the front windshield toward the now open barn door gently blowing in the breeze. Concern swept over his face then quickly turned to anger. He pulled up to the barn, got out of the Jeep with a mission in mind, and hurried toward the open door. He suddenly stopped just inside the doorway then slowly backed away with a horrified expression. He hesitated only a moment then quickly looked around outside, searching the property.

§

The police cruiser drove at a fast clip along the mostly dark back road with its lights flashing. Sheriff Dwight and Deputy Hauser watched the road before them as they neared Hawthorne's farm. Brodric's Jeep flew past in the opposite direction, heading for town. Both watched him pass at high speeds then exchanged looks of surprise.

"That was Brodric," Hauser announced.

"I see it was him," Dwight snarled.

The police cruiser made a sharp turn on the back road and chased after Brodric's Jeep with its siren wailing.

§

Sable sat at her desk grading papers despite the late hour.

Ally approached her desk while carrying a small stack of school newspapers.

Sable sat back in her chair, looked up at the young, gothic woman, and smiled. "There must be better ways for you to fill a Friday night."

"I could say the same to you, Ms. Renshaw," Ally teased. She patted the newspapers. "But the paper has to get out. Since everyone else had more important things to do, someone had to do it."

"That's very responsible of you, Ally."

"It'll be our little secret," Ally replied with a tiny smirk. "Wouldn't want anyone to know I'm actually responsible. It's difficult enough having a pastor for a father."

"Fathers are tough no matter what their occupation," Sable reluctantly replied and considered her own father at Ally's age. "Are you going to the dance on Saturday night?"

"Yeah, sure," Ally muttered sarcastically while rolling her eyes. "Nothing exciting ever happens at our school dances." There was an odd moment of silence as Ally stared at Sable. "Can I ask you something, Ms. Renshaw?"

"Of course, anything."

Ally fidgeted and appeared uncomfortable. "Do you think about Shauna?"

Sable tensed then sat forward and leaned heavily on her desk. "All the time."

"I sometimes dream of Tina. I see the burning church--" Ally shifted uncomfortably then held her head high. "I hate Brodric for what his brother did."

Sable stood from her chair, walked around her desk, and paused near Ally. She gave her a sincere look while sitting on the edge of the desk. "It's natural to displace blame in a traumatic situation like that."

"How can you not hate him?" Ally nearly choked on her words while fighting her tears. "How could I ever look at him and not wish him dead?"

Sable fidgeted and drew in a deep breath. "The next morning, after I'd heard what had happened, I refused to believe it," she gently informed her. "Once I accepted it, I wanted to hate Brodric too, because he was here and Haven wasn't. But then I realized how bad Brodric must have felt." She exhaled softly and relived the moment she'd heard Shauna was butchered. Sable snapped out of her trance. "Monsters aren't born, they're created. Placing blame and hatred on one who doesn't deserve it will only create more hate."

"Maybe one day, I'll understand," Ally replied softly and dabbed the corner of her eye. She sniffed then managed a tiny smile. "I'll see you Monday. Goodnight."

"Goodnight, Ally."

§

Ally left the school through the front doors and headed down the steps. A shadow seemed to follow her. Ally hesitated then looked behind her, scanning the mostly dark area where the parking lot lights didn't reach. There was no one there. She stared a moment longer with some apprehension then turned and nearly collided with Principal Dithers. Ally cried out with surprise, causing Dithers to jump as well.

"Oh, Principal Dithers," she gasped while clutching her chest. "You scared me."

He touched her arm and squeezed her elbow while smiling pleasantly. "I didn't mean too," he replied a little too cheerfully and offered a moderately creepy smile. "I was just on my way to my car. Would you like a ride home?"

Ally nervously pulled away from him, forcing him to release her elbow, and managed a casual smile. "No thanks," she announced while attempting to remain pleasant, although she was obviously distrustful of the principal. "I like to walk at night. My house isn't that far and it gives me time to think."

"All right," he replied, seeming slightly disappointed. "Have a nice weekend."

"Yeah, you too," she muttered while taking a few steps away from him. She watched him walk away then frowned her distaste for him. "Creep."

§

Sable collected some books and papers and set them on the corner of her desk within her nearly silent classroom. It was almost so quiet she could hear the hand on the wall clock ticking off seconds. An older janitor poked his head into the room.

"Going home soon, Sable?" Willard asked.

Sable collected her keys, flashed them, and smiled cheerfully. "On my way out now, Willard."

Willard pushed his broom into the room and immediately started sweeping. "Have a nice weekend."

Sable waved and left the room while gently swinging her keys. Willard inserted the tiny earbuds into his ears and listened to his favorite music while he swept. The music was so loud that anyone within a few feet of him would hear the tune. Despite being in his late sixties, the music was alternative modern rock.

As Sable walked along the hallway, she heard the clang of a metal locker as it slammed closed. She paused and looked behind her. There was no one there and, to her knowledge, no one else was in the building. A shadow moved in front of her while her head was turned. She looked in front of her. There was no one there either. Several yards away, she saw the fire door to the stairwell slowly shut. Sable eyed the door suspiciously then continued on her way toward the stairs. She uncertainly opened the door and peered into the stairwell. When she didn't see anyone, she shrugged it off as her weary imagination and headed into the stairwell.

Her uncomfortable shoes made a distinctive clatter as she headed down the concrete steps to the first floor. She passed through the fire door on the first floor and entered the hallway. The fire door clunked as it closed behind her, echoing throughout the building. Sable walked along the first floor hallway, listening to the echoing of her own shoes in the otherwise silent building. Out of the corner of her eye, she saw movement within the darkness through an open classroom doorway. Sable glanced into the classroom as she passed and saw a pair of glowing yellow eyes watching her. She froze with fear, although uncertain what she saw. The glowing eyes moved through the darkness toward her. Sable cried out with surprise and ran down the dimly lit hall toward the connecting lobby hall. She didn't know what came out of the room, but she wasn't about to stop and look either.

Brodric stepped into the hallway from the connecting lobby and raised his shotgun from beneath his long, black trench coat. Sable slid to a stop, staring at him with a look of horror. She attempted to turn and run the other way when she saw Haven approaching behind her. Her horror was indescribable at the sight of the man she believed to be dead. Sable cried out and dove to the side of the hall and into the lockers. Brodric's shotgun fired, echoing loudly throughout the once silent building. Haven leaped to the wall then back to the hall floor, avoiding the blast of pellets. Brodric ran past Sable and toward Haven as he leaped through a darkened doorway. Brodric slid into the open doorway then charged inside the dark auditorium after him.

Sable considered running from the building while screaming like a mad woman, but her curiosity got the better of her. She ran into the auditorium after them. Once inside, she paused near the doors and looked around the dimly lit assembly room. Brodric slowly walked down the side aisle practically in the shadows and kept alert, keeping his eyes on the ceiling and the stationary auditorium seats. Sable remained just inside the doorway and watched him as well as the darkened room.

"What--?" she attempted to speak.

Brodric held up his hand to silence her. He continued down the side aisle toward the stage. Sable saw something move within the shadows along the ceiling, although she was certain she was mistaken. Haven couldn't be on the ceiling. She squinted while watching the ceiling then took a step away from the door and into the side aisle for a better look. The shadow on the ceiling suddenly leaped down on top of her. Sable screamed as she was tackled to the carpeted floor. Despite the bad lighting, she was able to identify Haven on top of her, but he was no longer human. He had claws, fangs, and glowing yellow eyes. Sable screamed and fought the clawed hands tearing at her dress.

Haven attempted to subdue her hands while lunging for her neck with sharp teeth. Sable saw the menacing teeth and continued to scream while struggling against him. A thick liquid sprayed from his mouth, covering her face, hands, and arms in the sticky substance. Sable cried out with alarm and surprise to what she believed was her own blood from a bite she thought she hadn't felt. An overwhelming stench invaded her senses. As his teeth came at her, Sable blocked them with her forearm. Haven bit her lower arm causing a sharp, burning pain. She cried out and held him back with the arm between his sharp teeth. Brodric sprayed something resembling mace into Haven's face. Haven released Sable's arm with his teeth and bolted backward against the wall while screeching and holding his eyes. Brodric skillfully slung the shotgun into his right hand and squeezed the trigger with little hesitation.

Haven jumped away from the wall as pellets tore into the drywall. Haven leaped through the doorway with Brodric directly behind him. Sable clutched her bleeding arm and slowly sat up while watching the door. She heard a high-pitched screech. Brodric was suddenly thrown back into the auditorium through the doorway. He crashed into the seats and fell to the floor. Sable nervously looked from where Brodric fell to the doorway. She could hear the sound of shattering glass from the lobby. Brodric pulled himself to his feet, staggered a moment with disorientation, and approached Sable. He fell to his knees near her while gasping for air. He suddenly held his breath, made a face, and moved away from her.

"God! What's that smell?" he gasped.

Sable touched her shirt and neck. The thick, sticky substance clung to her fingers. She made a face and slung the substance from her hand. "Oh--yuk!"

They heard the sound of police sirens in the distance, sending Brodric into a slight panic. "We have to get out of here."

"Are you out of your mind?" she cried out. "We were just attacked! We're not the ones who need to run!"

Brodric grabbed her uninjured arm and pulled her to her feet behind him. "There's no time to argue," he snarled. "Now move it!"

# Chapter Eight

A police cruiser was parked outside the Hawthorne barn with its lights flashing while a young officer in his mid-twenties walked within the interior of the barn carrying his flashlight. Deputy McLean shined his flashlight along the floor, but there wasn't any sign of blood or dead bodies.

McLean shook his head with annoyance then held up his walkie-talkie. "Sheriff, I'm at the Hawthorne farm," he announced in a moderately bored tone. "There's no sign of those kids or any evidence of a brutal attack."

"Sounds like we have a couple of pranksters on our hands," Dwight was heard over the radio.

"What would you like me to do?"

"Get to the high school," Dwight responded through the hand radio. "There's been a break-in and Hawthorne's Jeep is parked out front."

"I'll be there in ten minutes," McLean replied then turned and left the barn.

A pair of glowing eyes looked down from the rafters, watching him leave, and then disappeared into the darkness. McLean climbed into his police cruiser and drove away from the farm. He pulled onto the back road and headed toward town. A few minutes after he vanished down the back road, Sable's car pulled out of the woods with its lights out. The headlights came on, and her car drove toward the private lane to Hawthorne's farmhouse.

§

Ally sat on one of the swings in the dimly lit playground not far from the newly built church. She lazily rocked on the swing while remaining deep in thought. While she remained in her own world, a shadow moved past her from behind. Ally sensed something, tensed, and looked around. There was no one there. It took only a moment before she returned to her thoughts. A twig snapped within the nearby woods. Ally jumped from the swing and looked around but again saw nothing. She turned toward the small house alongside the church and was about to head home when a shadow fell behind her. Before she could even react to the mild gust of wind, an arm caught her around the neck and was followed by a hideous snarl. Ally let out a startled scream and rammed her elbow backward, jabbing her attacker in the abdomen, then tossed him over her hip.

Jamie lay on the ground while holding his midsection. "Oh, God that hurt!" He then looked up at her with annoyance. "What's with you?"

She stared down at him with disbelief. "Jerk," she cried out. "What the hell are you trying to do?"

Jamie made an effort to jump to his feet, but he was obviously in some discomfort. "Just a little practical joke," he snapped back while rubbing his abdomen. "Lighten up."

"Lighten up?" she cried out with surprise. "Didn't you hear about Fuller and Elana?"

He gave her a puzzled look. "No, I was at the movies with Tonya," he remarked then showed some concern. "What about Fuller and Elana?"

"Izzy said they were killed in Hawthorne's barn," she replied then insecurely rubbed her chilled arms. "The police didn't find anything."

Jamie groaned and waved her off. "They're just playing around. Izzy's a big joker like me."

"That's not something you joke about."

"I'll give Izzy a call and straighten it all out. You'll see," Jamie announced with a hint of a smile. "Honestly, Ally, if I thought for a minute Brodric was dangerous, I'd never go near that place."

"But you said he's a psychopath--"

"You're so gullible," Jamie announced while chuckling.

§

Sable's car pulled up the driveway and parked in front of Brodric's farmhouse. Sable emerged from the driver's side while clutching her injured arm and stared at the once remodeled home now looking in sad condition. She drew a deep breath and looked at Brodric as he got out of the passenger side. He indicated the house with a wave of his shotgun, obviously having forced her to drive back to his house. She slowly approached the porch with him only a few feet behind her then entered the house. He flipped a light switch, which only operated the hall light. The large ceiling light only contained one bulb and barely lit the hallway. Sable looked around with surprise at the condition of the interior. Despite the once nice looking home hidden beneath, there were now holes in the walls, foul words spray-painted everywhere, broken objects, and cobwebs filling the corners.

Sable eyed Brodric as he locked the door behind them. "This is, uh, creepy."

Brodric glared at her. "No point fixing it when they keep destroying it," he announced then motioned her down the hallway toward the kitchen in the back.

Sable held the blood-soaked cloth to her injured, lower arm and nervously walked ahead of him down the hallway toward the kitchen. She glanced back at him several times with noted concern.

"If you let me go, I promise I won't mention any of this to the police," she insisted.

Brodric just glared at her. Sable appeared concerned and continued down the hall. He stopped her by a door before the kitchen and opened it. She looked down the dimly lit basement stairs and immediately panicked while looking back at him.

"Oh, no! I'm not going down there."

Brodric aimed the shotgun at her and showed little emotion. Sable stared at the shotgun, slowly turned toward the stairs, and walked down them. Sable and Brodric entered the well-lit basement, which was converted into a tastefully decorated studio apartment. There was an elegant living room, kitchen to the back, and bedroom and bathroom off to the side. Brodric closed a steel door behind him and locked it, placing the key in his pocket. He set the shotgun down on the kitchen counter and approached her. She backed up a step with a frightened look in her eyes. Brodric caught her wrist before she could bolt too far from him and examined her injured arm.

"That looks pretty bad," he informed her.

She had to convince herself he wasn't going to kill her and make a meal out of her. She attempted to relax and looked around the studio apartment.

"This is a lot nicer than upstairs."

Brodric didn't comment as his eyes strayed from the bite wound to the tears in her shirt. He reached out to examine the tears near her chest. She swatted at his hand. They exchanged glares. He released her wrist but maintained his glare.

"Any other injuries?"

She held her breath a moment while feeling her body start to relax. "I don't think so."

Brodric turned away from her with little interest. "Go soak in the tub," he muttered. "You smell like something crawled on you and died. I'll find you some clean clothes."

# Chapter Nine

Sable stood in Brodric's bedroom while nervously holding a towel wrapped around her slightly damp body. She looked around the tastefully decorated bedroom that didn't at all look like a man cave. Brodric had gone to great lengths to make his bedroom tranquil and inviting. Judging by the looks of the rest of the house, she expected him to be living like a barbarian. Brodric entered the room, startling her, and tossed a bottle of lotion and some clean clothes onto the bed.

He indicated the lotion in the unmarked bottle. "Rub that over your entire body."

His words sent a chill down her spine, as she reflected back on a movie with a similar line and a less than comforting ending. Sable picked up the bottle and smelled the contents. She made a face while wrinkling her nose.

"Oh, that's pleasant," she muttered and attempted to return the bottle. "I think I'll pass."

Brodric glared at her with limited patience. "That thing is after you," he snarled lowly. "Like it or not, it has marked its territory and you're it. Either you put that lotion on, or I'll put it on for you." He attempted to control his hostility and drew a deep breath. "Without it, it'll be after you until it gets you."

Sable stared at him then attempted a tiny smile. "Well, when you put it that way--"

Brodric left the room and shut the door behind him. Sable eyed the bottle and again sniffed the contents. She pulled away while making a face.

"Oh, that's nasty," she muttered. "I hope he's not secretly making a suit out of human skin."

§

Brodric stood alongside the small bar not far from the kitchen and played with an old police scanner. Sable appeared from the bedroom wearing a man's white button shirt with the sleeves rolled up and a pair of shorts that went halfway down her thighs. She subconsciously ran her hands over her skin.

"It stinks, but it makes my skin feel soft."

Brodric glanced back at her then indicated for her to take a seat. She uncertainly sat on the sofa, insecurely folding her legs beneath her. As Brodric approached, she tensed slightly then watched him sit on the coffee table before her. He reached for her wrist, causing her to jerk back slightly with concern. He glared his disapproval. She then allowed him to pull her injured arm toward him and watched as he applied some sort of cleanser to her bite wound. She cringed with discomfort as the cleanser stung the puncture wounds then stared at him while he concentrated on his work.

"So do you intend to tell me what I saw tonight, and why you felt the need to kidnap me?" Sable finally asked.

Brodric finished cleaning the cuts then wrapped her arm with a sterile wrap. "I told you, it wants you," he informed her. "If I would've left you, it would already have you."

She gave him a puzzled look. "Wants me for what?"

Brodric concentrated on his work and refused to look at her. "What do *you* think?"

Sable stared at him a moment then felt her entire body tense. "That was Haven, wasn't it?"

"What's left of him," he replied gently. "He's more of a monster now."

Brodric finished wrapping her arm and finally looked at her from where he sat across from her.

"And you knew he was alive the entire time?" she suddenly demanded.

"He was contained," Brodric firmly insisted. "Someone let him out." His eyes narrowed as a sneer crossed his face. "Undoubtedly one of your little parasite students."

"Contained?" she practically cried out. "Did you think that was good enough?"

"My way of containing is certainly more effective than Sheriff Dwight's method," he snapped. Brodric sprang up from the coffee table and turned hostile. "He can't be killed. I tried. And don't try to blame me for what happened tonight."

She stared at him with some surprise toward his sudden hostility. "I'm not blaming you."

Brodric fidgeted then walked away from her. He paused by the bar and poured himself a drink. Sable uncertainly approached him. There was a moment of silence as Brodric drained the entire contents of the glass.

Sable gently placed her hand on his, catching his attention. He cast a look at her but showed little emotion. "Thank you for rescuing me tonight."

Brodric looked away and slowly pulled his hand from hers. "I didn't rescue you," he scoffed. "I needed you for bait."

Sable suddenly frowned and appeared annoyed. "You're a real prick; you know that?"

"I was striving for contemptible bastard, but whatever works for you."

"Enough of hell night with Brodric Hawthorne," she lashed out then demandingly held out her hand while glaring at him.

Brodric casually eyed her but showed no sign of intimidation or cooperation.

"Give me my car keys and unlock the fucking door," she lashed out. "I'm going home."

"I'll take you home in the morning," he casually replied. "If he comes back for you, I can get another shot at him."

She allowed her hand to fall to her side while staring at him with disbelief. She wasn't sure what to say at that point. "I can't believe I actually had a thing for you once." Sable walked back to the sofa and cast herself onto it.

Brodric sharply turned and glared at her with a look of hostility and annoyance. "Oh, you want to bring *that* up? *That* was a cruel prank at my expense," he lashed out, turning hostile for the first time. "I saw your friend laughing."

Sable sat up straight and glared at him. She was actually surprised he even remembered the event. "She wasn't laughing at you. She was laughing because I'd never kissed a guy before." She heard the comment the moment it left her lips and instantly regretted sharing that personal information.

Brodric appeared surprised by the comment but his hostility quickly returned. "And I'm supposed to believe that?" he demanded. "Why me?"

"Because I liked you," she launched back then muttered, "I can't believe I still do."

Brodric turned back to the bar and refilled his glass. He took a quick swallow from the glass, remained silent a moment, and then set his glass down.

"If you knew me, you'd feel differently," he gently informed her. He recapped the bottle, composed himself, and then turned to face her. His hostility appeared to diminish before her eyes. "Why don't you try to get some sleep? I'm going to check the barn. Maybe he came back."

Brodric approached the door. Sable leaped up from the sofa and hurried to join him at the door. She was no longer angry but concerned.

"You can't go out there alone," she gasped, surprised that he'd even consider it. "I'll go with you."

"You're staying here," he insisted then gave her a quick once over with little emotion. "You're finally starting to smell better."

"I'm going with you."

"I said you're staying here," he announced and raised his brows. "Don't argue with me; you won't win."

Sable cast her back against the door, folded her arms across her chest, and glared at him.

§

Brodric slowly entered the barn with Sable behind him, clinging to his left arm. He held the shotgun in his right and indicated the light switch near her. They heard movement from within the barn. Sable practically lunged for the lights, brightening the barn interior. Brodric looked around the dark ceiling. Sable watched rats scurry across the floor and then witnessed a hawk gliding down to capture the rats. They heard Haven's soft snarl. Sable momentarily froze and hesitantly looked to her left. Haven stood alongside her. Sable screamed seeing him so close to her face.

Brodric turned with his shotgun leveled. Haven grabbed the shotgun, slung Brodric roughly, and tore the weapon from his hand. Brodric flew to the ground from the force. Haven slung the shotgun clear across the barn and lunged for Sable. She bolted from his path, resisting the urge to scream. Haven ran up the wall, flipped through the air, and landed in front of her.

Brodric scrambled across the barn floor for the discarded sling blade. Haven grabbed Sable as she screamed and struggled against him. He suddenly hesitated, smelled her, and then cringed. He smelled her again then snarled at her, exposing his sharp fangs. Haven shoved her roughly across the barn, casting her to the floor. Brodric sprang to his feet and swung the sling blade at Haven. Haven caught the wooden handle and shoved Brodric backward with it. Haven twirled the blade in his hands and prepared to slash Brodric. Sable gasped, sprang to her feet, and karate kicked Haven in the abdomen from the side. Haven stumbled back a step with surprise and some discomfort.

Brodric scrambled to his feet and faced his brother. Haven looked at Sable and growled deep in his throat. He once more smelled the air and bared sharp fangs at her while growling lowly. The growling sound sent chills down her back, but she didn't back down. He again turned toward Brodric and slashed at him with the sling blade. Brodric attempted to stop the blade by the handle but was once more thrown to the ground. Sable jumped between them and kicked Haven in the groin. Haven snarled, dropped the sling blade, and leaped for the wall. He sprang off the wall and disappeared out the open door.

Brodric stared at her with a look of surprise. "You're dangerous."

"You don't know the half of it," she remarked under her breath with irritation.

Brodric scrambled to his feet and retrieved the shotgun. "I have to stop him."

"Stop him?" she gasped. "He nearly killed you!"

"You don't understand," Brodric protested. "He's lost you as his mate. He's going to find another--tonight."

"Whoa! How do you know that?" she demanded with surprise. "I never heard him say that."

"He smelled my scent on you. He challenged me to get you back," he explained, speaking faster than usual. "You told him you'd chosen me. Now he's going to find another." Brodric headed for the door.

Sable hurried after him. "Where was I when all of this happened? What do you mean your scent?" A horrified look crossed her face. "What was in that lotion?"

Brodric hurried from the barn without offering an explanation. She followed him from the barn.

# Chapter Ten

The police cruiser was parked along the side of the road near the lane to Brodric's farm. It had been parked there for quite some time and nothing appeared to be happening. Deputy Hauser was bored as he stared at the quiet, private driveway. He finally removed the handset from the radio.

"Hey, it's Hauser," he announced into the hand radio. "Nothing is going on out here at the Hawthorne farm. I'm heading home. Over."

"Copy, Hauser," a woman's voice responded. "Have a nice weekend off. Out."

Hauser started the cruiser, turning on the automatic headlights. Haven stood within the headlights only a few feet from the vehicle. Hauser stared at the recognizable man from the past and nearly choked.

"Holy shit!" The deputy leaped out of the cruiser, took cover behind his vehicle door, and aimed his gun at Haven. "Hold it right there, Haven! Put your hands where I can see them!"

Haven grinned at the deputy with a humored look. He suddenly leaped out of the headlights with amazing speed and height. Hauser appeared horrified and looked at the sky and nearby trees with his gun aimed.

"What the hell--?"

Hauser turned around several times with his gun aimed to attempt to find the agile man. Haven was nowhere to be found. Hauser quickly turned for his open cruiser door. A shadow fell behind him along with a slight gust of wind. Hauser gasped while spinning around and saw Haven standing directly behind him. Before Hauser could aim his gun, Haven leaped on top of him, tackling him inside the cruiser. The vehicle rocked a moment as a struggle, possibly one-sided, took place. Hauser cried out followed by blood splattering inside the windshield.

Only a few minutes later, Sable's car barreled down the driveway and stopped at the end of the lane. The police cruiser remained alongside the road with the engine running, the driver's side door open, and the headlights shining. Sable and Brodric got out of her car and cautiously approached the vehicle. Brodric kept his shotgun raised and approached the driver's side.

Sable stopped near the front and stared at the blood on the inside of the windshield. She appeared horrified and held her hand to her mouth to stifle her gasp. "Oh, God--"

Brodric looked inside the cruiser and grimaced. He shut off the engine and returned to her.

"Is he dead?" she gasped, realizing how stupid the question sounded, considering the large amount of blood she'd seen.

"I'm convinced of it," Brodric remarked while looking around. "The body's gone."

"Gone?" she gasped. "What did he do with him?"

Brodric kept his attention on the trees and the darkened areas surrounding them. "Probably stashed him somewhere until he can return later and feast at his leisure."

"He eats them?" she nearly cried out.

Brodric glared at her with a look of impatience. "Where have you been?" he demanded. "Of course he eats them." Brodric took her arm and forced her back to the car.

She stared at him with horror. "But I thought that was just some sick joke."

The interior of the church was empty and dimly lit with candles at every pew and along the exterior wall. Ally walked up the aisle past the wooden pews. She headed toward the altar with the massive stained glass window beyond it. She looked around with concern and fear. Shadows seemed to crawl along the walls cast from the dancing flames of the candles. Pastor Milo stood at the altar with his back to her. He read passages from the Bible softly aloud. As Ally continued closer, she saw a young woman sitting alone in the first pew. She heard a scratching sound, alerting her to something else within the worship hall. Something dark scurried along the walls in the shadows, alarming her. She shivered slightly and looked at Pastor Milo standing before the altar with his back to her.

"Dad--?"

Milo continued to speak softly with his back to her. She slowly walked up to the altar.

"Dad, I really need to talk to you."

Milo turned around, revealing the deep scratches along his face, which bled freely. He continued to quote the Bible while staring blankly at her. Ally stared in horror at her father and backed away from him. Shadows continued to move along the walls. Black creatures seemed to close in on her. Despite her fear, Ally refused to cry out or run. She backed away from her father and turned away from the altar. She stared at the woman sitting alone in the first pew. It was Tina! Her sister was horribly burnt as she reached for Ally with a blackened, nearly fleshless hand. Ally gasped with horror and stopped in her tracks.

"Help me, Ally," Tina gasped while slowly standing as chunks of charbroiled flesh fell from her legs.

Ally now panicked. She bolted past her sister and down the aisle for the back doors. A dark figure wearing a black trench coat stood in the back of the church while holding a sling blade dripping blood. The shadows continued to close in. Ally stopped in the middle of the aisle and screamed.

Ally suddenly flew up in bed, her own scream waking her. The bedroom door opened, frightening her. She screamed again as the lights came on and brightened the room. Milo stood in the open doorway and stared at his daughter. The scars on his face from the scratches he'd received were a grim reminder of that horrible night Haven killed her sister.

"Ally, are you okay?" he asked with concern.

She stared at her father a moment while attempting to catch her breath. "Yeah, just a nightmare."

Her mother appeared in the doorway alongside her father and stared at her with concern. It wasn't the first time Ally woke the entire house with her nightmares.

"Want to talk about it?" Milo asked gently, assuming he knew which nightmare she'd been having.

"No, I'm fine," she replied gently. "Really."

Milo turned to Loren while closing the door. "Just a nightmare. She's fine."

"It's those kids she hangs out with," Loren remarked as the door closed, leaving Ally alone in her bedroom.

Ally snatched a quartz crystal on a rope and allowed it to spin over her bed. She pinched her eyes shut and held her breath a moment. "All good spirits watch over me," she whispered. "Clear the room of all evil spirits."

§

Cara tossed beneath her covers while she attempted to sleep. She softly cried out, gasped, and then looked around the room. She was relieved to discover she was still within her own bedroom. A shadow moved past her window, catching her attention. She looked at the window, uncertain what she'd seen, and climbed out of bed. She nervously approached the window, hesitated a moment, and then peered outside. Ally's face suddenly appeared in the window. Cara cried out softly before realizing it was only Ally. She exhaled with relief then opened the window.

"What the hell are you doing out there?" Cara demanded. "You scared me half to death."

Ally attempted to climb in through her window. "Never mind that. Help me get inside."

Cara helped pull her into the room. Ally fell to the floor with a thud then slowly stood.

"What are you doing?" Cara demanded while staring at her friend. "Haven't you heard of doors?"

"Do you really think your parents would let me in at one in the morning?" Ally asked softly.

"No, probably not," Cara replied then eyed her suspiciously. "Why are you here this time of night?"

Ally collapsed on the mussed bed and stared at Cara with a nervous look. "I had this horrible dream," she informed her with a serious look that conveyed dread. "Then it came to me."

"What came to you?"

"God."

"What?" Cara gasped softly while joining her on the bed. "You don't even believe in God."

"I do now," Ally replied softly without taking her eyes off her friend. "We have to send it back."

Cara was puzzled. "What are you talking about?"

"The evil," Ally informed her. "Haven." She fidgeted slightly. "I know a ritual that will send him back."

"I told you, he's not a spirit," Cara informed her. "He's alive. Of flesh and blood."

Ally held up a book on witchcraft. "We can do it. We just need to go out there."

"Go out there?" Cara suddenly gasped. "Because you had another revelation?" She vigorously shook her head. "No way. You didn't see it. You weren't there."

"We have to," Ally cried out, raising her voice slightly. "If we don't, who knows how many people will die."

Cara attempted to silence Ally's sharply raising voice. "You're out of your psychotic mind," she cried out in a whisper. "Besides, neither of us has a car. What do you suggest we do? Steal our parents' car or walk all the way out there?"

Ally shook her head then raised her brows. "Darrin has a car."

# Chapter Eleven

Tonya lay on her frilly bed with the phone in one hand and the television remote control in the other. Despite the late hour, she gossiped on the phone while attempting to find something to watch with little success.

"As well as expected," she replied with a bored sigh. "Jamie's crazy, but he has good weed." Tonya listened to the person on the other end then suddenly gasped and made a face. "You pig! No, I didn't do it with him." Tonya cast the remote aside, stood, and paced the length of her excessively girly room. "He couldn't pay me enough."

Tonya collapsed on the window seat among her collection of porcelain dolls and looked outside into the darkness. She saw Cara and Ally hurrying along the sidewalk in front of her house. Tonya jumped from her window seat and grinned slyly while spinning toward the television.

"Oh, my God! Freak alert," Tonya softly cried out with giddy delight. "Cara's with Ally. Looks like they're going to Darrin's house. I'll call you back."

Tonya disconnected the call, tossed her cell phone aside, and hurried from her room. A few seconds later, she ran out the front door of her house and snuck across the lawn to spy on the others.

Cara and Ally were already on Darrin's porch. Darrin slipped out and hurried them toward his old car. Tonya crept toward the bushes at the edge of her property.

"Where in the world are they going at this hour?" she muttered softly aloud to herself then appeared to pout. "And why wasn't I invited?"

As Darrin's car backed out of the driveway, Tonya attempted to flag them down, but they drove in the opposite direction. She frowned then returned to her house and approached the porch. A shadow fell down behind her. Tonya suddenly hesitated, having sensed something, and turned around with concern. Haven stood before her and smiled charmingly. Tonya let out a startled scream. As Haven leaped for her, Tonya bolted from his path and fell from the porch. She landed roughly in the flowerbed but recovered quickly. She looked behind her and screamed as Haven leaped for her. Tonya scrambled to her feet and narrowly avoided him. She ran along the front of her house, hoping to make it around the side for the back door.

Haven leaped onto the porch roof while Tonya ran around the side of the house. A nearby tree suddenly shook, startling her. Tonya skidded to a stop and looked up. Haven pounced down upon her, knocking her to the ground. She struggled and screamed against the terrifying man on top of her. The interior house lights came on, which were quickly followed by the outside lights. Tonya's mother and father stepped onto the front porch in their housecoats. Both looked around. Her father walked across the porch and scanned the entire front of the house. He didn't see anyone. Her mother and father looked at each other with bewilderment, shrugged, and returned inside.

Cara, Ally, and Darrin nervously entered Hawthorne's barn, which remained dimly lit from the earlier incident. They looked around the silent interior with nervous anticipation. Ally hurried to the center of the barn, kicked away some old hay, and drew a symbol in chalk on the floor. Darrin moved a bale of old hay aside, saw the blood on the floor, and then nervously looked around.

"I don't like this idea," he announced under his breath.

"Sit within the symbol," Ally ordered, ignoring his concern.

Cara and Darrin appeared uneasy and looked around the barn, keeping watch on the dark corners and the even darker rafters.

"Seriously," Darrin informed them while shaking his head. "This was a bad idea."

"Maybe it was just Izzy playing a joke," Cara informed them. "The police didn't find anything."

"Sheriff Dwight couldn't find his ass if it wasn't attached," Ally announced. "Come on, guys. Let's get this over with. I'm getting bad vibes."

"Your vibes are right," Darrin remarked then sharply eyed her. "We should be running from here."

Cara pulled Darrin toward Ally and the center of the barn. They reluctantly joined her on the floor in the circle. Droplets of blood hit the floor just behind Darrin, although he didn't notice. High above them within the dark ceiling, Fuller, Elana, and Hauser's mutilated bodies hung by their ankles from the rafters.

§

Sable's car pulled into the abandoned school parking lot, which remained lit throughout the night. Brodric pulled her car alongside his Jeep where he had left it when he abducted her. Sable nervously looked at the school through the windshield then back at Brodric where he sat behind the wheel of her car.

"What are we doing back here?"

Brodric shifted her car into park and casually looked at her. "It's going to be light in a few hours. I'm sure he's already found a quiet, dark resting place," he informed her. "I'll follow you back to your house so that you can get some sleep." Brodric shifted slightly. "I'll leave your place around sunup. I doubt we'll see him again until sundown."

"He won't come out during the day?"

"He could, but it's not likely," he replied.

Sable stared at him a moment then became tense. "You seem to know an awful lot about his condition," she commented. "You know what happened to him, don't you?"

"It's more information than you really need or want to know," he replied.

Brodric got out of her car without further explanation. Sable quickly sprang out her side as well. She didn't care; she wanted answers. As Brodric approached his Jeep, Sable followed him. She leaned against his door, preventing him from opening it.

He groaned and glared at her. "We've danced to this song before."

"Let me help," she boldly announced. "You need to trust someone. You don't have to do this alone."

"I'm used to fighting my own battles," he informed her. "Besides, I'm not entirely sure I can trust you. There's no telling what you might do with the information."

Sable gently placed her hands on his chest and looked into his eyes. "I'm still here, Brodric. I'm here because I care about what happens to you," she announced gently and suddenly realized she was touching him. She fidgeted. "I'm afraid if I walk away, you might wind up like Shauna. I can't go through that again."

Brodric eyed her hands on his chest then gently touched her face. He kissed her warmly but briefly on the lips, surprising her. He pulled away and met her gaze.

"If you knew me, you wouldn't like me," he informed her with little emotion. "It's probably best if we didn't get any closer."

She stared at him with some surprise to the comment. "And if I don't agree?" Sable allowed her hands to fall to her sides and leaned against his car behind her. "I could tell you I don't mind the age difference, and I don't blame you for what happened to Shauna." She then hesitated while staring into his eyes. "I could even say, quite sincerely, that I don't mind that you're some sort of alien creature from another planet."

Brodric's stare was fixed on her. Although he barely reacted, he fidgeted slightly and raised his brows. "Well, I suppose that's coming right out with it."

"Doesn't take a genius to put it together," she casually informed him. "My only real question would be--are you and Haven the same beneath it all? I mean, you won't start craving human flesh, will you?"

"Certainly not." Brodric fidgeted and placed his hands insecurely in his pockets. "After we were stranded here, Haven began to overindulge." He reconsidered the comment. "I suppose in a way, I did too, but I craved knowledge." He frowned with a look resembling disgust. "He craved booze, sex, and drugs. I don't know what he took that night, but it did something to him." Brodric sighed and appeared to relive the horror. "Stuart denied giving him drugs that night, but I know he did. He *always* did."

"So the drugs fried his brain?"

"I'm not sure. Back at the beginning of our evolution, our ancestors were more wolf-like," Brodric informed her and raised his brows dramatically. "Carnivores." He snorted a soft laugh, although it didn't seem funny. "Nasty ones at that. It's our primal state. I can't be positive, but I think he regressed backward."

"More like a wolf-bat, if you ask me," she remarked. "I saw him scaling walls and ceilings."

Brodric frowned with defeat. "I just know I'm not fast enough to stop him."

"How did you capture him the first time?"

"Sheer luck," he announced and nearly laughed. "He almost killed me as I tossed him into one of the cryo tubes from our ship." He subconsciously rubbed his left arm, indicating where he may have been injured. "The good and evil of our kind is we're amazing healers. It saved me, but it also kept him alive. Locking him in there and freezing him was the only way I could keep him contained."

"Nothing can kill him?"

He snorted a soft laugh. "I wasn't about to reopen his tube and find out."

She studied him a moment in silence then fidgeted. "None of this could have been easy for you."

"I manage, I suppose," he replied with little reaction. "Now you know where I'm coming from. I'm an emotionally dysfunctional alien with a bad attitude." He raised his dark brows daringly. "Still want to know me?"

Sable straightened from where she leaned against his Jeep and moved closer to him. "I think the answer's pretty obvious," she announced while fidgeting slightly. "In spite of it all, you're all I could think about while I was away at college."

Brodric attempted to hide his grin. "I'd be lying if I said I hadn't thought about that little scene beneath the tree at the church picnic," he replied while reverting back to his shyness from that day. "My first kiss from an Earth woman."

There was silence between them as their eyes locked. Both were now tense and somewhat embarrassed.

Sable offered a warm, tiny smile. "Maybe we could pick up where we'd left off."

Brodric's expression dropped slightly at her forwardness. He then smiled gently and pulled her into his arms. Sable stared helplessly into his eyes while feeling her heart racing with anticipation of his response.

"I'd like that," he replied softly. His look then turned serious. "Right after you get back."

She was surprised by his comment. "Back from where?"

He shrugged without care. "Wherever you intend to go until I stop Haven."

Sable frowned and pushed him away from her. "I'm not leaving you," she snapped. "You'll get yourself killed!"

"And you'd be able to do little more than watch," he bluntly informed her. "Some part of him remembered you with me. If he can use you to get to me, he will. If you really care, you'd do as I ask."

Sable groaned and rolled her eyes.

Brodric attempted to look into her eyes, but she avoided looking at him. "Hey, it's bad enough I have to fight my own brother, but watching him kill you certainly wouldn't help matters."

She finally looked at him. "We're wasting time."

"This is serious, Sable," he insisted. "I won't risk your life. He's my problem. I'll deal with him."

She raised her brows in silent suggestion. "You need bait, remember?"

He groaned softly at the comment. "Not one of my most convincing lies."

"Just get in the car," she ordered. "We can argue about it on the way back to your place."

# Chapter Twelve

Within Brodric's barn, Cara held hands with Ally and Darrin where they sat within the chalk symbol. Darrin was growing more impatient or just nervous the longer they remained within the creepy barn. Despite Ally's determination, Cara was becoming increasingly frightened by the strange sounds she was hearing. Her eyes suddenly opened and she darted looks around the dimly lit barn.

"I heard something--"

Ally remained still with her eyes closed. "Don't break the circle. He can't harm us."

Darrin and Cara exchanged looks, doubting Ally's assessment of what could and couldn't harm them. They heard movement from outside.

Darrin suddenly tensed and looked around with concern. "I heard it too."

Ally pinched her eyes shut while attempting to ignore their paranoia. "Concentrate."

Darrin yanked his hands from theirs and sprang to his feet. "Screw concentration."

Darrin pulled Cara to her feet, causing Ally to look up with surprise.

"We're out of here," Darrin launched with hostility. "Gather your broomstick and black cat. The bus leaves now!"

Ally sprang to her feet as Darrin pulled Cara to the barn door with little protest. The barn door opened before they reached it, causing all three to scream with horror while jumping back. Brodric stood in the barn doorway with his typical look of hostility and annoyance.

"What the hell's going on here?" he demanded.

Both girls clung to Darrin while hiding behind him. Darrin shoved Ally in front of them, startling her. All three stared at Brodric with horror.

"He can't hurt us if we stay together," Ally insisted.

"What a relief," Darrin snarled. "Please be sure to tell *him* that."

Sable entered the barn and stared at the three with a look of surprise. "What are you doing here?"

All three saw her and were able to breathe again.

"Oh, Ms. Renshaw--thank God," Cara gasped.

"Be careful," Ally announced with wide, horror-filled eyes. "You don't know what he's up to!"

Sable looked back at Brodric, who glared at them with a sinister look. She smacked him in the midsection. His evil look vanished as he eyed her.

"What?" he cried out.

"Stop trying to scare them," Sable scolded.

"Bad habit," he muttered.

"Find a new bad habit."

Sable took his hand and led him toward the frightened kids. They watched with wide eyes and backed away.

"I want you to apologize to Mr. Hawthorne for entering his barn without permission," Sable firmly instructed her students.

All three stared with surprise, uncertain how to react.

Darrin was the first to do as he was told. "We're sorry, Mr. Hawthorne. It won't happen again."

"Yeah, we're sorry," Cara replied a little softer.

Ally folded her arms across her chest and refused to look at him. "I'm not."

"Ally," Sable scolded. "If it wasn't for Mr. Hawthorne, I might be dead right now."

Cara's eyes suddenly lit up. "You saw him? He came after you?"

Sable stared at Cara with some surprise. "Were you here earlier tonight?"

Cara nodded with a frightened look while clutching her chilled arms. "That man locked in the room beneath the barn killed Elana and Fuller."

Sable appeared horrified and looked back at Brodric. "He killed my kids?"

Brodric frowned. "I wasn't sure what had happened. The trapdoor was broken and I saw him take off," he informed her. "That's when I followed him to the school."

Sable shut her eyes and allowed her head to fall onto Brodric's shoulder as sorrow consumed her. He held her in his arms and placed his cheek on her head.

"I'm sorry, Sable," he whispered.

All three watched with surprise at the intimacy between their teacher and the local legend. They exchanged stunned looks.

§

An hour later, Ally and Cara slept on the floor in Brodric's basement apartment with throw pillows beneath their heads. Darrin slept slouched in a chair with his feet propped on the coffee table. Brodric sat in the corner of the sofa with Sable laying against him as he held her.

"Your students are devoted little parasites," he muttered. "I'll give them that much."

"They're good kids."

"When they're not setting killers free."

Sable strained to look up at him from her reclined position. He returned the look with a raised brow. She ignored his comment and placed her head back on his chest.

"Do you have a plan to find him before tonight?"

"Finding him will prove difficult," he informed her. "I'm not exactly the celebrated citizen in town."

Sable once more looked up at him and raised her brows. "Then maybe the town will need an adjustment," she announced. "I'll go with you."

"I wouldn't invest much stock in your future if you're publicly seen with me."

"Honestly, I don't care what other people think," she informed him.

"It's your funeral," he muttered then groaned. "He'll be someplace dark and quiet with limited traffic. Possibly a basement of some sort."

"Plenty of those around town."

"The sad truth is, we probably won't find him until he comes out at night to feed," Brodric reluctantly replied. He pulled her head to his chest and stroked her hair. "It's nearly daylight. You should try to get some sleep."

Sable gently caressed his chest, enjoying the way his body felt against her. "You should too," she replied softly. "We have a long day ahead of us."

"I'm quite content right here."

Sable lifted her head, met his gaze, and smiled. Brodric returned the smile then leaned down and kissed her warmly on the lips.

# Chapter Thirteen

Early the following morning, the small police station had several cars parked outside. It seemed as if every space was occupied, which was unusual. Within the sheriff's office, several irate parents stood in front of Sheriff Dwight's desk. They all seemed to talk at once while Dwight attempted to keep them calm and prevent the madness from spreading.

"I assure you," Dwight announced above the chatter. "All your children were out together somewhere last night. They'll either show up later today, or we'll find them wherever they're hanging out." His words didn't convince any of the parents. "McLean is checking the usual hangouts, and we'll contact you when we find them. Please go back home."

Sheriff Dwight ushered them from the office and out the front door. He returned to his desk and collapsed behind it with a look of exhaustion. Deputy McLean hurried into the office and approached Dwight's desk.

Dwight glared at him. "I hope you have more information on Brodric and those kids," he muttered. "I have a bunch of panicking parents on my hands."

"His Jeep was last seen this morning parked outside Sable Renshaw's house," McLean informed him. "Her car wasn't there and no one answered the door."

Dwight groaned softly and allowed his head to fall back against the back of the chair. "Now that gives me a rash." He straightened and glared at McLean. "What's that girl up to? I thought she had more sense than that?" He shook his head with disgust. "We need a search warrant for his house. I want every inch of his place searched until those kids are found."

McLean fidgeted slightly. "Sheriff, maybe he had nothing to do with it," he remarked, reluctant to share his feelings. "We keep putting all our efforts into Hawthorne when it could be someone completely different."

"I've been dealing with this guy longer than you've been in town," Dwight growled and stood abruptly from his chair. "He's trouble." He collected his emotions and straightened proudly. "What did you find at the school?"

McLean appeared slightly irritated. "Nothing more than what we knew last night," he replied. "We should speak to Sable. See if she saw anything."

"I'm not sure I trust that one," Dwight remarked defiantly. "She's up to no good--hanging out with Hawthorne. That always happens when these girls run off to college. Come back all high and mighty."

McLean frowned his disapproval but didn't dare say anything. "Should I go out to Hawthorne's farm?"

"No. Wait until we get the warrant," Dwight replied and collapsed into his chair. "Call Hauser. See if he wants some overtime."

"I already tried," McLean informed him. "He must've already left for his fishing trip."

"Figures," Dwight muttered.

§

It was already early evening. Ally, Cara, and Darrin sat on the swings at the playground near the church in virtual silence while watching several children play in the sandbox and on the jungle gym. The three appeared exhausted from their long day of searching the town for signs of Haven's new lair.

"Did your parents freak out about last night?" Cara asked her exhausted friend.

She groaned with disgust and shook her head. "They wanted to have a doctor check me for bruises and hickies." Ally looked at the sky and shifted uncomfortably. "It's going to be dark in a few hours. Hawthorne seems convinced Haven will come back out at night to feed. I wish we could have found some clue to where he was hiding."

"We've searched half this town," Cara announced, seeming contented to sit on the swing and relax. "People are starting to give us strange looks."

"We haven't checked that abandoned grist mill near the lake," Darrin informed them, although lacking enthusiasm at the thought. The place was secluded.

"Creepy," Cara muttered.

"Get Hawthorne to go out there," Ally snapped with irritation. "It's his brother."

"What's up with Ms. Renshaw and him anyway?" Darrin finally asked. "I saw them sleeping together on the sofa. They looked awfully cozy this morning."

"It's obvious she's dating him," Cara insisted.

Ally muttered, "And people say I'm strange."

"You are," came a familiar voice from nearby.

All three turned to see Tonya standing near them with a broad smile on her face. She was dressed slightly more provocative than usual and had a strange look about her. Tonya tossed her hair back and leaned against the swing support.

"Jamie was looking for you," Cara informed her. "He's half frantic."

"Jamie has to get over it," Tonya announced then seductively walked around them while maintaining her strange grin. "I met the most wonderful guy."

"You did?" Cara asked with surprise then wrinkled her nose at the stench coming from their usually fresh smelling friend.

"Apparently he's not from this town," Ally muttered.

"Hey--" Darrin squawked defensively.

"Sorry, Darrin," Ally remarked then muttered under her breath. "Forgot you were there."

"Anyway," Tonya continued. "You have to meet him. He's tall, dark, and incredibly mysterious."

"Does he go to school near here?" Cara asked.

Tonya giggled while giving them a look that was moderately disturbing. "He's not in school. He's older."

All three eyed one another with the same distrust as if coming to the same, strange conclusion.

Cara glanced back at their friend and forced an uneasy smile. "So when do we get to meet him?"

"You're coming to the dance tonight, aren't you?" Tonya asked while running her hand along Cara's shoulder.

Cara shuddered from her touch. Their friend was definitely not herself. Darrin noted her behavior as well then smelled the air and made a slight face.

Ally sneered and looked away. "Dances suck." She then seemed to notice the strange smell as well and looked around while sniffing the air.

"I hardly think we should have the school dance," Cara remarked, stating what the others were thinking.

"Why?" Tonya demanded with irritation. "Because Elana and Fuller are out getting high somewhere?"

Ally leaned toward Tonya and sniffed the air. She suddenly made a face but didn't comment, although she did grimace and turn her head away.

"I'm going to call Izzy," Darrin announced. "He'll know if it was just a prank."

"Then it's final," Tonya announced with a flirty smile. "I'll see you guys tonight at the dance."

As Tonya walked away with a strange swagger to her walk, they saw the scratches on the back of her neck and arms. Ally stared a moment longer and appeared curious.

Cara again shuttered. "Anyone else think she's acting strange?"

"Have you met Tonya?" Ally scoffed. "She's the queen of strange. What the hell was that smell?"

"I don't know, but it was pretty bad," Darrin remarked. "Did you see her back?"

"Yeah, it looked like she did the nasty in a briar patch last night," Ally muttered.

"I think there's something seriously wrong with her," Cara announced with concern. "We should find Ms. Renshaw."

§

Wally's Country Bar had several cars parked outside for the early evening hour. Brodric and Sable entered the half-filled bar and immediately received several looks. Sable caught a particularly nasty stare from Stuart, who was among the regulars. Wally approached the couple from his position behind the bar and grinned when he saw Brodric.

"Hey, Brodric," Wally announced cheerfully. "What brings you here on a Saturday evening?"

"Just a few unpleasant details, Wally," he announced with limited enthusiasm.

Wally glanced at Sable and grinned his approval. "Certainly not from where I'm standing."

"Have you met Sable Renshaw?" Brodric asked while indicating her to the bartender.

"Briefly a few years back," Wally replied.

Sable smiled warmly and greeted Wally.

"I need to borrow a few things from you," Brodric announced while fidgeting.

Wally eyed him suspiciously. "Nothing illegal, I hope."

"No, just need help catching some pesky critters in my barn," Brodric remarked.

"Bats again?" Wally announced with a groan.

"Great big ones," Brodric muttered.

"Everything's in the back," Wally announced. "Take what you need."

Brodric guided Sable toward the back with a door marked 'private'.

Stuart suddenly turned on his bar stool and eyed Brodric with a drunken smile. "Well, well, if it isn't Brodric Hawthorne," he announced. "Rumor has it they found some dead kids out at your place."

Brodric refused to look at him. "I don't want to get into this with you, Stuart."

Stuart eyed Sable, giving her a quick once over. "Yes, wouldn't want to frighten away the lovely young lady." He then focused his attention on Sable. "Do you know what sort of monster you're dealing with?"

Sable glared at Stuart with limited patience. "You're the guy who sells drugs to kids, aren't you?" she suddenly demanded. "Who's the real monster?"

Stuart attempted to grab Sable's arm in anger from the comment. Brodric suddenly caught his wrist and twisted it down, knocking him from his bar stool and to his knees. Stuart cried out in pain and cursed.

"Don't touch her," Brodric snarled while locking eyes with the drunken man.

He released Stuart's wrist then guided Sable to the back room. Stuart sprang to his feet and pulled a bully stick from his pocket. A gun was heard cocking. Brodric and Sable turned. Wally had a .357 Magnum aimed at Stuart. Stuart stared at the large gun and slowly lowered his stick.

"Get out of my bar," Wally growled.

Stuart appeared hostile then stormed from the bar.

Brodric smiled and shook his head at Wally. "Remind me not to cheat at our Friday night poker games."

Wally chuckled softly. "Man, you can't even bluff without feeling guilty."

They entered the backroom, shutting the door behind them. Sable looked around the cluttered room and examined several objects with confusion. The place was a catchall room with objects she couldn't even fathom.

"Not much of a housekeeper, is he?" she remarked.

Brodric held up a chain on a pole and examined it. If Sable had to guess, it looked to be something used by crocodile hunters. She gave him a curious look.

"Just a few tools of the trade," he informed her. "Wally used to work down south removing alligators from pools, snakes from basements, bats--you name it."

"Do you think this stuff will help?"

"Anything's worth a shot," he replied then sighed softly. "Haven won't be very happy to see either of us again."

Sable lifted a large machete and studied it. "Crocodile hunting, huh?"

Brodric eyed the machete. "He spent some time in South America as well. Used for cutting through vegetation," he informed her. "Very interesting guy, that Wally. Obsessed with flesh-eating creatures." Brodric removed the machete from her.

"Maybe we should take him with us tonight," Sable muttered.

Outside Wally's bar, Brodric shut the trunk on Sable's car after stowing their borrowed tools. Darrin's beat up car pulled alongside them in the parking lot. Cara and Ally practically jumped from the car and ran for Sable.

"Ms. Renshaw, we think we know where to find him," Cara announced excitedly.

"We saw Tonya," Ally informed them. "She had scratches on her neck and arms. She smelled bad too."

Sable stared at Brodric with concern as he eyed the three kids.

"Where is she?" he asked.

"She's going to be at the dance tonight," Ally informed them. "She said she has a new *boyfriend*."

Brodric looked back at Sable with increased concern. "We need to look around the school before the dance. We have to find him or those kids could be in danger."

"I could talk to Principal Dithers about canceling the dance," Sable suggested.

"See what you can do," Brodric announced. "I'll take your car to the school. Meet me there."

Sable nodded and hurried with the kids to Darrin's car.

# Chapter Fourteen

The high school was alive with activity that evening before the start of the school dance. Several cars were parked outside belonging to those setting up for the dance, which would be starting in only two hours. Within the gym, several students set up a refreshment stand near the main entrance while Jamie set up his flashy sound system to provide entertainment. There were enough speakers along the walls to blow the roof off the gym. Erica approached Jamie while he frantically attached cords.

"Will you be ready in time?" Erica asked. "Couldn't you find anyone to help you set up?"

He looked up at his attractive teacher from his position nearly beneath the sound table and frowned. "Izzy never called back," Jamie remarked. "He was supposed to help me tonight. He's been acting really strange lately."

"Well, I'm sure someone will help you if you need it," Erica replied.

Erica saw Stuart enter the gym from one of the side doors. He seemed preoccupied as if looking for something or someone. Erica immediately fidgeted then looked back at Jamie and forced a smile.

"I'll ask around," she announced then hurried across the gym and met Stuart before he could get more than a few feet inside the gym. It was obvious he was drunk. "Damn it, Stuart," she scolded. "You can't be here."

Stuart smirked and gave her a quick, lustful once over. "Relax, sweetie; I'm not here to ravish you." He looked around with more than a passing interest. "I followed Brodric here."

Erica stared at him as her mouth fell open with surprise. "Brodric?" she gasped. "Why would he be here?"

"Not for you, I promise."

She folded her arms across her chest and glared at Stuart. "As if I would want him--"

"Come on. The entire town knew that you wanted to get into his pants," Stuart mocked her then grinned drunkenly. "Ironic that *he* turned *you* down.

"I never chased him."

"Sure you didn't," he replied with a throaty chuckle. "Just like you'd never get in the back seat of a car with me." Her face turned red and angry. He ignored her embarrassment and continued to scan the room. "I saw him with Sable earlier. Guess old habits die hard."

"Brodric and Sable?" Erica gasped with surprise then attempted to cover what was almost certainly jealousy. "He has to be ten years older than her."

"She had a thing for him before she went away," Stuart remarked and gave her another quick once over. "You ask me, they've picked up where they'd left off."

"You really can't be here, Stuart," she again insisted. "You're going to have to leave."

"I will," he retorted. "Just as soon as I settle a score with that prick."

"I mean it, Stuart," she lashed out. "Don't make me call Sheriff Dwight."

"You do, and I'll tell Principal Dithers to drug test you," he announced with a devious grin. "Wait until he sees what's in your system."

Erica glared at him then fidgeted and hurried away. Stuart laughed at her hasty departure then left the gym and walked along the nearly silent hallway. The main hallway near the lobby was lit, but the other hallways were fairly dark. A gate that had been closed toward the back hall to keep kids from roaming around the rest of the building was now partially open. A man walked along the back hallway and headed into the cafeteria. Stuart saw the man and hurried for the gate. He slipped through the opening and jogged down the hallway after him, entering the dimly lit cafeteria. The tables had chairs stacked on top of them, indicating the floor had been cleaned earlier. As he looked around, he realized the cafeteria was empty.

"Brodric? I know you're here."

Stuart walked across the cafeteria between rows of tables while looking around. The shadows on the wall moved. Stuart eyed the walls with a strange look. He removed his bully stick from his pocket and gently slapped it against his hand.

"Come on, Brodric," he announced while grinning. "I just want to talk to you."

A shadow fell down behind Stuart. Stuart hesitated from the slight gust of parting air then quickly turned with the stick raised, prepared to strike. To his horror, he saw Haven standing behind him. Haven grabbed him by the throat while sinking his claws into his neck. Stuart attempted to cry out as blood seeped from under the sharp claws. With one hand, Haven effortlessly slammed Stuart backward onto a table. The chairs scattered and the table broke from the sudden force. Stuart's body twitched a moment then become motionless.

Haven kneeled over the motionless man and inhaled deeply. He reached into Stuart's interior jacket pocket and removed a small bag of cocaine. He popped the entire bag into his mouth and ate it. Stuart slowly regained consciousness and moved with a soft moan. Haven exposed his sharp fangs and dived for Stuart's neck. Stuart saw the fangs coming at him but couldn't even scream. He attempted to struggle and gasped as the teeth penetrated his throat. As Haven's fangs tore into his neck, Stuart thrashed a moment then tensed and stopped moving. Haven ripped out his throat and lapped up the blood as it poured from the gash.

Students crowded into the lobby from outside, entering in herds to the dance already in progress. Loud music pulsated from the gym where students mostly socialized while a few actually danced. Several teachers were monitoring the dance, including a now tense Erica. Sable entered the gym with Cara, Darrin, and Ally. All four nervously looked around the nearly filled gym. She turned to her three students.

"I have to find Brodric," she informed them with concern. "At the first sign of trouble, I want you to get everyone out of here. Got it?"

"If I pull the fire alarm now, everyone will be out real fast," Darrin informed her.

"Unfortunately, the principal will also have you suspended," Sable reminded him. "Wait for signs of trouble."

"Believe me, if I see Haven, I'll be pulling that alarm myself," Cara insisted. "Screw Principal Dithers."

"I barely remember what Haven looks like," Ally remarked while looking around as well. "How will we know him?"

"He'll be the one slashing throats, Ally," Darrin mocked.

Ally glared at Darrin.

"Be careful," Sable warned them.

Sable left her three students in the gym then headed back into the lobby and toward the back hall. As she walked past the boy's bathroom, she was suddenly grabbed and pulled inside. Sable let out a startled scream and came face-to-face with Brodric. Her scream appeared to have startled him.

"Shh," he attempted to silence her. "Do you want to bring the entire school in here?"

"Was there a less subtle way to get my attention?"

"This place is crawling with teenagers," he launched hotly. "What happened to getting the dance canceled?"

"Principal Dithers was more interested in getting me into a corner than listening to me," she muttered.

Brodric gave her a bewildered look then frowned with disgust. "Wonderful role model," he muttered then became tense. "I found evidence of Haven's new home in the basement. Unfortunately, I don't think he'll be back there before morning, especially since there's a teenager buffet in the gym."

"What are we going to do?" Sable gasped.

"I have to find him," he announced. "I need you to stay with the students and watch for him. If you see him, clear out the building."

"You can't fight him alone."

"You can't help, Sable," he reminded her. "I've been preparing to fight him for five years. You're no match for someone like Haven."

"But I--"

"Please don't make this any more difficult than it already is," he insisted. "If something happens to me--"

Sable was about to interrupt him.

Brodric silenced her. "I want you to promise you'll leave town and never come back."

"You want me to turn tail and run?" she suddenly demanded.

Brodric placed his hands on her shoulders and stared into her eyes with a serious look. "Listen to me, damn it," he growled softly. "Once I'm dead, he's coming after you. Kill your enemy and his mate. Get it?"

She could barely contain the horrified look on her face. "That's pretty twisted." Sable drew a deep breath while staring back at him. "Please, Brodric. I want to go with you. I can help."

"If you care about your students, you need to look out for them."

She frowned at his words. "It sounds so logical when you put it that way."

Brodric kissed her quickly on the lips then smiled warmly. "I'm coming back for you, Sable."

She tried to be brave and nodded. "I know."

Brodric hurried from the bathroom. Sable sank into thought and tapped her fingers nervously to her arms.

# Chapter Fifteen

The school dance was a success with a record number of students attending, which was unfortunate. Students danced together in small groups while others collected by the walls and socialized with their friends. Teachers patrolled the dance like sentries on duty. Sable entered the gym through the main doors, which remained open, and observed the room from a distance. She scanned the dim walls and ceiling. Every shadow looked suspicious to her. Erica appeared as if out of nowhere, startling the already jumpy Sable. She gave Sable an arrogant once over.

"I'd heard you came tonight," Erica remarked in a slightly snobbish tone. "You aren't on the chaperone list."

"Can never have too many chaperones," Sable muttered then looked back at the high, dark ceiling and corners.

Erica folded her arms across her chest and raised an arrogant brow. "Rumor has it you brought a date."

Sable didn't respond nor pay much attention to the attractive teacher.

Erica was quickly losing patience. "So where is he?"

"Who?" Sable asked as if suddenly realizing Erica was speaking to her.

"Your date," she huffed. "Brodric Hawthorne."

Sable glared at Erica and the strange look she was receiving. "I don't know what you're talking about."

Erica allowed her arms to fall to her sides. "Fine, then I'll just have a look for myself."

As Erica turned and left the gym, Sable watched her leave and gave the comment some consideration. If Brodric had been caught inside the school, it wouldn't look good. Sable felt alarm sweeping through her and hurried after her. Erica walked along the dimly lit hallway while Sable hurried after her and continued to scan the darkened areas.

"Erica, this is ridiculous," Sable scoffed attempting to replace her concern with annoyance. "You're supposed to be chaperoning the dance not running around the hallways."

"Brodric isn't supposed to be here," Erica informed her without looking back. "I'm sure Principal Dithers and Sheriff Dwight would be very interested to know that he's running around the halls of a school building filled with children."

"He's not running around the halls," Sable insisted then thought up a quick lie that sounded plausible. "He's waiting outside in my car. Are you happy?"

Erica suddenly stopped, looked back at her, and smirked. "Nice try, but I'm not buying that." She then spun on her heels and entered the boy's locker room.

Sable cursed under her breath and followed her.

Izzy suddenly appeared in the gym doorway holding his wrapped, injured arm and looked around with a strange almost psychotic look on his face. He saw Jamie toward the back of the gym playing disc jockey then hurried across the crowded room to join him. Jamie saw Izzy as he approached the table and removed his headphones.

"You're late," Jamie shouted above the blaring music while rounding the table to join him on the other side.

Izzy suddenly grabbed Jamie by both arms and gave him a frightened, psychotic look. "We have to get everyone out of here, man!"

Jamie stared at him with surprise while attempting to loosen his grip. "What are you on?"

"He's here," Izzy cried out and shook his friend. "He's after us!"

Jamie pulled away from him and gave him a strange once over while gingerly rubbing his sore arms. "Yeah, okay, Izzy. Whatever you say."

Izzy lunged for the sound equipment and shut off the music. The gym fell silent as everyone turned to see why the music had stopped.

"Everyone has to get out of here," Izzy cried out. "He's after us!"

The students stared at Izzy then began talking among themselves, undoubtedly commenting on Izzy's outburst. Several male teachers approached them.

Izzy saw them approaching and attempted to bolt away from them while shouting his dire warning. "You have to listen! You're all going to die!"

The teachers cornered and captured Izzy, pulling him kicking and screaming from the gym. Jamie could only stare along with everyone else then resumed the music to draw the crowd's attention away from his psychotic friend. Some students resumed dancing while others stared at Izzy as he was forcibly removed from the gym.

"Run," he was heard screaming as they pulled him through the doors. "Get out of here!"

§

Sable followed Erica along the rows of lockers within the boys' locker room. While Erica continued to look for Brodric, Sable nervously scanned the ceiling. She knew Erica was taking this personally, but she didn't understand why. She made it perfectly clear she didn't trust Brodric and detested him. Why not just call Principal Dithers and let him handle it. It didn't seem to make much sense.

"You're wasting your time, Erica," Sable informed her while attempting to sound calm. "He's not here."

Sable had to admit, she was concerned that Erica might find Brodric roaming the halls where he didn't belong, but she was even more concerned they'd find Haven instead. Brodric suddenly appeared before them causing both to jump with surprise. Brodric eyed them with some frustration. Sable knew the look was directed mostly at her.

Erica glared at Sable and raised a cocky brow. "You were saying?"

Brodric wasn't in the mood to hear what either woman had to say. His stern glare shifted to Sable, scolding her with his eyes. "You shouldn't be down here."

"Neither should you," Erica launched back, taking it personally as if the comment had been directed at her. "Give me one good reason why I shouldn't call Sheriff Dwight?"

Brodric looked at Sable with an 'is she for real' look. He looked back at Erica with limited patience, knowing they had bigger problems. "Several students were concerned about a strange man lurking around the school," he informed her. "As a favor to Sable, I agreed to check it out."

"And I know who that strange man is," Erica snapped while glaring at him as her arms crossed her chest. Her carefully manicured nails tapped her bare arms. "May I have a word with you in private?" It was more of a command than a request.

"I really don't have time for this--"

Her look was threatening. "You'll have less time sitting in jail for trespassing," Erica launched back.

Brodric glared his disapproval as Erica walked past him and toward the shower area. Brodric eyed Sable, sighed with defeat, and reluctantly followed the irate woman. Brodric entered the large, dry shower area only a few steps behind Erica. He casually placed his hands in his pockets and stared at her with an annoyed look.

"I don't appreciate being threatened."

Erica turned to face him, smiled lustfully, and slipped her arms around his neck while caressing his shoulders. "I've been thinking about us a lot."

Brodric pulled away from her and gave her a strange look, obviously surprised by her sudden mood swing. "What us?" he practically demanded. "There was never an 'us'."

Erica again moved against him, pressing her body into his, and smiled warmly while running her hands along his chest. "I never stopped wanting you, Brodric."

As her arms again slipped around his neck, he attempted to remove them, but she clung to him with more determination, refusing to let him go.

"You don't want some young girl who barely has a clue on how to please a man," she cooed seductively.

Without warning, Erica kissed him passionately and with aggression. Brodric broke off the kiss and pushed her away from him with a little more vigor.

"I didn't care for your advances five years ago, and I care even less for them now," he scoffed.

Her lustful smile turned hostile. "Fine," she snarled. "I'm calling Sheriff Dwight. He'll have your ass in jail so fast--"

Sable stood in the shower room doorway with her arms across her chest and glared at Erica. "You go ahead and call Sheriff Dwight," she scoffed in an angry tone. "Brodric's here with me. I invited him. If you don't like it, you can take it up with Principal Dithers."

Erica glared at Sable, displaying her rage and hostility. "Fuck you." She stormed past Sable and into the locker room. "Fuck you both!"

Brodric looked at Sable and gave her a slightly humored smile. "Now I have women fighting over me in shower rooms," he teased. "Who would've thought I'd be so popular?"

Sable hid her humored look. "We should probably keep an eye on her."

The lights within the shower and locker room suddenly went out, causing both to look around with concern. Within the locker room, Erica stopped in the darkness and attempted to look around.

"Not funny, Sable!"

A large shadow passed above her head, rumpling her hair. Erica ducked and let out a startled scream. She looked around with concern. Sable and Brodric hurried into the darkened locker room, looking at the walls and ceiling. They could see Erica standing near the lockers with a look of fright. Erica was suddenly grabbed and pulled up to the top of the lockers, screaming the entire way. Sable and Brodric ran for her. Brodric scaled the lockers and disappeared into the darkness above them. Sable nervously watched, although she couldn't see anything.

Erica plummeted to the floor and almost landed on her feet, falling harshly onto her backside. Brodric and Haven were thrown in a massive ball to the floor, landing on one of the heavy wooden benches. It cracked beneath their weight. Haven, having landed on top, sprang off Brodric and ran up the side of the lockers, vanishing into the darkness. Erica screamed hysterically and witness Haven running out the door into the hallway. Sable ran to Brodric's side as he unsteadily moved to his feet. Barely taking time to recover, Brodric bolted across the locker room after Haven.

Erica ran to join Sable and grabbed her arm with fright. "What was that?"

"Just your average, man-eating monster," Sable muttered then pulled Erica across the locker room.

Sable and Erica ran into the hallway after Brodric and skidded to a stop just outside the locker room. Brodric stood by the open stairway door while staring up the steps then looked back as Sable attempted to calm the hysterical woman alongside her.

"He went upstairs," Brodric informed Sable. "Get everyone out of here."

Sable nodded and pulled Erica along the hallway toward the lobby area. Brodric disappeared into the stairway.

# Chapter Sixteen

Sheriff Dwight and Deputy McLean entered the principal's office and approached two male teachers standing over the nervously rocking Izzy, who chewed on his fingernails and stared at the floor.

"Damn it, Izzy, what's going on now?" Sheriff Dwight demanded. "Monsters eating more of your friends?"

Izzy looked up at the sheriff with hostility. "Have you found them?"

"No, we haven't found them," Dwight replied.

"Then don't be an ass and just believe me," Izzy snapped hotly. "I'm not lying!"

"Alien attacks, psycho killers at the mall, thieves who steal designer jeans. I've heard it all from you before," Sheriff Dwight announced. "Why should I believe you now when you say you released a monster that's eating your friends?"

"It wasn't just any monster, it was Haven Hawthorne," Izzy cried out becoming animated. "He tore out Elana's throat! I saw him do it!"

Deputy McLean glanced at Sheriff Dwight with a concerned look. "Isn't that what happened to Shauna Decker five years ago?" the deputy asked.

"Don't encourage him, McLean," Dwight scolded.

"All I'm saying is, maybe we should check into it," McLean questioned.

Sheriff Dwight cast a glare at his deputy. "It's my job to keep order in this town," he announced. "Until I have proof Haven is back, I don't intend to start a panic."

McLean frowned but didn't comment further.

§

Cara, Ally, and Darrin kept a watchful eye on the gym filled with students now slow dancing. Despite the soothing love ballad, all three remained tense.

"Do you suppose Izzy actually saw him tonight?" Ally finally asked.

"Nah, I think Izzy completely lost it," Darrin replied. "We'll just keep our eyes open."

"Maybe we could talk to Sheriff Dwight. You know, defend Izzy a little," Cara suggested. "Maybe he'll listen."

"I've come to the conclusion that Sheriff Dwight has an ax to grind and isn't interested in anything else," Ally informed them, now looking bored.

All three froze when they saw Tonya approach. She wore a slinky, satin dress and a moderately creepy smile. All three became tense while watching her and the surrounding area, fearful that Haven may have been close.

"So, uh, where's your mystery boyfriend?" Ally asked.

"He's with some of the guys," Tonya announced cheerfully. "Come on. I'll take you to meet him."

"Take us where?" Darrin suddenly asked, obviously unwilling to go anywhere with the strange girl. "Where did he go with these other guys?"

Her giggle was enough to send chills down their spines. All three tensed then exchanged wide-eyed stares.

"There's a whole other party going on in the basement," Tonya offered. "Booze and pot. You coming?"

All three looked at one another with bewilderment. They knew exactly what sort of party Tonya was leading them to. A slaughter party.

Ally looked back at Tonya and smiled for the first time. "Yeah, sure. Sounds like fun." She casually shrugged. "This party's going nowhere. Why don't we meet you down there?" She grabbed Cara's arm, startling her. "Cara and I need to use the girl's room and Darrin has to find someone to relieve Jamie."

Both Cara and Darrin eyed Ally as their mouths fell open in response. Tonya nodded cheerfully, gave a tiny wave, and walked away.

Darrin suddenly glared at Ally and nearly jumped in place. "Are you out of your mind?"

"I'm buying just enough time for us to find Sable and Brodric," Ally informed them with irritation. "He wanted to find Haven. Now we know where he is, so let's go."

Darrin and Cara uncertainly followed Ally from the gym. Jamie appeared suspicious as he watched them leave from where he stood at the DJ's table.

§

Sable and Erica approached the lobby where they discovered Sheriff Dwight and Deputy McLean approaching from the principal's office with the slightly crazed Izzy. Erica pulled free from Sable and ran for Dwight. She grabbed the sheriff by the arm.

"Sheriff Dwight," she proclaimed. "I saw him! It was Haven! He attacked me!"

Dwight and McLean exchanged slightly surprised looks. Dwight indicated Izzy. "Take him to the squad car and call for additional backup." He then looked back at Erica. "Where is he?"

"He went upstairs," she cried out. "Brodric went after him to try and stop him."

"I'll bet," Dwight muttered.

"Brodric is trying to stop Haven," Sable informed him. "If he gets caught in the crossfire, I'll have you investigated and brought up on criminal charges."

Dwight glared at Sable and pointed a warning finger at her. "Your new boyfriend is being arrested for the murder of my deputy," he launched back. "A few hours ago, we found Deputy Hauser's police truck painted with blood near Brodric's house." Dwight glared at McLean and indicated Sable. "Take her down to the station and hold her as an accomplice." He then indicated Erica. "Escort Erica to the principal's office. She'll be safe there."

As Dwight turned and headed for the back stairs, McLean stared after him and shook his head. He then looked at Sable and sighed with defeat. "We'd better go."

"He's out for revenge on Brodric," Sable informed McLean. "You know that."

"There's nothing I can do about it," McLean replied with frustration. "The most I can do is call for additional backup."

"Maybe there's nothing you can do about it, but there's something I can do," she informed him. "If you want to stop me, you'll have to shoot me."

"You can't go after them," McLean insisted. "You'll get hurt."

"Stop me."

McLean stared at Sable a long moment then groaned and looked away, silently granting his approval. Sable turned and ran after Dwight, who had already disappeared into the stairwell. As McLean looked back at the hysterical Erica, he realized Izzy had taken off. He looked around for any sign of the teenager then groaned softly.

"Shit." McLean looked back at Erica. "Come on; let's take you to the principal's office."

§

Brodric stood in the darkened library doorway and removed a handgun with a silencer. He looked around the ceiling, walls, and darkened shelves before flipping on the lights. As the lights came on, Haven fell from the ceiling to the floor. Brodric darted across the library.

§

Tonya walked across the basement, casually approached the breaker box, and threw the main switch. Every light went out except for a few emergency lights. She grinned with satisfaction.

§

Within the gym, several students screamed as the lights went out and the music stopped. Once their startled screams subsided, they talked quietly. Teachers hurried around the gym, attempting to keep the students calm, which actually seemed to work. The students remained where they were and looked around waiting in darkness for the lights to come back on. An occasional girl's startled scream indicated some students were having a little fun scaring other students during the power outage.

§

Brodric stopped halfway across the library when the lights went out. Despite the darkness, he cautiously continued across the large room. He seemed less affected by the darkness than humans, allowing him to see better. He walked along several aisles while keeping a firm grip on his gun as he kept an eye on the top of the bookcases. He saw a large object nearby and jumped into the aisle with his gun aimed. There was no one there. Brodric uncertainly straightened with a bewildered look on his face. A shadow moved behind him.

"Drop it," Sheriff Dwight snarled.

Brodric tensed to the sheriff's gruff voice then dropped his gun and raised his hands in the air. "Sheriff, you have to listen to me. Haven is here."

"Shut up," Dwight growled. "I know what you're up to. Trying to cause mass panic and confusion while you settle old scores against those who opposed you and your brother."

Brodric slowly turned to face Dwight while keeping his hands in the air. He glared his annoyance at the sheriff. "You just don't get it, do you?"

"Oh, I get it all right," Dwight snarled. "You don't fool me at all."

A large shadow appeared behind Dwight.

"From the moment you moved into town, I knew you were trouble," he announced with hostility. "And even though I can't prove you killed my deputy or those kids, I know you're just as rotten as your brother!"

Dwight tightened his finger on the trigger with every intent on pulling it.

"It's no wonder this town has a bad attitude," Sable was heard from directly behind Dwight.

Dwight spun around, startled by her voice. Sable suddenly kicked him in the face then watched as he fell to the floor. She glared at the unconscious sheriff with annoyance.

"You're a bad influence, Sheriff," she snarled.

Brodric took a moment to breathe a sigh of relief then recovered his gun and pulled Sable away from the fallen sheriff. He hurried her toward the library doors.

"You're supposed to be evacuating the building," he reminded her.

"I couldn't let him shoot you."

"I'm far craftier than Sheriff Dwight," he insisted. "You had nothing to worry about."

"Didn't exactly look that way from where I was standing," she remarked with little confidence. "Where are the weapons you'd collected to fight Haven?"

"The janitor's closet downstairs," he informed her. "I didn't have time to go back for them."

"Come on, Mr. Crafty, let's get everyone out of here," she announced. "There's no telling where Haven is now."

Brodric suddenly stopped and looked around the library. "Are you noticing a pattern here?"

Sable appeared confused and looked around, not sure what he was implying.

"Darkness," Brodric announced. "The lights always seem to be dim or out when he attacks."

"Well, he is nocturnal," she reminded.

"Not just that. I feel more powerful myself," he informed her. "I think he gets power from the darkness."

"Then we should get the power back on."

"No, you can't go into the basement. I'm almost positive his mate protects it," he announced. "They're making a nest for her, and she'll kill anyone entering."

Sable stared at him with concern. "You can give me the good news anytime."

"Any offspring of his will be less human and a thousand times more dangerous," Brodric replied while hurrying her from the dimly lit library.

"The concept of 'good news' is lost on you, isn't it?"

# Chapter Seventeen

Principal Dithers walked along the mostly dark basement with his flashlight leading the way. As he approached the breaker box, there was a faint scraping sound almost like fingernails on a chalkboard followed by what sounded like a woman's high heels clopping against concrete. Principal Dithers turned around and shined the flashlight into the dark corridor.

"Is someone there?"

There was no response; although he didn't seem convinced he was alone. Dithers drew a deep breath then returned to the breaker box. He propped the flashlight on a nearby ledge, shining it into the box, and looked over the switches. The sound of high heels striking concrete was again heard.

Ally, Cara, and Darrin slowly walked down the dimly lit basement stairs with Ally leading the way. Cara and Darrin were less confident than Ally, who seemed to show little fear on their journey into hell. Her lack of concern was somewhat concerning in itself to her friends, especially with only the emergency lights barely brightening their path.

"Are you sure this is a good idea?" Cara whispered. "With the lights off, he has the advantage."

"You want to find him, right?" Ally remarked. "This is where we'll find him."

"And this is right where he wants us," Darrin muttered while attempting to look around with little success. "We wanted Brodric to do the dirty work, remember?"

Cara pointed to a faint light ahead of them near the fuse box. "There's a light up there."

They approached the aisle and saw the principal standing with his back to them in front of the fuse box. The flashlight remained propped on the ledge near him, shining into the box. All three were relieved to see him and quickly approached.

"Principal Dithers," Cara gasped. "Thank God--"

Cara touched his shoulder. His head fell backward only held on by some flesh and tendons. His open eyes stared at them from an upside down position before his body collapsed to the floor. All three screamed. Tonya stepped out of the shadows from nearby. She smiled slyly while seductively swinging a blood-covered scalpel possibly borrowed from biology class.

"Never liked him much," Tonya announced without care. "Always putting his hands where they didn't belong."

All three slowly backed away from Tonya while staring at the bloodied scalpel in her blood covered hand. Ally quickly looked around the walls and ceiling as if awaiting Haven's arrival. She didn't see any movement.

"Think about what you're doing, Tonya," Cara gasped while attempting to control her emotions, although it was proving difficult. "This isn't you. Cheerleaders don't kill people."

"Oh, Cara. You don't understand," Tonya casually informed her. "It's a matter of necessity. I need to eat." She smiled evilly. "Unfortunately, Principal Dithers is far too old and tough. But you, on the other hand, you look nice and tender."

Cara suddenly ducked behind Darrin and clung to his arm as they backed away. All three were frightened and mostly sickened by Tonya's chilling comment.

"Can we get the fuck out of here?" Darrin softly cried out.

"Any suggestions?" Ally gasped softly.

"Yeah, run!"

All three turned and ran for the stairs. Tonya ran after them, keeping pace despite her high heels. Tonya suddenly leaped on top of

Cara and tackled her to the floor, landing on top of her. Cara lay on her back and stared at Tonya as she hovered over her with the scalpel in her hand. Cara screamed and attempted to hold back Tonya's wrist. Darrin grabbed Tonya around the waist from behind and clutched her wrist with the scalpel, keeping her from getting any closer to Cara. He pulled Tonya off Cara, partially holding her in the air. Cara kicked Tonya in the abdomen as Darrin pulled her off. Ally helped Cara to her feet as she scrambled to stand. Both girls quickly backed away and watched Tonya fight Darrin's grip like a wild animal. Darrin wasn't even sure what to do with the wild girl fighting against his hold. He finally cast her across the basement. She hit the wall but seemed barely fazed. She caught her balance then ran for them. Darrin, Cara, and Ally screamed and ran up the basement steps. Tonya slashed at Darrin with the scalpel, nearly clipping him, and then ran up the steps after them. Ally, Darrin, and Cara ran through the basement door and slammed it closed behind them.

Darrin braced his body against the closed door. "Okay, now we do it my way," he cried out. "Ally, go to the principal's office and get Deputy McLean." He then looked at Cara. "Cara, pull the fire alarm. I'll keep her from getting out until Ally gets back with McLean."

Ally and Cara nodded and ran in opposite directions. The basement door vibrated harshly against Darrin. He gasped and attempted to keep the door closed. The vibrating finally stopped allowing Darrin to sigh with relief.

Tonya sobbed from the other side of the door, sounding frightened and pathetic.

"Please, someone help me," she pleaded. "I don't know what's wrong with me. I'm so scared."

"Give it up, Tonya," Darrin cried out while panting out of breath. "No one's buying it."

"Oh, Darrin," she sobbed softly. "Please, help me. He made me do it. You have to help me."

"Go to hell!"

Tonya let out a shrill cry as the door vibrated harshly, nearly tossing Darrin off balance. The door vibrated again. Darrin was cast away from the door as it was thrown open. He leaped toward the door to shut it. The scalpel slashed his lower arm. He jumped back with surprise and a startled cry while clutching his bleeding arm. The door flew open and hit him harshly. He flew back and struck the wall then collapsed face first to the floor. Tonya casually approached her unconscious friend. She lowered herself beside him, pulled his head up by his hair, and lowered the scalpel to his throat. A sly smile crossed her face. Izzy suddenly appeared around the corner, saw them, and gasped.

"Tonya--?"

Tonya released Darrin's hair as she looked up, saw Izzy, and sprang to her feet. She smiled sweetly at him as if nothing had happened. "Hi, Izzy."

Izzy quickly backed away, attempted an uneasy smile, and then turned and ran. Tonya ran after him. Izzy ran along the hall and skidded into his hall locker. He frantically worked on the combination on his locker while nervously looking down the hall. Tonya casually approached him while twirling the bloody scalpel. Her high heels were heard echoing along the hall in a rhythmic clatter. Izzy opened his locker, removed his gym bag, and then ran down the hall. Tonya picked up speed and ran after him. Izzy darted into the dimly lit cafeteria and immediately slowed.

The emergency lights allowed enough light to see Stuart laying on the floor in a bloody heap. Izzy stared a moment with horror at the dead man then heard Tonya's shoes clopping as she approached the cafeteria. Izzy stared at the door a moment while avoiding looking at the dead man and then hurried across the cafeteria. The door opened and Tonya casually entered. She looked around, not seeming the least bit affected by Stuart's butchered body. She walked across the dimly lit cafeteria with the bloodied scalpel clutched in her blood-covered fist.

"Izzy, come on out," she cooed almost seductively. "I'm not going to hurt you."

She looked around the cafeteria. Izzy appeared from the darkness and stared at her. She smiled, turned in his direction, and casually approached. Izzy suddenly raised his hand to reveal his football. He took a step back for a long pass and hurled the football directly at Tonya. She appeared surprised and let out a startled gasp. Before she could dive from its path, the football nailed her directly in the face, driving her to the floor. She writhed on the floor while clutching her bleeding nose. Izzy ran for her and kicked the scalpel from her hand.

He stood over her and sneered. "That's the touchdown for the game, bitch."

Deputy McLean disconnected his cell phone and turned toward Erica, who now held a flashlight, brightening the principal's office.

"Additional back up will be here soon," he insisted. "I want you to wait here while I go check on the students in the gym and see what's taking the principal so long with the lights."

Erica uncertainly nodded. McLean approached the office door and noticed a shadow appear before the frosted glass. As he reached for the door, his right hand touched the handle of his gun. Haven crashed through the glass, pounced on McLean, and knocked him to the floor. Erica screamed, dropping the flashlight, and ran behind the desk. Haven leaped off McLean and lunged for Erica. Erica jumped out of his path as Haven crashed onto the desk and slid across it to the other side. Erica screamed again and ran for the door. Haven glided across the walls and dropped down between her and the door. Erica jumped back a step and stared at him as he locked eyes with her while grinning.

"Haven," she gasped while trembling. "Haven, it's Erica. Remember me?"

Haven slowly stalked her, moving closer as she continued to back away.

Despite her fright, she attempted a smile. "Remember the fun we had, Haven?"

He licked his fangs like a hungry wolf. Erica appeared horrified when she saw his fangs and the way he looked at her. She backed into the desk and felt for objects behind her. She grabbed a paperweight from the desk and threw it at him. He sprang to the wall and out of its path. Erica bolted for the doorway. Haven leaped onto her back and knocked her roughly to the floor near the unconscious deputy. She managed to toss Haven off her and instinctively grabbed McLean's gun from his holster while moving to her knees. She aimed the gun, but Haven was gone. Erica stared across the room with alarm and fright. She uncertainly moved to her feet while holding the gun in her shaking hands. Haven dropped down behind her.

Cara ran down the hall and skidded to a halt near a red fire alarm pull station. She was about to pull it when her wrist was suddenly caught. She gasped with alarm as she was spun to face Sheriff Dwight. He appeared extremely upset.

"That would be a big mistake, little lady."

"Sheriff, thank God," Cara cried out. "Darrin has Tonya trapped in the basement. She killed Principal Dithers. Haven is here!"

He stared at her with disbelief and shook his head. "Are you all in on this together?" he demanded. "It's not Haven; it's Brodric who's after you."

"No, it's Haven," she cried out with frustration. "You have to believe me!"

"I've had just about enough of you brats for one night," he snarled and pulled her toward the gym.

§

Ally ran along the dimly lit hallway toward the principal's office when she heard a muffled gunshot. She slid to a stop before the office and threw open the door. She was about to enter then suddenly stopped and stared with horror. Erica lay on her back across the desk with her eyes open; her blank dead stare focused on the ceiling. Blood surrounded a bullet wound to her chest and her torn throat bled freely. Ally slowly took a step closer and stared at the deep gash across Erica's throat. Deputy McLean remained motionless on the floor, although he didn't have any visible injuries. It was possible he was just unconscious.

Ally lunged for the unconscious deputy when the door suddenly slammed behind her. She spun to face Haven and stared at him with horror. He smiled pleasantly despite the blood dripping down his chin. Ally couldn't take her eyes off his bloodstained fangs as he approached her. She backed up while clinging to her witch symbol necklace and stared almost helplessly. Something clicked and her expression suddenly changed to anger and hatred.

"You killed my sister!" Ally reached into her pocket and removed a thin, gold cross. She held it out before her. "You can go to hell!"

Haven suddenly stopped and stared at the cross in her hand, convincing her it had worked on stopping him. He cocked his head slightly, the twisted smile returning causing her to fill with alarm. Haven leaped forward and tackled her to the floor. Ally screamed and struggled against his clawed hands as he attempted to bite and scratch her. She continued to thrash violently and rammed the end of the cross into his eye. Haven leaped back as she pulled the cross free. He clutched his bleeding eye and screeched a horrible sound, briefly startling her. Ally scrambled to her feet and ran from the office.

§

Brodric ran across the dark gym filled with commotion and teachers attempting to keep students calm. He stopped in the center of the large room and looked around a moment.

"Listen to me--everyone!"

He received several looks and gasps. The murmur of voices increased at the mere sight of him.

"Everyone needs to leave here immediately and return home," he announced.

Dwight entered the gym with Cara then released her and hurried for Brodric while aiming his gun. "You're under arrest!" he cried out.

Cara took advantage of the sheriff releasing her and slipped from the gym. Ally suddenly ran into the gym from the front entrance while screaming hysterically without slowing. Everyone stared at her as she continued to run across the room.

"He's after me," she screamed. "Run!"

There was a slight commotion from the crowd of students as they stared at her with concern, although some thought her hysteria was funny.

"Stop this immediately," Dwight cried out while staring at the hysterical girl.

All eyes were now on either Dwight or Ally, so no one noticed a shadow bolting into the gym. It crawled up the darkened wall to the ceiling.

§

Cara ran along the hallway and skidded to a stop just before the first fire alarm pull station. Without hesitation, she pulled the alarm. It immediately wailed its warning. Cara exhaled with relief. She was suddenly grabbed by her shoulder from behind, causing her to scream and turn. Darrin held onto her shoulder for support while clutching his bleeding arm. A cut on his temple bled freely, streaking fresh blood down his face. He breathed heavily and appeared concerned.

"She got away," he gasped with horror.

# Chapter Eighteen

The fire alarm wailed as the fire doors automatically shut within the gym and the entire building. Everyone screamed while pushing and shoving to both exits on either side of the gym, causing mass confusion and preventing anyone from actually leaving. The teachers attempted to shout instructions above the alarm and the screaming students, but their shouts fell on deaf ears. Brodric suddenly looked toward the wall and saw a shadow moving along it. His body twitched as he considered risking Dwight shooting him in order to stop Haven. Despite that he hadn't actually moved, Dwight pulled the trigger, firing a shot at Brodric. Brodric leaped out of the way just in time to avoid being shot. The bullet hit the wall and narrowly missed one of the teachers.

Whatever order within the chaos the teachers had succeeded in gaining was suddenly lost as everyone screamed hysterically to the sound of gunfire in the dimly lit gym. Students pushed toward the multiple exits in a massive herd while the teachers shouted and attempted to stop the panic and hysteria. Brodric watched the walls and ceiling while eluding Sheriff Dwight, who was caught up in the mob of panicking students. Despite the running kids, Dwight had a clear shot. Sable entered the gym through the back door with the machete from the janitor's closet in her hand. She skidded to a halt and saw Dwight about to shoot Brodric.

"Brodric, look out!"

Brodric spun around to her cry. Haven leaped from the disc jockey table, knocking Jamie off his feet as he passed, and tackled Dwight to the floor, landing on top of him.

Dwight stared up at Haven with a look of horror and rage. "You!"

Haven grinned through bloodstained fangs. "Still mad about your girlfriend?"

Dwight aimed his gun at Haven from where he was pinned beneath him. Haven easily snatched the gun from him, straightened, and casually shot him. Everyone screamed and looked back while piling out the doors. Brodric suddenly leaped onto Haven. In one swift motion, Haven cast Brodric off him and across the floor. Sable ran toward Brodric and pulled him to his feet. As the room rapidly cleared, Haven leaped onto the walls and jumped through several shadows. Brodric and Sable attempted to keep track of him in the dim lighting, but the dark shadows made it nearly impossible to pinpoint his location. Cara and Darrin fought their way into the gym as the last of the students shoved their way out. The doors automatically shut behind the last of the students. Cara and Darrin nervously looked around the room. Ally and Jamie joined their friends alongside Sable and Brodric. They all looked at the dark ceiling and walls. A shadow moved.

Ally pointed to the ceiling. "There!"

They quickly looked to where she pointed. Nothing moved. Brodric walked across the gym and closer to the darkened area. While they all looked toward the corner near the ceiling, Haven leaped from the nearby wall and tackled Brodric to the floor. There were several gasps from the others as Brodric and Haven struggled and fought on the floor. Haven slashed at Brodric's face, but he was thrown off at the last second. Haven rolled across the floor and back to his feet as Brodric quickly straightened. Haven snarled and leaped for him. Brodric attempted to shoot him several times, but he missed each time until the gun clicked empty.

Haven roughly cast Brodric across the room and into the stereo system, breaking and scattering all Jamie's equipment. Jamie cried out with anger and leaped for Haven. Haven turned and easily cast Jamie back the way he'd come. Sable ran for Brodric and attempted to help him up as Haven stormed toward his barely moving brother. Sable attempted to pull Brodric to his feet, but Haven was nearly on top of them. Sable leaped to her feet, facing Haven with the machete in her hand and a wild look on her face. Haven stopped a few feet from her and sniffed. His nose wrinkled as he growled lowly then attempted to circle around her. Sable remained between Haven and Brodric.

Haven leaped to the wall and once more vanished into the darkness. Everyone again looked at the ceiling. Haven suddenly dropped down between Sable and Brodric. The kids all screamed a warning to them. As Sable spun around, Haven knocked the machete from her hand. She kicked him in the groin then kicked him in the face, tossing Haven sideways. He caught his balance, looked back at her, growling a warning then turned away from her and focused his attention back on Brodric. Sable punched Haven in the ribs and kicked his legs out from under him, surprising him. Haven sprang to his feet and circled around her with exposed fangs, although he seemed unwilling to harm her. Sable again kicked out. Haven attempted to leap away, but he was clipped in the hip and once more fell to the floor. She attempted to punch him, but he caught her wrist and dropped her to her knees, causing her to wince in agony. Haven once more smelled her and snarled with something resembling annoyance.

Sable kicked him in the side several times while using his hand on hers as leverage, then swept his legs out from beneath him. Haven sprang to his feet with even more annoyance as Sable jumped to her feet as well. He snarled at her but still didn't attack. Brodric slowly pulled himself to his knees and watched as Sable again kicked at Haven. Haven caught her ankle and cast her off balance, throwing her harshly to the floor. It took her a second to recover and pull herself to her feet. Brodric suddenly leaped for Haven and they roughly struck the wall. Haven cast Brodric away from him then growled and charged him. Brodric ran from him and toward the wall, surprising everyone as he scaled it and flipped backward landing on his feet behind Haven. Haven slammed into the wall then sharply turned, looked back at Brodric, and growled.

Haven climbed the wall and into the shadows. Brodric looked around with anticipation. As Haven leaped down for him, Brodric bounded from his spot, forcing Haven to strike the floor. He again leaped for Brodric, who then jumped for the wall and ran up it with Haven following him. The others stared in amazement as both raced along the walls and ceiling, defying gravity while fighting each other. They rolled down the wall together and crashed to the floor. Haven slashed at Brodric, slicing skin while Brodric punched Haven. Haven leaped up and ran back for the shadows. Brodric snatched the machete from Sable and chased after him.

The gym doors were suddenly thrown open. Izzy entered with his arm locked around Tonya's neck, holding her in a helpless position against him and the scalpel to her throat. Tonya looked at the ceiling along with the others. They heard the growls and scuffling from the darkness. Haven suddenly fell behind Izzy and cast him away from Tonya. Brodric fell near him, swinging the machete, but Tonya attacked him, and tackled him into the wall. Sable pulled Tonya off Brodric and slung her across the floor, giving Izzy another opportunity to pounce on top of her and subdue her. Haven became enraged and leaped for Izzy. Brodric coiled back and swung at Haven, but his brother leaped away, avoiding the swinging machete and returned his attention to Brodric. Brodric swung several times but missed the quickly moving monster. Haven again disappeared into the darkness. Rather than chasing him, Brodric held the machete before his face, lowered his head, and shut his eyes.

Izzy again held Tonya before him with his arm around her neck and the scalpel to her throat. Izzy looked around the darkness of the ceiling.

"Come on you fuck shit! You want your girlfriend?" Izzy cried out. "Come and get her!"

Brodric remained perfectly still as they heard movement from the shadows. Everyone looked around with increasing concern and complete silence. Haven leaped out of the darkness for Izzy as Brodric suddenly swung the machete. Haven landed near Izzy holding Tonya and suddenly stopped with a strange look on his face. His head toppled from his neck. Haven's body stood motionless a moment then collapsed to the floor. Tonya screamed then passed out in Izzy's arms. Everyone stared at Haven's fallen, beheaded body. The gym door was thrown open. McLean entered with some unsteadiness and his gun aimed. He looked around with bewilderment and disorientation.

"Is everyone okay?" he cried out.

Before anyone could respond to his question, McLean sank to the floor, once more out cold. They all stared at the unconscious deputy.

The police and ambulance were outside the school along with the crowd of students and teachers assembled in the parking lot. Izzy and Jamie helped Tonya to the ambulance. She held her abdomen with a slightly sickened look and appeared disoriented.

"I really don't feel well," Tonya gasped softly. "I wish someone would tell me what's going on."

First responders escorted Cara, Ally, and Darrin to their awaiting parents. Deputy McLean tried to maintain control and order while an EMT attempted to tend to the deputy's injuries. Sable and Brodric sat on her car hood and watched the entire scene from a safe distance.

"Is it over?" she asked.

"Yes, unless he's able to grow back his head."

"How were you able to do that?" she asked with surprise. "Climb the walls like that?"

"Apparently Haven wasn't the only one able to do tricks," he replied. "The first time I'd caught him, I couldn't remember how I was able to do it, but I think it was similar to tonight, except I wasn't armed the first time."

"You won't, uh, start eating people, will you?" she asked with concern.

"No, of course not," Brodric replied. "The drugs made him crazy. I'm positive of that." He eyed her. "You still trust me, don't you?"

Sable clung to his arm and smiled warmly. "Of course I do." Her look turned serious. "There is something that has me puzzled though."

"What's that?"

"Why wouldn't Haven attack me?" she asked. "He went after everyone except me. Even when I attacked him, he wouldn't fight back."

"That lotion I gave you produced the scent of a pregnant female," he informed her. "As barbaric as my species had been, they were unable to harm pregnant females. I was hoping that would apply in this case as well, but I couldn't be sure."

"Oh--?" she replied but didn't seem convinced. "What was in that lotion?"

Brodric avoided looking at her and slid off the car hood. "It's late. We could both use some sleep." He took her by the hand and pulled her off the car hood as well.

She glared at him with concern. "Brodric, tell me."

He smiled warmly and kissed her quickly on the lips. "It's classified."

Sable glared at him. He assisted her into the passenger side of the car and shut the door behind her. Brodric rounded the car and got into the driver's side.

"Brodric, tell me," she insisted as he got into the car, joining her.

He leaned across the seat toward her and whispered something in her ear.

Her eyes widened in horror as she stared at him and gasped. "Oh, that's disgusting!"

The car pulled away.

# The End

# Cemetery Stalkers

# Chapter One

The old cemetery seemed peaceful in the darkness on the secluded back road. The only sound heard was the main gate creaking open and closed in the gently blowing breeze. The crypt located amongst hundreds of headstones was moderately creepy despite its cared for condition. A police car drove past the main entrance located on the road side of the cemetery. The police car stopped before the open, main gate. An officer in his early forties, who was riding in the passenger side, peered through the side window of the squad car into the cemetery then looked at his partner behind the wheel.

"Why do people insist they see things in cemeteries at night?" Ryan remarked. "These places give me the creeps."

The officer behind the wheel eyed the cemetery with fewer jitters and casually shrugged. "Sometimes kids play in there," Dan announced. "You know, practical jokes, drinking, and sex."

"Seriously?" Ryan remarked with surprise. "Kids go to those places to have sex?"

"You were a teenager once," Dan reminded him. "Horny boys only need a place and time."

"Sometimes a girl helps," Ryan muttered.

Dan chuckled at the comment. A shadow moved within the cemetery, catching their attention. Both officers strained to have a better look.

Dan sighed and opened his car door. "Guess we'd better check it out."

"Give those kids a little scare of my own," Ryan muttered as he got out of the car as well. "Dragging me out in a cemetery after dark--"

Both officers approached the open gate and entered the cemetery with their baton flashlights. They shined the lights across the headstones as they walked along the main path through the cemetery toward the crypt.

"Beloved wife," Ryan read from the headstone he passed. He looked at Dan. "Amazing how everyone was so beloved after they die. I'd like to see *money hungry bitch* engraved on my ex-wife's headstone."

"Just let it go, Ryan," Dan said with a bored sigh. "You're like a broken record."

They approached an open grave. Both men stopped and shined their lights around the area. The ground lay alongside the grave in a large pile. Dan stepped a little closer and shined his light into the massive, freshly dug hole. The closed vault could be seen deep within the pit.

"That's unusual," Ryan announced while keeping his distance. "I thought they usually filled them in right away."

Dan shined his light upon a discarded shovel. "They do," he replied with added tension. "We'd better call for some backup. Looks like we have ourselves a gravedigger."

"A gravedigger?" Ryan asked as he stared with surprise. "You think someone's digging up the bodies? Does that sort of shit really happen?"

There was a strange scraping sound from the nearby crypt. Dan shined his light toward the small building. Ryan followed the light to the creepy, marble crypt. The crypt door was partially open. Ryan's eyes suddenly widened.

"Oh, no," Ryan announced firmly while shaking his head. "You're not getting me to go in there at night in the dark."

"Stop being such a wuss," Dan remarked and removed his gun from his holster. "Cover me."

Ryan removed his gun as well and followed his partner toward the crypt. Dan approached the partially opened door, gently pushed it inward, and then shined his light inside the dark building.

"Oh, Jesus," Dan scoffed and straightened with a look of annoyance.

Ryan looked into the crypt as Dan stepped away and removed his radio. The solid stone encasements were torn away and several caskets lie on the crypt floor. The old caskets had been jimmied open, although the lids remained shut. Dan talked into his handheld radio.

"This is Officer Milner; we need assistance at--" Dan began while looking around the cemetery. His eyes suddenly widened. "Oh, Jesus!"

Ryan turned away from the crypt opening and shined his flashlight in the direction Dan stared. A cloaked figure stood in front of Dan, like some mystic archangel. Ryan's mouth fell open with surprise and horror at the image. The sharp tip of a dagger burst through Dan's back as he cried out. Ryan could do little more than stare with horror as he stumbled backward while raising his gun. His expression conveyed his shock and fear while his finger tightened on the trigger. The cloaked figure spun Dan around, allowing the nearly dead officer to take three bullets to his back. Ryan gasped with horror, having shot his own partner. The cloaked figure discarded Dan's body and lunged for Ryan. Ryan took a step back while aiming his gun once again. He stumbled over something and fell to the ground just before the crypt doorway. The cloaked figure lunged on top of him and plunged a fifteen-inch dagger through Ryan's throat.

§

The following morning, a police line surrounded the cemetery and the distant crypt. A chain locked the cemetery gate along with a 'keep out' sign posted in front. All signs of police vehicles had diminished with the darkness, but it was apparent that there had been quite a disturbance sometime during the night. Connecting to the cemetery property was an old, renovated farmhouse. Its detailed exterior had been restored to a nearly mint condition. A young attractive blonde woman in her early twenties sat on the porch railing and stared across the yard at the cemetery. Amber Willow was a tall, slender girl. Her fashion sense indicated she was usually a fun-loving, party girl, although not this particular morning.

A Jeep pulled into the driveway and up to the house. Amber sprang from the porch and hurried to the Jeep. Another young woman in her early twenties got out of her vehicle and looked toward the cemetery as well. Despite being the same age as Amber, Samantha Krosby dressed more business and less flirty. Sam was equally attractive but with a somewhat sophisticated appearance with light brown hair worn in a stylish ponytail. Although not nearly as tall and lean as her friend, Sam had more curves in the right places. Amber approached Sam's Jeep with a look of exhaustion on her youthful face.

"You are not going to believe the night I had," Amber announced while hurrying to the passenger side.

"What happened next door?" Sam gasped while casting looks at the cemetery.

"Neighbors got a little rowdy," Amber retorted. "What does it look like?" She shook her head and jumped into the Jeep.

Sam stared at the cemetery a moment longer then climbed back into her vehicle.

§

Sam's Jeep stopped just outside the local funeral home in town. Once the vehicle parked along the curb, Sam turned in the driver's seat and stared at Amber with shock and surprise by the story she'd been told.

"I can't believe what practically happened in your backyard," Sam said with a firm shake of her head. "It's no wonder you didn't get any sleep."

"The police were no help either," Amber informed her while attempting to stay awake. "My brother went into the cemetery to find out what was going on, and they wouldn't say more than two officers were killed. Didn't do much to ease our worries. I mean, there could have been a psychopath running around our yard. Considering there are only two houses on that entire stretch of road, you'd think they'd at least give us something."

"That's just too much," Sam replied in disbelief. "You live next to a cemetery, and you work in a funeral home. It's a wonder you ever sleep."

"Come on, Sam. There's nothing scary about either," Amber replied. "I help my uncle with the funeral home because someone has to take care of departed loved ones. And a cemetery is just a resting ground, not some cursed place. You can't allow things like that bother you."

"I know," Sam said with a soft sigh. "But after hearing two cops were killed in the cemetery next to your house, it's enough to give me some serious creeps."

Amber laughed nervously. "I'll agree with you there." She opened her passenger side door and looked back at Sam. "Wanna meet for lunch today?"

"If you're up to it," Sam replied. "What time?"

"It's going to be a busy day. Why don't you just walk over when you're ready," Amber informed her simply. "I can leave whenever."

Sam shifted uncomfortably then forced a tiny smile. "Why don't I call you on your cell phone instead?"

Amber smiled gently and groaned. "You are a funeral home phobic."

"There is no such thing," Sam said while grinning. "See you later."

# Chapter Two

A two-year-old boy in a sailor outfit sat on a rocking horse and cried. The mother shook a stuffed animal and made kissy noises to catch the child's attention, failing in her mission. Sam stood behind the camera in the portrait studio and squeezed a squeaking stuffed animal with the same goal as the little boy's mother. A lanky man in his late twenties entered the studio wearing a clown nose and orange wig. The little boy stopped crying and watched Sam's boss, Dawson Dean, skip around the room. The little boy began to giggle. Sam snapped several photos then sighed with relief when it was all over. Several minutes later, in the outer lobby, the mother carried her little boy from the studio.

Sam turned to Dawson and shook her head while marveling. "You certainly have a way with kids," she remarked.

"Yeah, too bad I don't have the same luck with women," Dawson teased while smiling cheaply.

Sam shifted uncomfortably. She feared where the conversation might be leading. It wasn't as if her boss wasn't somewhat attractive, he just wasn't her type. His being her boss didn't do anything to increase her feelings for him either.

"How about lunch today?" Dawson asked, his cheerful mood returning.

"Sorry," Sam replied. "I'm meeting Amber for lunch."

Dawson frowned at the response. "I'd invite myself along, but I don't particularly care for Amber."

"I don't know why the two of you don't get along," Sam remarked. "She's a nice girl."

"She works in a funeral home," he replied. "Seems pretty creepy to me."

"I doubt that's the reason," Sam muttered.

The front door opened, alerting them to potential customers. A man in his early thirties entered the studio and paused just inside the doorway. Dawson eyed the man wearing sunglasses then looked back at Sam.

"And speaking of creepy," Dawson snorted softly but loud enough for the man to hear. "It's back."

The handsome man removed his sunglasses then eyed Dawson and raised a dark brow. "Don't you have anything better to do?" he scoffed.

Dawson sneered at the man and walked from the lobby into the back studio. Sam approached the handsome dark-haired man and smiled pleasantly at him.

"Mr. Colbert," Sam announced cheerfully. "What can I do for you today?"

Murphy Colbert leaned against the front counter and grinned teasingly. "For starters, you could call me Murphy."

Sam hid her embarrassment and leaned on the counter near him. She couldn't help taking in a sweeping glance of his handsome features and toned athletic build. "I don't think my boss would appreciate that too much."

Murphy shrugged without care. "Your boss is an arrogant asshole," he replied then removed a business card from his pocket. "I'd like you to take some pictures around my house. I want to send photos to my niece in New York. She's going to do some interior decorating for me and suggested some landscaping."

Sam glanced at his business card then looked back at him with a gentle smile. "Mr. Dean was pretty upset that I took those photos of your dog last week. I don't think he'd be too happy if I took pictures of your house."

"I'm not bringing business to Dean's photography shop," Murphy informed her simply. "I'd like you to do this on the side. I'll pay you whatever you think the job is worth."

Sam fidgeted and stared at him. "You're putting me in a rather awkward position," she informed him. "You know Mr. Dean doesn't like you."

"I don't care what Dean likes or doesn't like," Murphy replied. "Do you want to spend the rest of your life taking the same five photos of screaming kids? Come on, Sam, you're better than that.

You should be free-lancing. Start your own business. This will never bring you success or appreciation for your talent."

"That's kind of you to say, uh, Murphy," Sam said with some hesitation, feeling awkward calling him by his first name. "But free-lancing is a pretty unstable job. I still have to pay back the loans from my photography classes."

"If it doesn't work out, I'm sure you can find another job that pays more than your cheap boss pays," Murphy announced. "Nothing ventured, nothing gained."

Sam smiled and nodded gently. "You're right, Mr. Colbert, uh, Murphy," she said in an attempt to stop the debate. "I suppose I could take the photos on my own time."

"When do you think you can stop by for the shoot?" Murphy asked with a curious tilt of his head.

"I don't have any real plans this weekend," Sam said with a slight frown then managed a smile. "I suppose early morning or later in the evening would work best for outdoor shots."

"Great," Murphy replied with a pleasant smile. "Why don't we make plans for Saturday around five o'clock, that way you can decide where you want to start. Are you familiar with the area?"

Sam looked at his card and studied the address with some surprise. She looked back at him and managed a tiny laugh. "This is just down the road from my friend, Amber. She lives next to the cemetery."

Murphy's expression dropped at the comment. "I heard there was some sort of trouble out there last night. I couldn't see much from my place."

"Yes, there was," Sam replied and shivered at the thought. "Apparently two police officers were killed. Must have been chasing someone. Gives me the creeps."

"There's been some controversy surrounding that cemetery for the past few months," Murphy informed her. "Your friend better keep her doors locked at night." He managed a smile despite the morbid conversation. "I'll see you tomorrow evening then." He then turned and headed for the door.

Amber entered the studio as Murphy was leaving. Murphy held the door open for her then proceeded out, returning his sunglasses to his face. Amber paused just inside and turned to watch Murphy leave. She spun on her heels and looked at Sam with a bright smile plastered on her face.

"Oh, he's one, hot stud muffin," Sam announced with an exaggerated gasp.

Dawson stood in the open doorway to the studio with his arms folded across his chest and a disapproving glare while staring at the outer door.

"He's an asshole," Dawson interjected and straightened.

Sam returned to the sign-in book to check on her next appointment then eyed Amber with a tiny smirk. "He has to be ten years old than you," she informed her friend.

"So?" Amber announced with a devious smile. "Maybe I like my men older and more experienced. Who is he?"

"Actually, he's your neighbor," Sam informed her.

"He's some rich, eccentric jerk," Dawson remarked lowly. "He comes in here at least twice a week and makes eyes at Sam. What's the creep luring you in with this time?"

Sam groaned and placed the card in her pocket. "He's not a creep, and he's not luring me into doing anything. He's paying me to take some photos of his house for his niece."

"Sure," Dawson snapped and moved next to her. "He just wants to get you into his bedroom. Trust me I know his type. Rich and full of himself."

Sam walked away from her boss and approached the front door. Amber hurried after her appearing confused by the turn the conversation took. Sam turned to face Dawson from across the room.

"He's not interested in me, Dawson. He's interested in my portfolio. Give the guy a break, huh?" Sam remarked in Murphy's defense. "I'm going to lunch. I'll be back in an hour."

Sam and Amber left the studio. Amber trotted alongside Sam with a childish grin on her face.

"Tell me all about him," Amber announced enthusiastically. "Is he *really* rich?" Amber suddenly gasped with excitement. "I wonder if he owns that big, expensive looking home? The one that looks like a mini-castle. Of course, he does! That's the only other house on my road." She bounced alongside Sam. "Oh, you have to introduce me. Can I come along to his house? Please!"

"My goodness, Amber," Sam interjected. "You're worse than a schoolgirl."

"He's drop-dead gorgeous," Amber replied with enthusiasm.

"I think there should be some sort of law against mortician's using that term," Sam muttered lowly. "Only if he doesn't mind that I bring you along. I'll have to ask him if it's okay."

"It should be," Amber remarked then raised a devious brow. "Unless he *is* planning something romantic."

"You're just as bad as Dawson," Sam snapped. "I'd think I'd know if he was flirting with me, and he definitely wasn't flirting with me."

"And if he was?" Amber asked while grinning lustfully.

"If he were, I'd have to tell him he's too old for me," Sam informed her simply. She then laughed softly. "Besides, could you imagine me with the rich, pompous type?"

"No," Amber replied with a teasing grin. "You're more of the local, country boy type." Amber then grabbed onto Sam's arm. "Speaking of which, you're still coming over tonight, right? My brother is cooking his world famous stew."

Sam laughed and nodded. "Yes, I'll be over around six or so."

# Chapter Three

Sam walked onto Amber's porch and promptly knocked on the door. While she waited for her friend to answer, she looked toward the cemetery just beyond the front yard and stared at the police line remaining around the crypt. Sam shifted uncomfortably and looked back at the door. The door opened to reveal Amber's tall, lean brother. Baxter was a moderately handsome man in his mid-twenties with sandy brown hair. He stood in the doorway with a puzzled look on his face.

"Can I help you?" Baxter said simply.

Sam smiled and tilted her head with a humored look. "You invited me, remember?"

Baxter continued with the game. His eyes narrowed as he considered her comment. "Hmm, sorry. Don't know what you're talking about."

Sam pushed Baxter aside and entered the house. Baxter laughed and shut the door behind her.

"You're such a pushy person, Sam," Baxter teased while grinning as he followed her down the hallway with a lively spring in his step. "I love forceful women."

"You'd love any woman with a pulse," Sam remarked with a teasing smile.

"True," Baxter said with a soft laugh. "But keep that between us. I have a date tonight."

Sam stopped in the hallway and turned to face him. "And you actually brought her home? This is a first."

"Have to get serious some time." He appeared to reconsider then smiled and casually shrugged. "Or maybe not."

§

All four sat around the elegantly set dining room table in the neat but old room. Venus was an attractive, large bosomed blonde woman possibly over the legal drinking age. Baxter had a type, and his type consisted of beautiful women with limited intelligence and ample cleavage refusing to be contained. Amber and Sam exchanged looks several times as Venus attempted to keep her cleavage within her low-cut, form-fitting shirt. It was obvious she wasn't wearing a bra indicated by her high beams poking through her thin shirt. Baxter practically lay across the table while talking to her in a soft, romantic voice.

"Such a fascinating life you've led," Baxter remarked with a dreamy sigh. "I don't think I've ever dated an underwear model before." He paused for effect then grinned. "Do they give you free samples?"

Venus giggled. Amber and Sam rolled their eyes and looked back at their plates.

"Isn't this the best beef stew ever?" Amber announced loudly, reminding Baxter that he and his date weren't alone.

"And the wine selection is exquisite," Sam added while holding up her glass. "How ever did someone like your brother develop such great taste?"

Baxter held Venus's hand and looked deep into her eyes while responding to Sam's sarcastic remark. "It's a gift. I'm full of surprises."

Venus giggled again. "This is one of the best meals I've had in a while," she announced. "I think it's romantic when a man cooks for me."

"That's me, Mr. Romance," Baxter remarked in his sexiest voice, attempting to woo his date.

Amber leaned closer to Sam. "It's getting deep in here," she muttered.

"Guess we don't need dessert," Sam replied. "There are enough sweet nothings at the other end of the table."

"What happened at the cemetery?" Venus asked, switching gears on Baxter.

Baxter released her hand and straightened with a broad grin. "Another ghost attack," he informed her then raised his brows deviously. "There are always strange noises coming from that cemetery. The dead are very restless."

Venus giggled at the comment. "You'd say anything to make me laugh."

"True," Baxter replied then turned serious. "But I'm not kidding. I actually saw someone lurking around the cemetery on more than one occasion. When I went outside to see who was hanging around, I never found anyone."

Amber frowned while glaring at her brother. "You have not. That's not funny, Baxter," she scoffed. "Two police officers were killed there last night."

Baxter glared at his sister with irritation. "I wasn't trying to be funny," he snarled back. "Why won't you believe that I've seen ghosts? Just because you refuse to believe it, that doesn't mean it's not real."

Venus looked at Amber with large, curious eyes. "Have you ever seen ghosts in the cemetery?"

"Certainly not," Amber announced firmly and tossed her napkin down. "Even if I did believe in ghosts, I'd certainly never believe they'd be capable of killing two men."

"Suit yourself," Baxter remarked simply. "But when you wake up and find some zombie hovering over your bed, just remember that I was right."

"If I ever wake up and see a zombie standing over my bed, it'll be you. I promise that'd be the last time you ever scare me again," Amber informed him in a threatening tone.

"Enough joking around," Sam announced simply and set her wineglass down. She cast a look at Baxter. "You're going to scare Venus into leaving." She raised her brows. "And I *know* you don't want to do that."

Baxter stared at Sam a moment then quickly looked at Venus and attempted a smile. "I was just kidding. I have a great sense of humor," he announced and attempted to lighten the mood. "Wanna watch a movie in the game room?"

Venus smiled warmly and nodded. Baxter jumped to his feet, took Venus's hand, and led her to the dining room door. He paused in the doorway and looked back at Sam and Amber.

"I made dinner," he announced simply then wagged his finger at the two of them. "You two get to clean up."

"Figures," Amber muttered as Baxter disappeared through the doorway with his bombshell vixen. "Anytime he cooks, there's always a catch."

"It's only fair," Sam replied simply.

"Oh, but you should see how he leaves the kitchen after he cooks," Amber remarked and stood. "I swear he uses every piece of cookware. Once, I found marinara sauce on the ceiling fan."

§

Amber and Sam sat on the front porch of the house later that evening and enjoyed the night air. The full moon allowed just enough light to see the headstones within the cemetery and the chilling police line around the crypt. Sam sat on the railing and stared across the yard at the cemetery.

"Very creepy," Sam remarked under her breath as she rubbed her chilled arms.

"Not usually," Amber remarked. "But since the murders, I've looked at that place from a different perspective."

"I didn't see anything in the paper," Sam remarked. "I guess they didn't find the killer yet. That would make me more nervous than anything."

Baxter and Venus walked onto the porch with a blanket, a flashlight, and a bottle of wine.

Amber glared at Baxter. "What do you think you're doing?" she demanded to know.

"We're going for a little romantic interlude," Baxter replied while raising his brows cleverly. "Venus wanted to see the crime scene, so I thought I'd give her the personal, guided tour of our cemetery."

"That's sick," Amber snapped with a look of disgust at her brother.

"Well, a little kinky, maybe," Baxter replied as Venus clung to him in a giddy mood, receptive to the remark. "But I don't know if it qualifies as sick."

Baxter and Venus walked off the porch and headed for the cemetery. Amber and Sam looked at each other and grimaced at the thought.

"I think that's my cue to leave," Sam informed Amber and stood from where she'd sat on the railing. "If I see your brother getting it on in the cemetery, I'll be violently ill."

"Me too," Amber muttered and stood as well. "Let me know what Mr. Colbert says about tomorrow."

"I will," Sam replied and left the porch.

# Chapter Four

Baxter and Venus stood before the police line within the cemetery and strained to see the area surrounding the crypt. Markers indicated where the bodies had been found and the ground remained soaked with dried blood. Baxter looked back at her and smiled deviously.

"Creepy, don't you think?" Baxter asked then offered a creepy laugh.

Venus appeared concerned and ran her hands along her chilled arms. "A little," she replied timidly. "Why don't we find another spot?"

"Good idea," Baxter interjected cheerfully.

They walked through the cemetery with their blanket, wine, and flashlight. Baxter held the light to his face and began laughing in a macabre manner. Venus smirked, but she appeared to lose her thrill for their morbid interlude.

He gave her a puzzled look. "You aren't scared, are you?" Baxter asked.

"No," Venus replied a little too quickly as she nervously looked around.

Baxter spread the blanket out near several older headstones. "The whole thrill is the fear factor," he informed her. "Makes for stimulating sex."

Venus managed to smile warmly, although she no longer seemed convinced. Once they sat on the blanket, Baxter poured them some wine. She sipped the wine and looked around with a tiny, nervous smile.

"This certainly is different for me."

"Like I said, it's stimulating," Baxter announced then leaned forward and kissed her.

She returned the kiss that quickly turned passionate as he slowly lowered her to the blanket. They made out on the blanket for a few minutes before Baxter ran his hand firmly along her body. The sound of leaves rustling caught her attention. Venus suddenly stopped his hand and lifted her head.

"I heard something," she announced firmly and looked around.

Baxter continued to run his hand along her side and pushed her back down on the blanket. "You're just imagining things." He kissed her neck. "Just relax, baby."

He kissed her along her neck and down the opening of her shirt to her ample cleavage. Venus attempted to look around, unable to relax. Baxter pinned her to the ground with his body, not allowing her much room to survey the area. The snapping of a twig alerted her. Venus gasped and sat up, nearly knocking Baxter over.

Baxter sat up with a groan and stared at her. "It's just your imagination," he informed her with less patience. "There's no one out here but you, me, and a bunch of dead guys."

"I think we'd better go back," Venus announced firmly and stood.

Baxter groaned with disappointment and allowed his face to fall into the blanket. "Okay," he breathed lowly then looked back at Venus.

Venus looked around nervously and rubbed her chilled arms. The cloaked figure stood behind her with a dagger raised in its gloved hand.

Baxter's eyes widened with horror. "Oh, shit!"

Venus spun on her heels, saw the cloaked figure behind her, and screamed hysterically. The dagger was thrust down into her throat. Baxter stared in horror while scrambling backward on the blanket then looked up to the cloaked figure as it approached him, its dagger dripping blood.

Amber entered the photography studio the following morning as Sam was ringing up a woman's photo purchase. The woman collected her purse and her envelope and left the studio, politely nodding to Amber. Amber approached the front desk and leaned on it with exhaustion.

"What brings you here so early on a Saturday morning?" Sam asked while eyeing her weary looking friend.

"Can you believe I was called in to work early this morning?" Amber announced with a sigh.

"I swear I've been working every Saturday since the beginning of time," Sam muttered.

"Dawson around?"

"He's in a photo shoot," Sam replied.

"Good, then I can escape before he's finished," Amber stated with little enthusiasm to see Dawson. "Did you talk to Mr. Colbert yet?"

"Yes, he called this morning to confirm our appointment for this afternoon," Sam replied. "He said it didn't matter if you wanted to come along."

Amber jumped around excitedly. "Oh, I can hardly wait. Hope I'll have some energy left this afternoon."

"So how did Baxter's cemetery date go last night?" Sam asked while raising a curious brow.

"Oh, I'm sure he got lucky, as usual," Amber replied. "I left before he got up. He usually sleeps until noon after a full night of meaningless sex." She sighed and leaned on the counter. "At least someone's getting some."

"Are you on that again?" Sam groaned.

"I haven't had a good date in months," Amber informed her. "Or even a bad one, for that matter." She straightened and smiled with enthusiasm. "Maybe Mr. Colbert can change my unlucky streak for me."

"And if he's not interested in you?" Sam asked.

"I know the type," Amber remarked while grinning. "He's looking for someone young and vibrant. I qualify. Besides, once he finds out you're not interested, he'll be all over me."

"I still think you're way off base with that," Sam remarked. "He's not interested in me. If he were, he wouldn't have agreed to let you tag along this afternoon."

"I'll bet you five dollars he is," Amber announced with a cheap smile.

"Okay, and suppose he is," Sam interjected. "What makes you think he'd switch gears and go after you?"

"Because," Amber replied while straightening proudly. "I'm more outgoing than you are. I know how to turn them on." She smiled slyly. "Baxter's not the only one who inherited the gift of seduction."

Dawson appeared from the studio along with an older couple. "I'll have those proofs for you by Monday morning," Dawson informed them.

They nodded and left the studio. Dawson eyed Amber and approached the counter.

"Hey, what brings you here on a Saturday?" Dawson asked, surprised to see her.

"The funeral home has been kind of busy lately, and they asked me to work," Amber replied.

"Yeah, people are just dying to get in there," Dawson announced with a grin.

Amber smirked at the old joke. "If I had a dime for every time I've heard that one."

Dawson looked at Sam and offered a warm smile. "So what are your plans for tonight?"

"Sam and I are going to Mr. Colbert's house," Amber informed him with a teasing smirk. "For a threesome."

Sam rolled her eyes at her friend's idea of humor.

"I don't think that's such a good idea, Sam," Dawson announced. "You don't know what that guy's up to. I don't trust him."

"I was teasing about the threesome," Amber huffed.

Dawson glared at her then returned his attention to Sam. "This is serious."

"I'll be fine," Sam informed him without care. "Amber's going with me."

"I heard he's into some pretty weird stuff," Dawson informed her. "He has a collection of medieval weaponry."

"Who told you that?" Sam asked while giving him a strange look.

"Mr. Johnson," Dawson replied. "Apparently they have a long history."

"You mean Mr. Colbert's gay?" Amber gasped with a look of horror.

Dawson glared at Amber. "No. That means they don't get along. In fact, they hate each other." He then focused his attention back on Sam. "Mr. Johnson told me a lot of things about Mr. Colbert."

Sam studied Dawson with an odd look. "And you're just telling us today? Why didn't you say something yesterday?" she practically demanded. "Or did you just find this out yesterday when you told Mr. Johnson that Mr. Colbert was in here talking to me?"

Dawson fell silent and seemed reluctant to respond.

"You just don't want me going to Mr. Colbert's house," Sam remarked simply.

"No matter what my reasoning, Sam," Dawson announced, "I don't think you should trust that guy. There were two murders not far from his house. How do you know he's not involved? The guy's creepy."

Sam rolled her eyes and turned defensive. "I'm tired of your unfounded jealousy, Dawson. I can date whomever I wish, and that includes Mr. Colbert."

Amber suddenly took an interest in the conversation and stared at her friend, obviously offended. "Wait a minute--"

# Chapter Five

Sam's Jeep pulled up to the impressive, yet sinister looking mansion only a quarter of a mile from Amber's house. The front drive was decorated with marble statues of gargoyles and strange looking plants. Both Sam and Amber got out of the Jeep and paused a moment to stare at the mansion.

"Wow," Amber said with a look of surprise. "This guy must *really* be loaded."

Sam removed her camera bag from the Jeep and joined her friend as they approached the house with some hesitation. Murphy appeared on the porch. His large Belgian Malinois dog ran from the porch and happily greeted both women. Amber was a little intimidated by the fierce looking teddy bear of a dog. Sam greeted the dog with great affection, having spent time photographing him the previous week at the studio.

"I'm so glad you could make it," Murphy announced cheerfully as he approached, calling the dog back for Amber's comfort.

As they approached Murphy and the house, Amber suspiciously eyed the creepy gargoyle statue near the porch.

Murphy caught her concerned look and laughed softly. "Don't mind the gargoyles; they don't bite."

Sam studied the exterior of the house then looked back at Murphy with a nervous smile. "This is an interesting place you have here, Mr. Colbert, uh, Murphy."

Murphy looked around as well and beamed with delight. "Do you like it?" he asked cheerfully then chuckled. "I get mixed reactions to my eccentric sense of style. Can't please everyone, I suppose."

He led them onto the porch and paused before the front door. The marble doorknocker was in the image of a gargoyle as well, making the women wonder about his bizarre fascination with the hideous creatures. As he opened the door for them, Sam and Amber looked at each other as if debating who would have to go first. Sam finally entered and paused in the foyer. The grand hallway was a masterpiece of detailed carved wood while the floor was a light gray marble. Antique furnishings, suits of armor, swords, shields, and unusual paintings lined the walls, lending a heavy medieval feel.

"Now this is twisted," Amber announced bluntly.

Sam glared her disapproval at Amber's blunt comment spoken aloud.

Murphy shut the door behind them. "I used to be a medieval folklore professor."

Sam looked back at Murphy and smiled warmly. "Really? Why don't you teach anymore?"

"I had a disagreement with the Dean," Murphy replied and walked down the foyer steps then looked back at them with a teasing grin. "Apparently there was some offense taken to medieval torture. I didn't invent it; I was just explaining it."

"You and my brother would certainly find a lot to talk about," Amber remarked lowly.

They followed him down the foyer steps and into the hallway itself. His dog disappeared into one of the rooms then returned with his favorite squeaky toy and dropped it at Amber's feet. She eyed the heavily chewed toy and grimaced slightly. Murphy picked up the slimy toy and tossed it down the hall. The dog ran after it. Murphy returned his attention to Sam.

"I'll give you the guided tour, and then you can decide where you'd like to begin," Murphy announced. He led them to the first door on the left.

Sam glared at Amber. "So, is he acting like a guy intending to seduce me? I think you owe me five bucks."

"Give him time," Amber remarked gently.

They followed Murphy into the first room. Sam stared at the elegant study with its stained-glass windows, wood carved fireplace, bookcases, and a large, detailed antique desk and chair. The only modern thing in the room was the computer on top of the desk.

Murphy turned and leaned casually against the desk, although both women found his pose quite sexy.

"Of course, you'll stay for dinner," Murphy informed them simply. "Since you'll be here a while, that is."

"We'd love to," Amber interjected quickly.

Sam elbowed Amber while hiding her embarrassed look. "We don't want to put you to any trouble."

"No trouble at all," Murphy announced a little too cheerfully.

§

While Sam snapped pictures in the library, Amber hovered over Murphy and asked him every imaginable question, even the embarrassing ones. Sam looked back every few minutes and rolled her eyes at her friend's misguided attempt at flirting. It was almost a relief when Amber excused herself to use the lady's room. Sam finished taking her last photo in the library and marveled at Murphy's home.

"I was a bit skeptical at first, but you really have a unique house, Murphy," Sam remarked.

Murphy approached her while smiling timidly. "Boredom and money make bad bedfellows," he replied.

"I wouldn't know," Sam replied with a humored laugh while glancing at him.

He stared into her eyes and smiled warmly. "I'm sure you've never been bored a day in your life."

Sam laughed at the comment then looked away with embarrassment. "Perhaps we should move on to the bedroom." Her expression dropped after she realized what she had said and how it sounded then quickly attempted to cover for her blunder. "To photograph."

Murphy grinned and backed away from her. "Whatever you want," he replied gently and showed her to the door.

They left the library and headed up the elegant staircase that seemingly climbed to heaven. Sam looked at the lower level as they climbed the stairs.

"Certainly get a workout in this house," Sam remarked while laughing.

"Saves money on a home gym," he informed her with a teasing grin.

Sam paused at the top of the stairs and looked to the foyer and hallway below. "Quite a view from up here."

Murphy stood alongside her by the railing and studied her with some concern. "Do I make you nervous?"

Sam looked at him with some surprise. She then realized how close he had been standing and attempted not to notice. "No, of course not. Why do you ask?"

"You've appeared uncomfortable since you've arrived," Murphy replied then fidgeted. "I was hoping my eccentricity didn't concern you."

"No," Sam began then hesitated and smiled gently. "Well, maybe a little, at first. It's been my experience that wealthy, eccentric men have an invincibility thing going on. Think they can do whatever they want without consequences."

"That's not the case, I assure you," he said gently. "The simple truth is I like you." His look turned more serious. "I like you a lot."

Sam stared at Murphy a long moment with some surprise. "I don't know what to say--"

Murphy smiled gently and moved closer to her. "You could start by saying you'd like to go out with me."

Sam turned away from him and fidgeted with her camera. "I really hadn't expected them to be right."

Murphy leaned against the railing and studied her. "Expected who to be right about what?"

She turned and fidgeted slightly. "Dawson and Amber," she replied gently. "They thought you brought me here as a ploy to get me alone, but I didn't believe it. I thought you were really interested in my talent as a photographer."

"I am interested in your photography," Murphy replied. "This wasn't a ploy to get you alone, Sam. I'll admit, it's easier to talk to you here then it would've been at the studio, but that was just an added bonus not the motive."

"I'm not into casual dating and romantic flings," Sam informed him simply. "If that's what you're interested in--"

Murphy took two steps closer to her putting no distance between them. "I know you're not the casual type," he replied eagerly, seeming pleased with her response. "Neither am I. Will you consider giving me a chance?"

Sam stared into Murphy's eyes a long moment with some embarrassment then looked down at her camera and fidgeted. She finally met his gaze.

"I'm a little surprised to admit it, but I think I would like to get to know you better."

Amber was heard calling for them from downstairs. She could be seen roaming around the main hallway below. Murphy stepped away from the rail, avoiding being seen by Amber, and moved closer to Sam. He gently touched her cheek with the back of his fingers then pulled her into his arms and gently kissed her on the lips. Sam sank against him, allowed her free arm to slip around his neck, and returned the kiss. Amber could be heard coming up the stairs while calling for them. They released each other and put some distance between them. Sam fidgeted with her camera while feeling her cheeks redden then looked at the stairs just as Amber appeared at the top.

"Didn't you hear me calling?" Amber practically gasped.

"I guess not," Murphy replied while hiding his sly grin then nodded down the hall. "The master bedroom is at the end of the hall." He shifted with some tension and seemed to blush as well. "I should check on dinner. You can meet me downstairs in the lounge when you're finished up here."

Amber appeared disappointed while staring at the handsome man. "You're not going to join me--us in the bedroom?"

Murphy smirked as he walked toward the stairs. "That might prove embarrassing," he replied and headed down the stairs.

Amber glanced at Sam and pouted. "I wouldn't be embarrassed," she remarked.

"Maybe *he'd* be embarrassed," Sam replied then turned and walked down the hallway.

Amber hurried after her with a confused look on her face. "Why in the world would he be embarrassed? It's his bedroom."

"Precisely," Sam remarked.

She considered the comment. "Oh," Amber giggled. "He might have impure thoughts."

"He may not be the only one," Sam informed her simply.

"Oh, you know I have them already," Amber announced with a laugh.

# Chapter Six

After dinner, Sam finished taking her photos while Amber entertained Murphy with another round of flirting. Once she was finished taking photos, Sam decided to relieve Murphy of Amber's company. Murphy walked with Sam and Amber to the double foyer doors and held one side open for them.

"Well, ladies, it's been a pleasure having you both over for the evening," Murphy announced then glanced at Sam with a sly smile. "I'm glad it didn't have to be all work."

"I've had a great time, Mr. Colbert," Amber announced cheerfully, practically falling over herself. "We should get together again sometime soon."

"That's a wonderful idea," Murphy replied then looked at Sam. "Have you decided what I owe you for the photos?"

"I'll wait for you in the car," Amber informed Sam, taking her business cue, then left the house.

"It's not necessary to pay for my time," Sam informed him while attempting to hide her reddening cheeks. "Just pay for the photos. That'll be enough."

"Don't be ridiculous," Murphy announced boldly. "I'll make up my own number and get you a check tomorrow."

She held back her laugh. "I'll see you tomorrow then," Sam replied.

Although she meant to leave, they stared at each other a long moment. Sam couldn't seem to pull herself away despite knowing she was sending a strong signal. The signal was eagerly received.

Without hesitation, Murphy pulled her into his arms and kissed her passionately. Even though she was taken by surprise, Sam returned the kiss without thinking twice. She didn't know what came over her, but she couldn't tear herself away from his warm embrace or the passionate kiss. Murphy broke off the kiss and pulled back just enough to meet her gaze, although refusing to release her. Both heard the door gently creak, causing them to pull away and look toward the partially open door. They were relieved to discover no one was there.

Sam smiled with embarrassment. "I should go."

"Yes, of course. Goodnight, Sam."

§

Sam pulled up to Amber's house and stopped her Jeep. She looked at Amber, who sat quietly sulking in the passenger seat. She hadn't said a word on the two-minute trip back to her house on the other side of the cemetery.

"You've been awfully quiet," Sam commented. "What's wrong?"

Amber glared at Sam with a fire in her eyes. "What's wrong? I saw you kissing Colbert," she snapped. "You didn't even want him until you knew I was interested in him."

"No," Sam replied. "I wasn't interested in him because I really didn't believe he was interested in me. He wants to go out with me, and I'd like to go out with him."

Amber sprang from the car and hurried up to the house. Sam got out of the Jeep and ran after her.

"Amber," Sam called after her and ran onto the porch behind her. "You're not being fair."

Amber entered the house and shut the screen door behind her. "I'm not being fair? You knew I liked him, and you went after him anyway!"

"But he likes me," Sam announced. "You like a different guy every week."

"Do not!"

"First there was Dawson, now you can't even come to the studio without the two of you having an uncomfortable moment," she lashed out. "Then there was that doctor you wanted to cozy up to, so you rolled in poison ivy just so you could meet him. Who can forget the cop that you ran a stop sign to meet, and then the judge you had to appear before to contest the ticket," Sam informed her. "That was just the last few months. If I waited for a man you didn't like, I'd never date."

Amber slammed the door and locked it. Sam groaned and walked off the porch. "And then there's me who always seems to pick crazy friends." She approached her Jeep. "My luck, Murphy will turn out to be a psychopath." Sam paused before her Jeep and looked at the back tire. It was flat. She shook her head. "What started out as a beautiful evening has quickly gone sour."

Sam removed her cell phone and attempted to find a strong enough signal, but typical for the back woods, there wasn't one to be found. She wasn't even sure why she bothered. She'd never gotten a cell phone signal at Amber's house. Sam turned and walked back to the house then promptly pounded on the front door.

"Amber, I have a flat. I need to call my dad." There was no response. She pounded again. "Come on, Amber. You know I don't have a spare tire."

She hoped if she made enough noise, Baxter would hear and assist her. His car was still parked out front, so he could even give her a ride home. He had to be more reasonable than his sister was. Sam waited a moment longer, but when no one answered the door, she threw her arms in the air.

"Fine! Leave me stranded, but this is it!" Sam stormed off the porch and walked down the driveway.

Amber stood before Baxter's bedroom door on the second floor and knocked urgently. "Baxter," she announced firmly. "Baxter, I need to talk to you." There was no response. She opened his door and looked around the dark bedroom. The room was a disaster, but it apparently always looked that way. "Baxter?" Amber left the bedroom and walked down the hall toward the stairs. "Baxter? Where are you?"

Amber walked down the stairs and headed toward the kitchen. The cloaked figure appeared from the darkened dining room behind her with a dagger clutched in his hand. The sinister creeper approached her from behind her and raised the dagger in the air. Amber suddenly paused with an odd look on her face. She turned around, saw the frightening figure, and screamed.

§

Sam walked along the dark, back road past the cemetery toward Murphy's house and muttered to herself while playing with her car keys.

"Some friend," she snapped lowly. "Making me walk in the dark. If I get hit by a car, she'll never forgive herself, the bitch." Sam looked at the cemetery to her left and suddenly became concerned. "I must be insane," she remarked softly under her breath.

She looked up the road. Murphy's house could be seen in the near distance. She picked up the pace and walked faster past the cemetery. She could see the police line around the crypt just up ahead to her left.

"I'm never going to forgive her for this."

Sam walked as fast as she could past the old cemetery. Although she didn't see it, the cloaked figure ran across the cemetery in the same direction she was walking. Sam shivered slightly and looked back at the cemetery. There was nothing there. Dark shadows from the headstones lent an eerie atmosphere to the already creepy lot. Sam continued past the open front gate and stared at it with bewilderment. She would have sworn it was chained shut on their way to Murphy's house that afternoon. Just after she passed, the cloaked figure appeared by the gate. Sam looked back and saw the menacing figure a couple of feet behind her with the dagger in his hand. Sam cried out in surprise and ran for Murphy's house. The cloaked figure chased after her, swiftly gaining ground. Sam was tackled to the stone alongside the road. She screamed and flipped herself over as the cloaked figure coiled back with the dagger. Sam screamed again, slipped her foot between them, and thrust her attacker off. She scrambled to her feet in the loose stone and continued her sprint for Murphy's house.

The cloaked figure sprang to his feet and chased after her. Sam looked behind her only to see her attacker was nearly on top of her again. The dagger slashed at her. Sam screamed and threw herself to the ground to avoid the large dagger. As she scrambled to her feet, he backhanded her across the face. She was thrown backward and struck the iron gate, hitting her head. Sam clutched her head as she swayed a moment then sank down the gate.

§

Murphy paced the grand hallway with the cordless phone against his ear waiting for someone to pick up on the other end. He paused when the call was answered.

"Hello, Mr. Krosby," he announced into the phone. "This is Murphy Colbert. I hope I didn't wake you. I was just wondering if Sam made it home safely. Would it be possible to talk with her?" His smile faded with some surprise. "Oh, she's not home yet?" Murphy appeared disappointed then fidgeted. "Could you ask her to call me when she gets home?" He attempted a smile. "Thank you." Murphy disconnected the call, ran his fingers through his hair while fidgeting, and looked around the hallway. "If I only knew Amber's last name--"

Murphy walked out the foyer door and stepped onto the front porch. He strained to look down the road past the cemetery toward Amber's house but couldn't even see as far as the crypt. He tapped his fingers on the cordless phone while contemplating his next move. Murphy frowned and walked back inside.

"Don't be an idiot stalker," Murphy muttered. "She's probably hanging out with her friend before heading home." He shut the front door and looked at the clock in the hallway. He frowned and again tapped the cordless phone. "Why do I have this uneasy feeling?" he muttered then sank into thought. Murphy set the phone down on the small, antique table and removed his car keys from his pocket. He nodded. "Okay, I'm officially a stalker." He headed out the front door.

Murphy hurried across the driveway to his Bronco and jumped inside. He started the vehicle and drove down the driveway. As he passed the cemetery, Amber's house came into view. Murphy slowed near the cemetery and stared at Sam's Jeep parked in Amber's driveway. He appeared relieved to see her Jeep still at her friend's house. Casting a look into the rearview mirror, Murphy saw the cloaked figure in the back seat. He gasped and slammed on the brakes.

The cloaked figure sprang forward between the seats and grabbed Murphy around the neck. Murphy gasped and fought the hand now crushing his throat. As they struggled, Murphy's foot slipped off the brake onto the gas. The Bronco flew forward and struck the iron fence surrounding the cemetery. Murphy was thrown forward, the air bag cushioning his blow. The cloaked figure struck the dashboard before hitting the windshield. Murphy appeared a little stunned but gathered his wits enough to reach for the door. The cloaked figure flailed in the front passenger seat then kicked Murphy with a booted foot. Murphy's head struck the driver's side window, knocking him unconscious.

# Chapter Seven

$S$am woke with some disorientation within a damp and dreary basement. The sound of dripping water was almost deafening in the otherwise silent room. She slowly looked around from where she lay on a metal table. The room gave the appearance of a 1920's medical examiner's lab. Leather straps held her wrists down. She immediately fought the leather restraints. She then heard voices from the next room. Sam listened a moment then pulled against the straps. The old leather was soft enough that she was able to slip her hand from one strap. Sam sat up despite her dizziness and unbuckled the second strap. The voices became louder, indicating her attacker would soon be in the room with her. Sam jumped off the table, clutched her injured head, and swayed with some dizziness. A small metal table next to the exam table contained strange tools and objects, some stained with blood. Sam stared at the table with a look of complete confusion. She didn't know where or what the place was, but she knew she needed to escape. She hurried to the partially opened door and peered into the next room. There was no one there.

Sam cautiously entered the next room and paused. There were several sheet-covered tables lined along the room. It would appear as if she was in a morgue, but that didn't make any sense. Sam stared at the nearby table, hesitated, and then pulled back the sheet. To her horror, she stared at Venus. Her skin was ash gray and there was no denying the large hole in her throat, now cleaned of blood, came from the dagger carried by her attacker. Sam gasped softly and jumped away from the dead woman then looked at the other tables with sheets covering them. The same form was beneath each sheet, indicating each contained a body. Filled with panic, she ran from the room and entered the next room over. Sam suddenly froze while staring at the old, dingy living quarters.

Well-preserved dead men and women sat on the dusty furniture in perfectly natural positions. Sam stifled her scream and quickly backed out of the room. She ran into someone, let out a scream, and spun around. The cloaked figure stood before her with the dagger in his hand. Sam backed away with horror and fought her urge to scream hysterically. She needed to keep her wits about her and becoming hysterical served no purpose. The cloaked figure lowered his hood to reveal Amber. Sam's eyes widened in horror as she stared at her best friend.

"Amber," she gasped. "What's going on? What have you done?"

Amber smiled with a look of insanity in her expression. "Bet you wish you'd never kissed Murphy now."

"I don't understand," Sam gasped as she nervously looked around.

"Nobody ever could," Amber replied while twirling the dagger. "Just a little hobby of mine." She looked around the room as well. "Some people collect stamps. I collect people."

"You're sick," Sam lashed out and backed up a step.

"You don't know the half of it," Amber announced with an evil chuckle. "Your newly found boyfriend is about to become my next addition."

"Murphy?" Sam demanded as her eyes widened. "What have you done to him?"

"Nothing yet," Amber replied while grinning. "But I'm going to let you watch while Murphy and I make love."

"He'll never touch you," Sam snapped.

"He won't have to," Amber replied with a twisted smile. "He won't even be alive for it."

Sam stared at her with a look of complete horror then suddenly lunged for Amber. Amber swung the knife as Sam tackled her against the wall, forcing the dagger from Amber's hand. Sam punched her repeatedly in the face until her friend fell to the floor. Sam ran from the room and up the old steps for the only door. She threw open the basement door and realized she was standing in Amber's modern kitchen. Sam was momentarily surprised by what had been happening just one floor beneath a house she'd spend so much time visiting.

She hurried for the back kitchen door and threw it open. The cloaked figure stood before her with a dagger in his hand. Sam cried out and turned to run. Amber appeared in the basement doorway, touching her bleeding lip.

"You're going to pay for that," Amber growled lowly.

Sam looked back at the figure in the doorway. The cloak was removed to reveal Baxter grinning slyly.

"And I'm going to take great pleasure in carrying it out," Baxter announced cheerfully.

Amber glared at her brother with some surprise and irritation. "Where's Murphy?" she demanded to know.

"He was gone by the time I got there," Baxter informed her firmly. "What the hell? Didn't you tie him before you came back to the house?"

"With what? I didn't exactly have any rope on me," Amber snapped. "We have to find him."

"He's probably already back at his house," Baxter snarled. "We can't be running around if he's called the police. We need to prep Sam. We may not have much time."

"Damn it; I want him!" Amber cried out in anger. "He's mine! You said I could have him!"

Baxter pointed his dagger at Amber. "You will, but it'll have to wait for another time. Right now, we have to dispose of her. Let's do this!"

Amber appeared to sulk. Baxter forced Sam back to the basement door. Sam considered her next move, but none of them seemed to have a very happy ending for her. She reluctantly did as they instructed.

Sam entered the sitting room with the preserved bodies lounging on the furniture. She cringed then looked back at Amber and Baxter. Baxter shut and braced the door with a bar.

"If you're thinking someone might find you," Baxter announced with a cheap grin on his face, "you're *dead* wrong. The passageway in the wall is very natural looking, so even if someone did come down here looking around, they'd never find this room."

"But no one's ever come snooping around anyway," Amber informed her. "We've been entertaining our guests for a few years now."

Sam expression remained placid. "What do you intend to do with me?"

Baxter shrugged with a broad grin. "Add you to our collection. But don't you worry about a thing. You'll have much more fun once you're embalmed. It's a fetish of ours."

Sam looked from Baxter to Amber. "You kill people then embalm them like you do in the funeral home? Does your uncle know about this?"

"Why don't you ask him?" Amber asked with a teasing smile then pointed across the room to a dead man positioned in a recliner, appearing to be asleep.

Sam held back her gasp, shut her eyes, and looked away. "You're both sick!"

Baxter waved the dagger around. "Watch your temper there, Sam. We might decide to torture you *before* we embalm you."

Sam glared at Baxter with loath in her eyes. While she should have been frightened, she could feel her anger taking control of every nerve in her body. She knew she was about to do something stupid, but her fate seemed pre-determined already. Perhaps stupid was her only option.

"I want to torture her anyway," Amber sulked then turned angry. "She stole Murphy away from me."

"Oh, stop with Murphy," Baxter snapped and rolled his eyes. "You sound like a broken record."

"You always get the ones you want," Amber launched.

"And I let you play with them too," Baxter replied. "You want her to play with uncle? Would that make you happy?"

"No, I want to embalm her alive," Amber exclaimed then grinned with enthusiasm.

Baxter cringed and gave her a disgusted look. "You know I hate the screaming."

Sam nervously looked around the room while Baxter and Amber argued lightly. The doorbell could be heard ringing from upstairs. Both Baxter and Amber stopped talking and looked at the ceiling.

"Someone's here," Amber whispered.

"No shit," Baxter remarked lowly. "It might be the police if *your* Murphy called them." He darted looks at Sam. "You stay down here and keep her quiet. I'll check the door. Give her something to silence her."

Amber nodded as Baxter walked toward the door. She removed a bottle of chloroform from her pocket while Baxter shed his cloak. Baxter opened the door to the secret room while Sam kept careful watch over both, waiting for her moment. She'd strike when Baxter left the room. As Baxter stepped through the doorway, Sam felt her body twitch, prepared to take on her armed friend. Baxter suddenly cried out and staggered backward into the room while holding his bleeding midsection. Amber screamed with horror and ran to her brother. Murphy stepped into the doorway while clutching a medieval sword dripping with fresh blood. He had dried blood on the side of his head and a psychotic look in his eyes.

Amber screamed like a woman possessed, raised her dagger, and ran for Murphy. Murphy cried out while swinging the sword, connecting with Amber's neck. Her head flew across the room, rolling past Sam. Her headless body collided with Murphy, knocking them both to the floor. Murphy threw her slightly twitching body off him and scrambled to his feet. Sam's entire body sagged with relief. She ran to Murphy and threw her arms around him. He held her against him in a long embrace and breathed a sigh of relief. He slowly pulled away and searched her for injuries.

"Are you okay?" he asked gently.

Sam nodded and sighed. "I am now."

He looked at Amber's severed head several feet across the room. "I'm sorry I had to kill your best friend."

Sam managed a nervous, uneasy laugh. "I was thinking about finding a new one anyway."

Murphy reclaimed his sword and guided Sam from the room. "Let's get out of here before something else happens."

"How did you find me?" Sam asked as they headed up the stairs.

"I followed that bastard here after he'd come back to finish me off," Murphy informed her. "He left the back door unlocked. I followed the three of you down here and nearly lost my opportunity when he locked the door."

"But how did you ring the doorbell while standing outside the basement door at the same time?" Sam asked as they entered the kitchen.

"I rewired the doorbell to the basement to make it ring when I touched the wires together," Murphy informed her then smiled. "I'm more talented than I appear."

"Talented isn't the word," Sam replied with a tiny laugh.

"More like stupid," came Baxter's voice from behind them.

Both spun around with surprise. Baxter tackled Murphy to the kitchen floor, knocking his sword across the room. They struggled for the dagger, now hovering over Murphy's face.

"Don't you know you never leave the killer unless you're certain he's dead?" Baxter cried out with a crazed psychotic look in his eyes while on top of Murphy.

Murphy kicked Baxter off him. Baxter flew across the floor then scrambled to his feet. Murphy crawled across the floor and retrieved his sword. He flipped himself over into a sitting position with the sword clutched in his hands, but Baxter was already thrusting the dagger for him. Sam appeared behind Baxter and plunged a butcher knife repeatedly into his back. She screamed like a wild woman with every thrust. Baxter managed to turn around while the assault continued. Sam released the knife within Baxter's back, stunned he had the strength to face her. He was about to strike her with the dagger when Murphy suddenly kicked his legs out from underneath him. Baxter fell backward and struck the floor, embedding the knife deeper into his back. Baxter gasped several times as blood seeped from his mouth. He took his final breath and stared at the ceiling. Sam gasped several times before she was finally able to relax.

Murphy scrambled to his feet, reclaimed his sword, and approached Sam where she stood over Baxter's body. There was an odd silence as both stared at the dead man. Murphy suddenly chopped downward with his sword and severed Baxter's head from his neck. Sam cried out with surprise, jumped back a step, and stared at Murphy. Murphy panted several times, attempting to catch his breath, and stared at Baxter.

"Thanks for the advice, bastard," Murphy casually remarked. Murphy grabbed Sam's hand and pulled her from the kitchen through the back door.

§

Police cars were parked in front of Amber's house with their lights flashing. It was already sunrise. Sam and Murphy were finally able to leave and walked along the road past his mangled Bronco smashed against the cemetery fence. Murphy looked at his vehicle and held Sam against him while they walked.

"God, what a night. I can't wait to take a hot shower and sleep for a week," Murphy muttered softly. "I'm sure your parents will be happy to hear from you. They must be worried sick."

"I'll call them and tell them I'm okay," she replied softly with a tiny smile.

"You don't want them to come and get you?" Murphy asked as he looked at her. "That was my only car."

"I'm so tired; I just want to sleep," she informed him then stared at him with some apprehension. "And when I wake up, I want to wake up in your arms."

Murphy smiled and held her against him. "I'm glad to hear that." There was a moment of silence as they continued toward his house. "Of course, now I don't feel like sleeping."

Sam clung to his arm and laughed softly. "Me either."

Murphy stopped, turned her to face him, and kissed her warmly but passionately. They slowly pulled away and looked at the cemetery ten feet away. Both became uneasy. Murphy grabbed her hand and hurried her away from the cemetery.

# The End

# Other books by Holly Copella!
## Reviews left on Amazon are appreciated!

## "The Battle for Andrea Maria"

**A cruise ship attack turns six survivors into overnight celebrities after they take credit for the heroic act of a stowaway who died saving them.**

The cruise is just what Jess needed--a bit of harmless fun far from her daily grind. But what begins as a relaxing vacation turns into a desperate fight for her life when terrorists take over the ship and start piling up bodies. Teaming up with a mysterious stowaway, Jess attempts to send out a distress call but knows they cannot wait for help to come. If she or the few remaining passengers have any hope for survival, Jess must act now. The papers dub it "The Battle for *Andrea Maria*," but to Jess it is the moment she fought side-by-side with her enigmatic Romeo, saving the ship--and losing him. She thinks the story ends there, but really, the nightmare is just beginning...

## "Insanely Deadly"

**When the dead return to life, it's up to an admiral's daughter and a mildly insane, former war hero to save their small town.**

Jetta Cross, a Navy Admiral's daughter, is tasked with keeping her father's comrade, a former war hero turned town crazy, grounded in the real world. Capt. John Hunter is still fighting the war in his head, where imaginary dead people are part of his world. When a viral outbreak brings about a zombie uprising, Hunter is left to his own devices. He must resume his role as a one-man commando unit in order to destroy the ravenous undead. With Hunter still fighting his own inner demons as well as the undead, the townspeople fear their zombie neighbors may not be the only threat. Stranded at the island's luxurious resort with a handful of workers, Jetta is forced to live up to her father's reputation and take charge of the deteriorating situation at the hotel. She must wage her own war against the infected before the government declares her hometown a total loss.

## "Deadly Institution"

**A town recluse suspected of killing his wife teams up with a young woman in order to stop a killer.**

After being accused of murdering his wife, Konrad Asher turns his back on the town that once adored him. Ten years later, he still holds his grudge and the title of the most feared man in town. With the reopening of the burned mental institution, where his wife had died, former employees are now murdered one-by-one, throwing suspicion back on Asher. A young local reporter, Jacey, is forced to reveal her long-time friendship with the infamous recluse in order to clear his name not only in the recent murders but to exonerate him in the death of his wife as well. Will Jacey's relationship with Asher invite the killer closer to her? Or is the killer already in her life?

## "Screenplays: The Island Collection"
## "Jungle Princess", "A.L.F. Resort", "Brighton Island"

**Discover how romance and fun in the sun can be downright *chilling*!**

*"Jungle Princess"* is a romantic/thriller that leaves a teenage girl stranded on an island with two male shipmates and a creature of "unknown" origin. She soon discovers the island is home to an abandoned prison with several prisoners roaming free. What really killed over one hundred prisoners? And is it still out there--?

*"A.L.F. Resort"* is a romantic/thriller set on an island resort with Artificial Life Forms as the main draw. At this resort, all your fantasies come true...until a malfunction removes safety inhibitors on the A.L.F.'s. Zombies, biker gangs, and mobsters run amuck, turning fantasies into nightmares. A young reporter gets more of a story than she anticipates, but will she survive long enough to write the story?

*"Brighton Island"* is a romantic/thriller set on a private island. When the owner's niece brings her psychic friend to the mansion, his presence awakens the spirits' tortured souls. As the psychic attempts to solve the old murders, the niece is confronted with the possibility that she's next to join the mansion ghosts. Stranded on the island with a crazed killer, her uncle wages his own war to save them. Will his "shock and awe" tactics actually save them or get them killed?

## "Death Displacement"

**A grief-stricken man travels back in time to seek revenge on the woman who murdered his girlfriend but inadvertently falls in love with her.**

Kane is about to marry the woman he loves. His life is perfect. A few weeks before the wedding, a vindictive woman from his girlfriend's past mysteriously arrives and kills her. He learns of a traumatic accident that happened five years earlier, which triggers Riley's hatred for his girlfriend. Distraught over his girlfriend's death, Kane uses an antique time machine to travel into the past in order to find and destroy the woman responsible. When he runs into Riley's younger self, he realizes she's not the monster she later becomes, and he can't bring himself to destroy her. With a little help from his oddball friend from the past, they formulate a plan to prevent the accident that sends Riley down her destructive path. Kane's plan backfires when he falls for the younger Riley. His new tortured existence is further complicated when future Riley, his girlfriend's killer, shows up with her own devious agenda that doesn't include him. Will he be able to stop the time ripple, which ultimately ends with his girlfriend's death? Or will future Riley take him out of the timeline forever--

## "Dead Village"

**After strange happenings isolate a small resort town from the rest of the world, nearly one hundred residents seek refuge at the closed hotel. Only eight survive the night. And that's just the beginning...**

One day after the entire population of Fox Ridge Village disappears, a car wreck forces several unsuspecting crash victims to seek help at the closed summer hotel. Within the hotel, they discover the grisly aftermath of a brutal slaughter. Crash victims Vander and Devon, a reluctant clairvoyant, team up to solve the riddle of the "haunted hotel" and the mass hysteria plaguing the remaining survivors. By the time they discover the hotel's secret, they're already drawn into the hysteria. As the body count continues to climb, it's a race to isolate the source and bring everyone back to reality before they kill one another. Will Devon be able to communicate with the traumatized spirits before their fate becomes her own?

# "Misfits, Inc."

**A seemingly ordinary, young woman meets four misfits who claim she has given them supernatural powers.**

While on a business trip to a remote island paradise, a bored secretary, Hailey, has her world turned upside down when her path collides with a psychic freak, Skyler. He attempts to convince her that they had met in his dreams, and she had chosen him as one of her four mystic warriors. After Skyler foresees a woman's death, they discover an unidentified creature has killed one of the guests. They are joined by a lounge pianist and a rich playboy, who also claim they had met her in their dreams. If Skyler's prophecies are genuine, the evil entity controlling the ravenous creatures needs to destroy Hailey to ensure its survival. Reluctantly accepting her fate, Hailey has to locate the last and most powerful of her chosen warriors, The Guardian. Their fate is in doubt when The Guardian turns out to be a self-absorbed, former cat burglar with a bad attitude. Can Hailey turn her company of misfits into an elite team of mystic warriors? Or will The Guardian's secret agenda destroy them all?

# "Basement Dwellers"

**A viral outbreak at a hospital leaves a mortician, sheriff, and coroner fighting for their lives against a horde of undead and the CDC.**

After a massive car wreck leaves several survivors in critical condition at the local hospital, a surgeon uses experimental drugs on his critical patients and accidentally causes a zombie outbreak. When local mortician, Lexx, receives an infected corpse as her client, she becomes stranded in the hospital basement during CDC quarantine along with the local sheriff and the coroner. The infamous surgeon struggles to find a cure for his infectious blunder by using the other survivors as test subjects. Meanwhile, Lexx and the sheriff attempt to locate his missing sister, who's stranded somewhere in the battle zone that once was the emergency room. It's a race against time and the ravenous undead. Can they survive the undead before CDC sanitizes the hospital of all infection?

## "Witness Protection"
## Also available in audiobook!

**After witnessing an execution, a resourceful young woman attempts to disappear while being pursued by a hitman and a handsome federal agent.**

A helicopter pilot, Jackie Remus, reluctantly agrees to go on a date with one of her clients, but her date is unexpectedly cut short when she witnesses a man being murdered. After narrowly escaping with her life, she is placed into protective custody. When the safe house is breached, Jackie makes a daring escape from both the hired killers and the handsome FBI agent, who wants to return her to protective custody. With a little help from her sly and crafty friend, Monroe, Jackie is convinced she can disappear until the trial. While on her journey to meet with her friend, she solicits help from a few shady but lovable characters along the way. Although she manages to stay one-step ahead of the hired killers, the federal agent remains in hot pursuit. Will Jackie reach Monroe before she's captured by the FBI and returned to protective custody? Or will the hired killers silence her first?

## "Town Darling"

**After surviving a brutal attack that claims the lives of those she loves, a young woman seeks revenge on a corrupt town.**

Going back home is never easy, but for Casey, it means returning to her corrupt hometown where she barely survived a brutal attack. Accompanied by two family friends, she seeks justice for the night that destroyed her life. Her physical scars are nothing compared to her emotional ones, forcing the local sheriff to believe that the town darling is back for revenge. As the conspiracy for her revenge appears to be leading up to the coveted town fair, the sheriff is determined to stop her from fulfilling her vengeful scheme...but guilt over his role on that fateful night continues to haunt him. Will his desperate need for Casey's forgiveness be his undoing? Or will Casey's desire for revenge destroy them both?

## "Unconditional"

**A young woman puts her life on hold to care for an unstable, highly skilled combat soldier, who believes someone is trying to kill him.**

A botched military coup leaves a team of elite fighters injured with one clinging to life in a coma. When Harlan wakes from his coma, he's left with no memory of his past life. His commander's daughter, Indy, takes it upon herself to care for the fallen war hero. She's challenged with more than just his physical care as she combats with not only his memory loss but also his newly found desire for her. His infatuation with her becomes the least of her worries when he sinks back into his role of a combat soldier. Believing his life is in danger, his fighting skills surface, turning him into an unpredictable and dangerous man. Will his memory return to him before Indy is forced to commit him? Or will he finally find his nemesis, "the coyote", and possibly claim the life of an innocent person?

## "Witness Protection 2"
## The Return of Whiskey Tango Foxtrot

**Believing she holds the clue to millions in missing laundered money, a young woman is placed into the protective care of a former Navy SEAL team.**

Feeling sorry for her recently separated co-worker, Leeann invites Wiley to join her and her friends on their night out. Little does she know that finding her co-worker murdered is just the beginning of her nightmare. Leeann unknowingly holds the key to fifty million dollars in potentially laundered mob money. With hired killers pursuing her, the FBI places her into a different kind of protective custody. Former Navy SEAL team Whiskey Tango Foxtrot reunites to keep Leeann alive at their secret hideaway. What should be an easy assignment takes an unscheduled turn when secrets, lies, and betrayal threaten to derail their mission. Is the team prepared for a war on their own doorstep? Will Leeann's misguided trust endanger the lives of those sent to protect her?

## "Deadly Institution 2"

**When blackmail turns into murder, a young woman finds herself caught in the killer's crosshairs.**

The small town of Stony Ridge is no stranger to scandal and persecution of the innocent. When a brutal killing shakes the town's prestigious country club, Jacey McMurray seeks help from a self-proclaimed vigilante, Konrad Asher. As her professional and personal worlds collide, Jacey fears the stress of the country club killings have finally taken their toll on Asher. Can a stressed out vigilante stop the killer before he strikes again?

## "Witness Protection 3"
## Alpha Mike Foxtrot

**A helicopter pilot risks her life to help a team of retired Navy SEALs rescue two girls from a killer.**

When former Navy SEAL team Whiskey Tango Foxtrot asks for a simple favor, Jackie reluctantly offers her air-taxi services. What could go wrong? What begins as a search and rescue for two girls turns into a fight for survival against a heavily armed drug cartel. Wanted by the law with the cartel in hot pursuit and their home base breached, the team is forced to call in a favor from a questionable ally. Unfortunately, their new safe house isn't what it seems. Without knowing who the real enemy is, can Jackie and the team save their young witnesses from the hands of a killer?

## "The Pen Pal"

**In order to save her friend, she must enter the mind of a serial killer.**

When her best friend is abducted, no one believes Jolynn saw it in a psychic vision. With nowhere to turn, Jolynn reluctantly joins Agent Harris Slade and his team on their hunt for a sadistic serial killer known only as "The Pen Pal". Finally confronted with the killer, Jolynn realizes she must enter the mind of the psychopath in order to stop the brutal killings. But when her vision reveals a particularly disturbing death, can Jolynn sacrifice her lover for her friend?

# "Awaken the Dead"

**A grieving innkeeper struggles to keep her haunted hotel out of foreclosure.**

After losing her parents in a suspicious boating accident, Harley Brandon is determined to keep the family hotel out of foreclosure. Unfortunately, the hotel ghosts have other plans. Built with tainted money, the century old Horizon Hotel thrives on a tradition of murder, scandal, and suicide. As the paranormal activity increases to alarming levels, Harley discovers the truth about the hotel and its residents. Can Harley save her friends from the hotel's frightening hidden secrets?

# "Already Dead"
## Supernatural Collection

**From the already dead to the undead. Three supernatural tales of "things that go bump in the night".**

"Bloodletting" - A vampire themed resort allows guests to *participate* in their Bloodletting Ritual to celebrate the island's legendary vampires.

"Reaper of Souls" - A young woman must outwit an evil sorcerer in order to save her brother or become one of his minions forever.

"Already Dead" - When Flight 220 crashes, ten passengers make it to an isolated island, but only one man lives to tell the lie.

## "Witness Protection 4"
## O-Dark-Hundred

A simple assignment turns deadly when a retired Navy SEAL team uncovers a plot to kill a notorious mob boss.

When Whiskey Tango Foxtrot embarks on a simple stalking case, they're not prepared for a trip to a private island paradise owned by an infamous mobster. With one of their own suffering from traumatic head injuries, the team is left scrambling to decide what is real or imagined. The situation escalates even further when they uncover an assassination plot where everyone is a suspect. Now targets themselves, can the team survive their trip to paradise?

## "Witness Protection 5"
## Outside the Wire

After suffering several casualties on their last assignment, a retired Navy SEAL team discovers their misery is just beginning.

When Whiskey Tango Foxtrot returns home after suffering a devastating loss, they're hit with even more bad news regarding the rest of their team. Their grief is cut short when they discover their names are all on the same hit list. Hunted by relentless assassins, the scattered team must decide whether to remain safely hidden or find the man who put the price on their heads. Against the wishes of her teammates, Jackie strikes out on her own in order to save a friend who wants her dead. In a kill or be killed situation, will Jackie's emotions finally betray her?

## Coming Soon!
## "Once Upon a Disaster"

# ABOUT THE AUTHOR

Holly Copella has been writing since the age of twelve when her frustration at a book's poor plot drove her to author her own story. Over the last decade, she's written a number of screenplays, some of which she's now adapting into novels. Her fascination with zombies and other darker material lends an edge to her writing, which tends to lean toward horror. As a fan of Agatha Christie, she appreciates the craft of a good plot and the importance of creating significant characters.

Hailing from Pennsylvania, Copella lives in the Endless Mountains on a farm with her rescue horses and other animals. In addition to writing and reading fiction, she enjoys riding horses and traveling to Las Vegas and Disney World.

www.ingramcontent.com/pod-product-compliance
Lightning Source LLC
Chambersburg PA
CBHW071040250626
47159CB00012B/1252